Jack & Susan in 1933

Jack & Susan in 1933

Michael McDowell

FELONY & MAYHEM PRESS • NEW YORK

All the characters and events portrayed in this work are fictitious.

JACK & SUSAN IN 1933

A Felony & Mayhem mystery

PRINTING HISTORY
First edition (Ballantine): 1987
Felony & Mayhem edition: 2012

ISBN: 978-1-937384-39-5

Manufactured in the United States of America

Printed on 100% recycled paper

Library of Congress Cataloging-in-Publication Data

McDowell, Michael, 1950-
Jack & Susan in 1933 / Michael McDowell. -- Felony & Mayhem
edition.
    pages cm
ISBN 978-1-937384-39-5
1. Nineteen thirties--Fiction. 2. Marriage--Fiction. 3. Mystery fiction.
I. Title.
PS3563.C35936J34 2012
813'.54--dc23
                          2012045488

For Mr. Wilson, Ms. Goodman,
and Ms. Goodman-Wilson

The icon above says you're holding a copy of a book in the Felony & Mayhem "Wild Card" category. We can't promise these will press particular buttons, but we do guarantee they will be unusual, well written, and worth a reader's time. If you enjoy this book, you may well like other "Wild Card" titles from Felony & Mayhem Press.

For more about these books, and other Felony & Mayhem titles, or to place an order, please visit our website at:

www.FelonyAndMayhem.com

Other "Wild Card" titles from

FELONY&MAYHEM

MICHAEL McDOWELL
Jack & Susan in 1913
Jack & Susan in 1953

BONNIE JONES REYNOLDS
The Truth About Unicorns

SARAH RAYNE
A Dark Dividing
Ghost Song

Jack & Susan in 1933

The Revelers of 1933:

JACK, a well-placed lawyer in his father-in-law's firm, and a man with the wrong wife—

SUSAN, a young woman from the right side of the tracks, whose life has been derailed into Manhattan's cabaret life—

BARBARA, Jack's wife, and as delicious an enemy as Susan will ever encounter—

And then the black-and-white bundles of mischief *Scotty* and *Zelda*, pups of the period who become Jack and Susan's saving gift...

Part I

JACK

CHAPTER ONE

Should auld acquaintance be forgot
And never brought to mind?
Should auld acquaintance be forgot
And days of auld lang syne?

"WELL," SAID BARBARA Beaumont, dusting the glitter off her bare shoulders, "that was a bit of a dirge, wasn't it? You'd think the New Year's baby had died."

"So far as I'm concerned," said Barbara's husband, Jack, "it's a goner already." A little triangular hat of purple foil perched askew on his head.

Harmon Dodge, his eyes slightly crossed with alcohol, carefully aimed the glowing tip of his cigar stub at the skin of a balloon bearing the numbers 1933, and on the second try burst it.

The three were in the Villa Vanity, a New York City speakeasy on East Fifty-second Street. There had been a time when going to such places had been a thrill. You heard about it from a friend in a whisper. You went there by taxi and got out at the end of the street. One searched out the number while another watched for cops on the beat. You gave a secret knock and an absurd password. You went down into a dank cellar with sweating walls and joined the brightest and best of New York society. You tested the alcohol by sticking your thumb into the glass—if the nail didn't come off, it was potable. Then you drank yourself into an expensive stupor that next day became a rueful consciousness. But the thrill of lawbreaking compensated for the actual dreariness, and anyway, people had large amounts of money to spend on convivial vices.

Not anymore. Not in this Depression, when in New York alone half a million men were out of work. No longer. No one had any money, and no vice managed to be convivial. People drank juniper gin not to raise their spirits but to bury their spiritlessness a little deeper. It was also apparent, at this late date, that the Prohibition amendment was to be repealed. The police had better things to do than to close down nightclubs that sold food-colored alcohol in Coca-Cola bottles. The police herded the homeless about the city, quelled strikes among the unemployed, and stopped crazed men from beating their families in the extremity of their unhappiness. Speakeasies had become nightclubs and moved upstairs, where the apricot-colored bulbs in the chandeliers could be seen clearly from the street. A few even had discreet signs screwed into the brickfronts. Nobody cared anymore, and gone were the secret knocks, the absurd passwords, and the thrilling, if remote, anticipation of arrest.

Barbara Beaumont, née Rhinelander, leaned her elbows on the table, which was about the size of a salad plate, and looked bored. Barbara had made a perfect study of boredom, for it was the fashionable pose among her set. Barbara was so good at it, she could have looked bored at the Last Judgment. She had managed to look bored and act bored for so long and with such intensity that boredom itself had become boring for her—or so she languidly said—and now she did it out of habit. Barbara had a smile that expressed ennui, and a laugh that expressed lassitude, and even a kind of shriek, reserved for special occasions, such as coming across a disassembled body in a steamer trunk, that expressed nothing but a kind of convulsive weariness of life. At the same time, of course, she was, considering the human being as a piece of machinery, constructed of indefatigable steel.

"Don't do that, Harm," said Barbara languidly.

"Don't do what?" asked Harmon, trying to put together a match flame and the tip of a new cigar. He was drunk, which was his usual state for twelve o'clock at night, even when the New Year wasn't being welcomed.

"Tell him not to do that," Barbara said to her husband, Jack.

"Not to do what?"

"Not to smoke a cigar with the band still on. It's the most vulgar thing in the world. Once a man asked me to marry him," said Barbara vaguely, "and I refused because I once saw him smoke a cigar with the band still on."

Harmon, who had at last managed to get flame and tobacco in proximity, looked up and down the length of his cigar for a few moments, as if weighing in the scales of eternity whether it would be worth the trouble to pull the tiny gold band off the end.

"Here," he said at last to Barbara, "you do it."

He held out his cigar to her. She slipped off the band and dropped it into a pile of confetti that had accumulated on the table. The band continued its slurred version of "Auld Lang Syne."

Jack sat back, tried to find a place for his legs that wouldn't trip anyone up, and reflected how much of his life was like this. Drunkenness and conversations about cigar bands. Morose celebrations. Barbara's face, which was a very Ecclesiastes of world-weariness. In point of fact, most of his life was like this.

Barbara's father, Marcellus Rhinelander, was the head of the law firm of Rhinelander, Rhinelander, and Dodge, up in Albany. (Dodge and one of the Rhinelanders were dead.) Jack had started out his legal career in Albany, though not in the firm. He had met Barbara at the Club, and after a courtship of six months duration, had asked her hand in marriage. Jack's offer was accepted with a metaphorical yawn, and he'd immediately after wondered why he'd done it, though on the whole it continued to appear to have been a good idea. After the return from the honeymoon to a beastly place in Maine, Barbara had announced her intention of moving to New York City. She had spent her childhood and adolescence there with her mother, and now wanted to go back. Jack pointed out that his job was in Albany, but Barbara pointed out in return that Rhinelander, Rhinelander, and Dodge had a New York City office—under the direction of Harmon Dodge, son of the original Dodge of the firm. Marcellus Rhinelander complied with his daughter's wish, and Jack was placed in the New York office.

Jack had been there three years now, and the fact of the matter was, he did all the firm's work. After the Crash the firm had specialized in bankruptcies, so there was no lack of business. Jack had become expert in appeasing creditors, salvaging tiny pensions for broken businessmen, and seeing to it that young sons and daughters remained in college. Bankruptcies were emotional proceedings.

Jack's duties to the firm of Rhinelander, Rhinelander, and Dodge did not end at the threshold of the lower Fifth Avenue offices, however. Jack had gradually found himself responsible for the maintenance of the private life of his superior, Harmon Dodge. Only a year older than Jack, Harmon had two vices, two excitements, two failings, and two strengths. They were liquor and women. Jack and Barbara clubbed with Harmon four nights out of seven. Jack made sure that Harmon got home safely, spilled over sideways in a cab with a five-dollar bill stuck in his jacket pocket, and Barbara tried to make sure that he didn't sign power of attorney over his life to some hard-boiled baby he'd met under the influence.

So, for better or worse, Jack and Barbara Beaumont were part of café society. Barbara was well-born and beautiful after the fashion of the well-born, which is to say, her beauty was strong and built to last. Her features, which were graceful and regular, never softened. Her green eyes never went liquid, her light brown hair was never negligently tossed, her dress was always right but always calculatedly right. She invariably looked, even under the most appalling of circumstances, as if she had just come back from a photographer's studio.

Jack Beaumont was tall, and handsome after the fashion of the Arrow shirt man, which was, in 1933, very handsome indeed. He was blessed with strong features, cheekbones that produced shadows in certain lights, a jaw that would had done service to Moses setting himself up against the pharaoh, and eyes that were a quiet, liquid gray. The regrettable thinning of his light brown hair only made his high, intellectual brow higher and even more daunting. He appeared to best advantage when sedate and reposed and naked. For when he put on clothes, they invariably got wrinkled, and pulled in the wrong places, and were a tailor's dream of rips and snares. When he moved about, he was sometimes clumsy, owing to his height and the astonishing length of his legs. The condition got worse when he was tired. He was frequently tired because of how many late nights he spent in his superior's company.

Jack wasn't even allowed to feel animosity toward Harmon for keeping him up so late every night. Harmon, it was explained to Jack, couldn't have been a playboy if Jack didn't work so hard at the office, obviating the necessity of Harmon's doing any work at all. This was Barbara's reading of the situation, and she had never hesitated to state her opinion to Jack, to Harmon, or to the two when together. Even Harmon took up the call. "Jack, my dear fellow," he'd declaim in his cups, "I must tell you something—I've you to blame for this dissipation. You entirely. Entirely. If you didn't cover for me so splendidly at the office, why, I'd have to knuckle down and do a little business myself. But you are so damned conscientious that you don't leave me with a thing to do but to drink myself into oblivion every day, and"—here he'd glance at Barbara, and finish off euphemistically—"look for a little frilled company and solace."

So it was Jack's fault that his boss was a satyric lush.

Barbara's eyes dutifully scanned the crowd in the nightclub every few minutes, as if in bare hope something would prove worthy of comment. Finally, her eyes brightened a little, giving a tiny cold glint of reflected amber light. "That's why we're here," she said, smirking knowingly. "I see. I wondered why you'd picked this den of dreariness for our New Year's celebration, Harm. Now I understand. I don't sympathize, I'll never forgive you for dragging me to the Villa Vanity—never, in the entire of *ma vie*—but I do understand."

Barbara's drawled complaint gave Jack the time to look around the room for the woman who had brought Harmon Dodge, and in consequence himself and Barbara, to this out-of-the-way place. Jack knew it was a woman because it was always a woman. Harmon Dodge liked three kinds of women—those who worked in cloak checks, those who sold cigarettes from a tray around their necks, and those who leaned on pianos and sang.

Harmon's women—and there had been enough of them to secure a generalization—tended to be very pretty, at least when seen in the right costume, in certain lights, and through the watery red eyes of the inebriated. They were cunning rather than intelligent. The most that could be said about their background was that it had to be kept there.

This one was a singer.

After "Auld Lang Syne" the band had morosely packed up its instruments to a little scattered applause, and wandered off backstage severally. Then a tiny curtain was raised, revealing a tiny stage with a very large grand piano, behind which sat a dapper little man with thick spectacles, and before which stood a young woman with lustrous black hair and shining black eyes. She was dressed simply, in a black crepe sheath, with a red heart-shaped brooch on her left sleeve. Her skin was translucently white, and it fairly shone, as the moon shines, in the white spotlight.

"*Too* splendid an *ensemble*," remarked Barbara dryly in Harmon's ear. "So simple, yet so effective and affecting. And the heart on the sleeve—how dreadfully clever. Makes one want to run into the powder room and weep for the sheer splendor of it."

"I think she looks first-rate," returned Harmon, waving away the cigar smoke obscuring his vision of the vision in black.

Jack, too, thought the singer looked first-rate. In fact, he rather preferred the singer's outfit to Barbara's, which in his opinion was a little overdone—a canary-yellow gown with a slightly darker cape, yellow half-length gloves with a thick diamond bracelet outside, and a fur boa that dropped into Jack's Rob Roy, giving it a decidedly foresty taste.

"What was her name?" asked Jack, leaning forward. "I couldn't hear the announcer."

"Susan Bright," said Harmon with mystical reverence.

"Wonder what it really is," said Barbara. "Natasha Rambova's real name was Winifred Shaunessy."

"Susan Bright's her real name," said Harmon. "I asked."

Jack and Barbara exchanged glances which clearly said, *So. They've already met.* And attached the further opinion, *This one could be trouble.*

As the short, myopic, boiled-shirt accompanist began his piano introduction, the Villa Vanity gradually quieted.

It wasn't a respectful silence, Jack thought, but a weary one. No one wanted to think about the New Year. The only predictions that anyone was making was that 1933 was going to be worse than 1932. Hoover was out, Roosevelt would be coming in. But what could one man do? In a strange way, it was like the end of the world. Certainly it was the end of the world that all these revelers had known, and all these revelers knew it. So they listened to the singer because they wouldn't then have to talk about themselves and remember their unhappiness.

> Let us pause in life's pleasures and count its many tears
> While we all sup sorrow with the poor;
> There's a song that will linger forever in our ears;
> Oh! Hard Times, come again no more.
>
> 'Tis the song, the sigh of the weary;
> Hard Times, Hard Times, come again no more,
> Many days you have lingered around my cabin door;
> Oh! Hard Times, come again no more.

Her voice was sweet and melancholy. She had control over it. She didn't press against the lyric. The simple Foster words, however, were bitterly ironic considering that hard times had indeed come again—and with a vengeance.

"I imagine her parents were married, don't you, Jack?" said Barbara.

"Shhh!" said Harmon, not even looking around.

> There's a pale, drooping maiden who toils her life away,
> With a worn heart whose better days are o'er:
> Tho' her voice would be merry, 'tis sighing all the day,
> Oh! Hard times, come again no more.

"I'll bet her father plucked chickens in an Iowa grocery store. In fact," Barbara went on, "I'd stake any amount of money on it."

"She's from Boston," said Harmon. "Her father failed in the Crash."

"Oh dear," sighed Barbara, "she *would* have an interesting past, wouldn't she? Interesting pasts are always so...so...so *uninteresting*. People think that having an interesting past makes up for every other deficiency of character and intellect and social position and fortune."

Susan Bright smiled at Harmon. Jack saw that. Jack also saw that his wife smiled back a sickly sweet smile as if the signal had been meant for her. Barbara was always doing things like that.

'Tis the song, the sigh of the weary;
Hard Times, Hard Times, come again no more,
Many days you have lingered around my cabin door;
Oh! Hard Times, come again no more.

Jack ordered another drink. Barbara's boa fell into that one, too. The fallen ash of Harmon's cigar ignited the pile of confetti on the table. Barbara calmly poured Jack's Rob Roy over the flames, which only served to ignite the tablecloth. After the waiter had put out the fire, Jack ordered another drink. Susan Bright sang more songs: "The White Dove," "My Kahlua Rose," and "If You Were the Only Girl in the World (And I Were the Only Boy)." She ended her set with "Love for Sale." Barbara murmured, "How vastly appropriate..."

At one o'clock the curtain was lowered.

"Can we go now?" asked Barbara. "Harmon, you're stinking already."

"Let's go back to my place," said Harmon, enunciating his syllables clearly but with obvious effort.

"No," said Barbara.

"I had some champagne—some *real* champagne—smuggled down from Montreal."

"For a little while," said Barbara. "Only a little while. Then Jack and I will tuck you into bed."

"No," said Harmon, getting up from his chair unsteadily, "Susan will do that."

CHAPTER TWO

"PERSONALLY," SIGHED JACK as he leaned against the wall next to the elevator, "I'd like to investigate the rumor that there's no place like home."

The elevator doors opened, and Barbara stepped neatly inside. "We must see that Harmon gets home safely," said Barbara, and smiled the coldest and politest of polite, cold smiles at Susan Bright as the young singer stepped in alongside her.

Barbara Beaumont had a way of looking at you without focusing her eyes, as if you weren't quite worth the trouble of setting the optical muscles into operation. "And besides," she went on, grabbing Harmon's coat sleeve and dragging him into the elevator, "some poor soul spent his entire New Year's Eve smuggling a case of champagne down from Montreal."

"Braving snow and blizzard and a stint in a federal penitentiary," said Jack, coming in last.

The elevator doors closed, and suddenly Jack was overwhelmed with a close atmosphere of wet fur, alcoholic breath, cigar smoke, and Barbara's sickly sweet perfume Miracle, probably called that, Jack surmised, because it was a miracle that no one in the elevator was asphyxiated.

"George," said Harmon, clapping a hand on the shoulder of the middle-aged black man in a too-tight red jacket who was operating the elevator, "this is Miss Bright."

"How de do?" said George politely, turning his head only enough that he could see her out of the corner of his eye.

"Hello," returned Susan Bright with a discomfort that made Barbara smile.

"George," Harmon went on, "you are to let Miss Bright up to my floor anytime she pleases. Do you understand?"

"Sure do, Mr. Dodge," said George. Miss Bright's discomfort increased dramatically, as did Barbara Beaumont's smile. "Here your floor, Mr. Dodge. And Happy New Year to you all."

"Thank you, George," said Jack, slipping a two-dollar bill into George's hand. George deserved the tip, in Jack's estimation. When Jack wasn't around, George guided Harmon from the front door of the apartment building to the elevator, slid him down tenderly to the floor of the gold cage, lifted him up again when the cage had reached the twenty-third floor, and saw him to the door of his bedroom.

Harmon Dodge owned one of the topmost floors of an apartment building on Park Avenue. A few years before, it would have been unattainable by a mere partner in a law firm, but hard times had come to the owners of fine apartments, and Harmon had accepted the place in lieu of payment for his handling of a particularly involved bankruptcy case. Actually, in lieu of payment for *Jack's* handling of the case.

The apartment consisted of a massive living room with views of the East River, a large dining room on the opposite side of the apartment, an adjoining kitchen and maid's room, a large bedroom overlooking Park Avenue, and a gentleman's study where the gentleman stockpiled smuggled liquor. There were windows all round, and at each corner of the apartment was a small tiled solarium containing the dead flowers of the previous occupants of the penthouse.

Barbara had procured Harmon a live-in maid, and had scoured the employment agencies for just the right combination of efficiency, appearance, and demeanor. The right combination, in Barbara's estimation, turned out to be a two-hundred-pound black woman with asthma who wouldn't do anything but dust and cook breakfast. Barbara's reasoning behind this unlikely choice (when so many qualified women were available and wanting the work) was that a two-hundred-pound black woman with asthma was just about the only female in all of New York whom Harmon would not try to wheedle into matrimony. As Audrey could cook breakfast, and dusted now and then, and even sometimes consented to iron his shirts, Harmon realized the intelligence of Barbara's choice.

Audrey, her wheezing visage sullen beneath a glinting crown of bob pins, shuffled out of her bedroom in a ratty red housecoat, and fetched three bottles of champagne on a silver tray. Then, setting out four champagne glasses from an ebony and glass cocktail cabinet (another spoil of bankruptcy), the maid shuffled off to bed, pausing only to remark to Susan, "Keep him away from the windows, miss, 'cause he do have a tendency to fall out..."

Susan Blight's lower lip dropped a little, as if it took her a moment to understand the implication of this injunction. "Does she expect me to stay the night?" Susan asked Barbara in a low, surprised voice.

Barbara Beaumont laughed gaily, a gay laugh that might have meant any number of things, such as *Don't bother to play the innocent with us, Miss Bright* or *Whose lower limb are you attempting to manipulate?* Jack, as he unwrapped the first bottle of champagne, thought Susan Bright's confusion looked very real. It wasn't, of course, he was sure of that, for Miss Bright didn't actually blush. Jack himself blushed at anything—at the very thought of blushing, in fact—and even now could feel the blood rushing up through his neck and into his face. So if Miss Bright weren't blushing, then she wasn't ingenuous, and it was quite apparent to Jack that she was merely as good an actress as she was a singer. Here was Harmon, slouched on the sofa with his head thrown over the back, not quite comatose yet but on his way, and here was Miss Bright next to him, doing her best to look uncomfortable, probably in hope that Jack and Barbara would get the hell out of there so that she could get Harmon into bed before he was quite unconscious. Yet it was a good act, for Susan really did look uncomfortable.

"Thank you," she said quietly as Jack handed her a glass of champagne.

"Harmon, sit up," said Barbara briskly. "You're making a spectacle of yourself, which is not new to us but which is evidently making your friend extremely uncomfortable as you invited her up here and she was probably under some absurd notion that you intended to remain conscious for a few minutes, at least until we could toast the New Year properly, that is, with real champagne."

"Happy New Year," said Harmon, raising his head slowly from the back of the sofa, and taking the glass of champagne from Jack.

"To prosperity," said Jack, raising his glass.

"To solvency," said Susan Bright, raising hers with a small gesture suggesting a sincere skepticism.

"And may the coming year," said Barbara as if she were already bored with the proceedings, "be not quite so boring as the last. If the whole country, and us especially, are to be so confoundedly miserable and poor, let us at least have a year that is not so unremittingly dreary."

They drank.

Susan Bright's eyes shifted round the room. "I'm not so certain," she remarked with a little hesitant deference, "that you should think of yourself as 'confoundedly miserable and poor.' There are a great many people in New York who couldn't afford this champagne, or this penthouse, or—"

"Or what?" said Barbara with her menacing smile.

"There are people who can't afford anything," interrupted Jack. It was too late in the evening for a fight, and he knew that his wife would fight to the death with anyone who denied her the luxury of feeling miserable and poor.

"I suppose," said Barbara with her tiger-lying-in-wait smile, "that you were of a prominent family crashed in 'twenty-nine."

Susan Bright blinked. "Yes," she said.

"The Brights of Boston," said Harmon, sitting forward with his empty glass held out for a refill.

"I'm sure you were as high then as you are low now," said Barbara sympathetically.

Susan Bright looked as if she did not know what to say. A gold digger she was, but Jack wasn't certain that she deserved this.

"Excuse me please," the singer said, getting up and leaving the living room.

"A little tact," said Jack gently to his wife.

"Me? Me?" cried his wife, taking the bottle of champagne from Jack's hands. "I'm the soul of tactfulness."

"I know your tact," said Harmon, getting up and going up to the window. He fumbled with the latch. "I've seen it chip the furniture." He pushed open the window and thrust his face into the frigid night air.

"Don't you dare fall out," said Barbara. "For then we'd have to take that woman home, and she dresses as if she lived on Staten Island."

"She's a very nice girl," said Harmon, turning back from the window. There was a hint of clearheadedness in his voice, though he was looking at the second champagne bottle as if it might be a convenient way to smooth out this emerging lump of sobriety. "And I don't know how many times I've gone to the Villa Vanity to hear her sing, and I don't know how many nights I've gone to her dressing room to ask her to have dinner with me, and I don't know what I've spent on flowers, and I certainly don't know why she finally agreed to go out with me tonight."

"Because you'd never invited me to meet your friends," said Susan Bright from the doorway.

"What has that to do with anything?" said Harmon in genuine curiosity, meeting Susan at the sofa.

"It means simply," said Barbara, "that if you invited Miss Bright here to meet your friends, then you thought she was a little more than a cheap nightclub pickup."

"Barbara!" cried Jack.

Barbara smiled and held out her glass for more champagne. Jack poured, but as he poured, he was watching Susan Bright to see how she would respond to this insult. A cheap nightclub pickup would break a bottle over Barbara's head. A woman of a middle-class upbringing would get up and telephone for a taxi. A lady of true gentility would have pitched Barbara out the open window.

"Barbara is exactly right," said Susan Bright with perfect dignity. "As I do consider myself somewhat better than a cheap nightclub pickup, I refused to go out with Harmon until he treated me accordingly."

Exactly right, thought Jack. If this singer could stand up to Barbara, then Harmon might be in for real trouble. She was very pretty when she leaned against a piano, and now she turned out to be clever as well. It was a potent and dangerous combination.

"Let's dance," said Harmon suddenly, keeling over in the direction of the Amrad radio. (The company had gone bankrupt the year before, and Harmon had come away with the Aria, the Serenata, and the Symphony models.

He'd kept the Serenata, put the Aria in Audrey's room, and had the Symphony delivered to George the elevator man's Harlem home.) But as the radio was twenty feet away, and Harmon's outstretched arm came nowhere near the dial, Jack got up and tried to find a station playing dance music.

"'NXQ," suggested Susan. "Ted Lewis is broadcasting live from Chez Firehouse tonight."

It was easy to find the station, as Ted Lewis's tonsilly tenor crooned "Dip Your Brush in Sunshine." Harmon got slowly to his feet, discreetly assisted by Susan Bright. He draped his arms over her shoulders, and the two moved slowly across the living room floor.

Jack watched Harmon and Susan for a few moments as he opened the second bottle of champagne. Then he watched Barbara watching them. He wondered what his wife was thinking. Harmon was, for better or worse, their best friend. It had always been the hope of Harmon's father and Barbara's father that Harmon and Barbara should marry. And Harmon and Barbara had known each other quite forever, and once had even been engaged. But they'd known each other too well and too long, and Barbara wasn't the sort to want something she could have and that was good for her at the same time, and had broken the engagement. This satisfied Harmon as well, for he had established at a young age his abiding passion for young women of a certain type utterly distant from Barbara. After the broken engagement, the two were the greatest friends possible, and attained a kind of jocular intimacy. Harmon had been best man at the wedding. At the reception he'd broken a hundred-year-old punchbowl. Jack, though, wondered what Barbara thought as she watched Harmon Dodge dancing with the nightclub chanteuse.

"A penny for your thoughts," he said, coming to refill her glass.

"I'm certain she dyes," said Barbara in a whisper. "No one's hair is truly that black."

Barbara sipped her champagne, watching Susan Bright over the rim of her glass. Jack perched himself on the arm of her chair and put his arm around his wife.

"Don't sit there," said Barbara. "When you perch like that, you invariably tip over and spill your drink, usually on me. Why don't you ask me to dance?"

"Because I always step on your feet," said Jack.

"Yes, but at least my dress is safe." She reached over and turned out the lamp on the table beside her. Now the room was lighted only by the soft glow of the lights in the open cocktail cabinet, by the yellow dial of the radio, by the cold waxing moon shining through the windows at the end of the room, and by the softly glowing lights of the East Side.

Barbara rose, took Jack's champagne glass and set it safely aside. Then she placed her head against his shoulder—for Jack was quite tall, and Barbara only of medium height—and Jack put his arms about her. Holding his breath against a too-strong infusion of Miracle perfume, he brushed his lips against her cheek. "New Year's," he whispered. "Truce?" Meaning, of course, not a truce between them, but between Barbara and Susan Bright.

Barbara considered this. "Till the champagne gives out," she conceded.

The couples danced slowly in the darkened living room. Ted Lewis crooned on, assisted by the Boswell Sisters and a surprise appearance (some time after four A.M.) by Ethel Waters. Every song somehow sounded sad. The two couples continued to dance, pour more champagne, look out of the windows, lean against the radio, pick the leaves from the dead plants in the solaria, and became more and more melancholy thinking of the year that lay ahead, and the dismal hope that was so meager and groundless that it was no hope at all, that things would get better and not worse. When Jack inadvertently knocked over the last bottle, Audrey made a psychic appearance with a fourth bottle, uncorked it, poured four more glasses, and then crept back to bed, preserving them all for another while.

"An invaluable woman," Harmon remarked to Jack and Barbara over Susan Bright's bare white shoulder, "and if she didn't have asthma, and weighed half as much, and weren't in love with George, then I would have probably married her by now." Then he pulled back and looked tenderly at Susan, who didn't have asthma, weighed just about half as much as Audrey, and almost certainly wasn't in love with the gentleman who drove the penthouse elevator.

"*Is everybody happy?*" Ted Lewis called out on the radio.

"No!" cried Jack and Barbara, Harmon and Susan.

And then the first sun of the new year rose bleakly over the East River, spilling orange light over their drawn faces.

CHAPTER THREE

"I WANT A MORNINGCAP," said Barbara with her face turned away from the rising, unflattering sun, "and then I want to go home. Jack, pour something sharp into a glass and don't tell me what it is, would you?"

Jack poured dark rum into a glass and handed it to his wife, who was looking intently at a wall. Not because the wall held any intrinsic interest for her, but if she pressed closely enough to it, no one could see how drawn and tired her face was. At this point in the proceedings, Jack thought he wouldn't mind staring at a wall for a few hours or so, until Everything and Everyone went away, or the Depression was cured, or something else equally improbable came to pass.

Harmon had genially passed out on the sofa, with his legs thrown across Susan's lap. Susan's head lolled on the back of the sofa, her eyes were gently closed, and she softly sang a song that Jack didn't know. She looked up only when Audrey came sleepily out of her bedroom and tossed a blanket over Harmon's head.

"Pardon me," said Audrey as she fumbled in Susan's lap to pull off Harmon's shoes.

Susan obligingly raised Harmon's feet, and asked, "Won't he suffocate with the blanket over his head?"

"Hasn't yet," replied Audrey, heading back for her room. "And Happy New Year, y'all."

"Happy New Year," returned Jack.

"Happy New Year," returned Susan.

"I'll have another morningcap," said Barbara, still staring at the wall, though she'd moved down to a new patch.

"Miss Bright?" asked Jack. Susan now sat with Harmon's unshod feet in her lap. The blanket over his head muffled his rhythmic snore.

"No thank you," said Susan. "I really should be getting home soon."

"Oh," said Barbara, turning suddenly away from the wall, but ducking immediately into a cool shadow. "Oh, please do let Jack drive you."

Jack turned, with Barbara's glass in one hand and the bottle of rum in the other.

"Ah, yes of course," he said uncertainly, not sure what Barbara wanted out of this.

"No, of course *not*," said Susan. "If you are half as tired as I am, you'll want to go directly home yourselves. I can easily call a taxi."

"No, no, we insist," said Barbara. "You live on Staten Island, don't you?"

"No," returned Susan with a crinkled brow. "What made you think that? I live on Seventy-first Street, near the Hudson."

"Oh yes," said Barbara in a tone that suggested she had heard of the river that bordered the unfashionable side of the island. "Yes, yes," she mused, "the Hudson is a very pretty river, I believe, and we were at a party once—

do you remember, Jack, though it was ever so long ago—at an apartment building on that side of the park. You could see the Hudson from the maid's room's terrace."

"Actually," said Jack, in deference to honesty, "you know the Hudson quite well, darling. Your father's house is on it."

"Oh yes," said Barbara with apparent delight at the discovery. "They would be the same river, wouldn't they? Having the same name and all. I just never connected them before. At my father's house," she explained to Susan, "the Hudson is quite grand, and you can sail along it for many miles and see nothing but one splendid estate after another. And here, of course, it is quite narrow and dirty, I believe, and it is certainly not anything special to live along it, so I never quite made the connection that *your* Hudson and *my* Hudson were at all the same thing."

"I understand how you might have made such a mistake," said Susan dryly. "The similarity of names— *Hudson* and *Hudson*—must have been very confusing. Still, there's no reason that you have to see me home."

"Oh, *I* won't," said Barbara, "but my husband most certainly will. Jack, call me a taxi, and then I want you to get Miss Bright directly home."

A look passed between Barbara and Jack, a look that said, *This is not* pro forma *politeness, Jack. Take the woman home.* This glance was not lost on Susan Bright, Jack saw, and she no longer protested. Perhaps she wants to know what's coming, thought Jack. Jack wanted to know too.

"Excuse me for a moment," said Susan, getting up carefully and arranging Harmon's feet on the couch. "And then I'll be ready to go." She disappeared down the little corridor that led to the bathroom.

"Tell me what this one's about," said Jack to his wife. "It's six A.M. on New Year's morning, and I don't have enough mind to figure it out myself. And why are you grinning?"

"I'm grinning, darling, because we just prevented that dreadful young woman from going to bed with Harmon, who obviously would have awakened this morning with a proposal of marriage on his lips, which, it is perfectly obvious, is exactly what that dreadful young woman wanted out of this night."

"That part I understand," said Jack, who was actually wondering whether he wanted a morningcap of rum, too, or whether he simply wanted to crawl under the blanket with his boss and go to sleep until 1943, when things would almost certainly be vastly different. "But why should I have to drive all the way cross town to take her home?"

"Because I want to make sure she *goes* home. If we simply left now, she'd drag Harmon into the bedroom, undress him, undress herself, crawl in beside him, and when he woke up, say, 'Darling, you were wonderful last night. And yes, yes, I will marry you, anytime you say.'"

"She doesn't seem *quite* that type," said Jack.

"She is," said Barbara definitively. "Here she is," Barbara whispered. "I hope she wasn't listening outside the door. She's that type, too."

"I'm ready," said Susan Bright, drawing her coat over her shoulders.

"It was an immense pleasure," said Barbara with gaping insincerity.

"I assure you," returned Susan, "that it was every bit as much a pleasure for me. I wonder if we'll be seeing any more of each other in this coming year. I shouldn't wonder if we were."

Barbara said nothing, but smiled her cold, polite smile, which even Jack had to admit was fairly ghastly in the light of dawn.

Susan pulled down the blanket just enough to uncover Harmon's brow and eyes. Holding her coat closed at the throat, she leaned down and kissed his forehead. His eyes fluttered open, struggled to focus, gave up the struggle, and closed again. Susan pulled the blanket back over his head.

Jack's Lincoln LeBaron roadster was parked around the corner. It was a powerful car with a twelve-cylinder engine and was capable of a hundred and fifty horsepower. It cost a great deal more than the annual salaries of most men in New York. Jack himself couldn't have afforded the thirty-five-hundred-dollar price tag, but the car was yet another bankruptcy spoil given the firm of Rhinelander, Rhinelander, and Dodge in payment for services rendered. And as Harmon Dodge already had four automobiles, this one came to Jack. Jack was not ashamed to take the gift, for he had done all the work on the case and felt it was his due. He was enormously proud of the machine, and even if he had had his choice, he would have picked the same viridian the body was painted and the same black leather upholstery. The only thing he would have had different were the tiny initials on the dashboard cubbyhole. Instead of RBW—whatever poor bankrupt that was, he would have put JAB—John Austin Beaumont. But such a small matter was hardly enough to damage the enjoyment he felt in the car—after all, the letters were very small and hardly likely to be noticed.

"Who is RBW?" asked Susan Bright as soon as he'd come round to the other side. "Isn't your name Beaumont?"

"The former owner of the car," said Jack, his enjoyment in the automobile damaged. He really would have preferred that this young woman, who was obviously impressed with money, since she was doing so much to snag Harmon, think that he had bought the car outright. But at least she could still think that he had paid for it, even if he'd purchased it second-hand.

The morning was cold, and a drizzle sometime during the night had left the sidewalks and streets slick with a thin layer of ice. The car was cold, and the automatic starter, which had originally added over a hundred dollars to the price of the automobile, wouldn't automatically start. Susan huddled in her coat, and blew on her hands to warm them. She did not make polite conversation, though Jack reflected that perhaps she had had enough of Beaumont politeness in her exchanges with Barbara. As he repeatedly pressed the starter, Jack glanced sidewise at Susan and hardened his heart against her black hair, her translucent skin, her coat that was really too thin and not proper protection against January cold in New York.

"Your lipstick is the color of calves liver," he remarked entirely without thinking. Or, rather, that was exactly what he was thinking, but he hadn't considered that it might be the wrong thing to say aloud.

"And your hair is the color of rotting hay," returned Susan with perfect equanimity. "And you have all the politeness of your beautiful and well-bred wife." She opened the door of the car and stepped smartly out. She headed for the green and black Terminal taxi that was parked ahead of Jack.

She had her hand on the back door of the taxi at the very moment the automatic starter caught and the powerful roadster engine burst into frantic life. Unfortunately, Jack had neglected to shift into neutral, and the car leapt forward four feet into the rear of the taxi, smashing both of the cab's rear lights and knocking Susan to the ground with the impact of the collision.

"Oh God, not this *this* morning," Jack groaned, and crawled out of his car.

"Very well then," said Susan, picking herself from the sidewalk, "if you don't want me to take a taxi, I will walk home."

"No!" cried Jack.

"Mister," said the taxi driver, getting slowly out from behind the wheel, "this is not my taxi. This is my brother's taxi. My brother gets out of prison tomorrow. Do you know why my brother was in prison? He got sent to prison for mauling a guy who rammed his taxi from behind.

Tried to stick the guy's head in his glove box. So just tell me, what's your address? My brother'll be coming in on the Elmira bus tomorrow. He'll want to meet you."

Susan waved ironically to Jack as she turned the corner. Evidently, she really did intend to walk home, even though the wind was high and sharp and her coat so thin.

Barbara emerged from the wide double doors of Harmon's building. "Can't you do anything right?" she asked.

"There was an accident," Jack tried to explain. Jack was actually thinking, *I wish I were wearing different clothes.* A boiled shirt with champagne stains, trousers that were too tight in the crotch, opera pumps not meant for negotiating icy streets, and an overcoat with a torn lining that kept bunching up beneath his armpit. It was barely dawn, he had just smashed up the back of a taxi owned by a convicted criminal, and his wife had found a perfectly admirable excuse to be bored with him for the rest of the week.

"You'd better go after her," Barbara sighed. "If you don't, she'll catch pneumonia, which will only make her more interesting. Harmon will propose at the side of her hospital bed."

"Hey," said the driver of the mutilated taxi.

"Hey yourself," said Barbara. "I'll take care of you. Go on, Jack, go pick up that girl."

Jack obediently climbed back into the roadster, backed up carefully, and turned out into the street. Just when he was almost free of the space, however, his tires skidded on a patch of ice. He fishtailed his right fender against the rear door of the taxi, crumpling the door and mangling the handle.

"My brother will *kill* you, your wife, *and* your damn girlfriend!" Jack heard the driver scream as he drove on. He did have complete confidence that Barbara would handle the man and his complaints.

Jack turned uptown on Sixth, and drove slowly, looking for Susan. He was also thinking about the damage that must have been done to his rear fender and the grille. The car had been a Christmas bonus, and already...

It wasn't hard to find Susan. On the very early morning of New Year's Day 1933 there were few people about. With her black coat wrapped tightly about her, she walked quickly along the west side of Sixth Avenue, going north, hugging the sides of buildings against the driving wind. Jack pressed the horn several times. Once she glanced around, but recognizing the automobile, she forged ahead even more quickly, and turned the corner onto Fifty-eighth Street.

Jack was determined not to lose her. Though the street signal clanged warningly, the metal finger about to change from Go to Stop, Jack did not hesitate to turn left across three lanes of the street—and luckily there was no traffic in the oncoming lanes. However, so sudden was the turn and so icy the street that the roadster skidded to the right and the back of the car bumped up over the curb. A lamppost embedded itself a couple of inches deep in the passenger door.

"Damn," said Jack, entirely giving over the modest mental calculation he had been making of the cost of repairs to the new automobile.

He pressed on the accelerator and tried to disengage himself from the lamppost, but that wouldn't do. Susan, who was doubtless laughing, moved farther on up the street toward Seventh Avenue. Jack threw the car into reverse, stepped on the accelerator, and spun back out into Sixth Avenue—though there now *was* traffic coming south—a large black Studebaker President, being carefully driven by a woman in a fur coat whose husband, in crushed top hat, was slumped on the front seat beside her. Jack was able to make out this much detail because the President smashed into the rear of his roadster, caught on the bumper, and shoved him halfway down Fifty-eighth Street. Jack finally succeeded in getting the car into forward again, and then he turned sharply left and slammed on the accelerator in an attempt to get free of the Studebaker. This, rather to his surprise, worked, and he spun onto Sixth Avenue with no more damage to the roadster than smashing one of its headlights (which hadn't been broken when he hit the taxi) against the side of a parked milk truck. Crashing the same red light at Fifty-eighth Street again, he turned a sharp left and sped on toward Seventh. He caught sight of Susan on the other side of the avenue, headed along Fifty-eighth Street toward Broadway. A quick glance to the right and left on Seventh showed no more than two taxis, a beer truck, and a chauffeured limousine in his path. He weaved the roadster across, his thumb on the horn, and continued along Fifty-eighth Street.

Finally he caught up with Susan, just before she was about to turn onto Broadway. He slowed the car, rolled down the right-hand window, leaned across the seat, and called to her.

"Miss Bright!"

She turned, as with dread.

"Please go away," she said.

"Let me drive you home," said Jack politely.

"In that? Let me point out, Mr. Beaumont, that you are driving the wrong way on a one-way street. Even-numbered streets go east."

She then turned north on Broadway.

Jack hurriedly turned the corner, just as a Terminal taxi took the same corner toward him. The taxi blew its horn, and Jack frantically blew his. Much to Jack's satisfaction, there was no collision and no further damage to his roadster from the Terminal taxi. Right behind that vehicle there was a Yellow Cab, and the Yellow Cab blind-plowed into the back of Jack's roadster. Jack heard two of his tires explode, and he felt the wheel lock in his hands. The car jumped the Broadway curb and made a quasi-hop through the air.

Through the windshield Jack caught sight of Susan Bright directly in front of his roadster. Her face bore an expression that said quite clearly, *I might have known...* Jack pulled the hand brake, but even before Jack's brain had had the leisure to remember that brakes don't take against the air, Susan's face had disappeared beneath the nose of the roadster, and the roadster itself had crashed into the facade of an insurance building.

CHAPTER FOUR

"ARE YOU ALL RIGHT?" Jack called breathily as he attempted to peer over the top of the steering wheel. He couldn't get up because the impact of the crash had jammed the steering wheel quite deeply against his stomach.

"I am most certainly not all right," said Susan Bright, slowly rising from a crouch in front of the car. She had taken refuge in a small recessed doorway in the facade of the insurance building. That refuge had saved her life. The car had smashed on either side of the narrow recess, and she was pinned there now. "Back up, would you please, Mr. Beaumont?" she said in a voice of half growing anger and half fading terror.

"If I could, I would," said Jack as he carefully picked a shard of windshield glass from his neck. "But I'm afraid I can't move. This wheel's embedded in my stomach. Also," he said after a moment, "the door won't open. Perhaps," he

35

suggested, "since I don't seem to be able to help you, you should climb over the hood."

"The hood is covered with broken glass," Susan returned. "And besides, it's smoking. Is this one of those automobiles that blows up?" she asked in a tone of voice suggesting that she wouldn't be surprised to hear that it was.

"I don't know," said Jack. "That's one of the things they don't tell you when you get a car from a bankrupt. Why don't you just open the door and go inside the building, and that way you'll be out of danger if there's an explosion."

"It's locked," she said after a moment's experimentation. Jack wasn't surprised to hear it. It was, all things considered, that sort of morning—and it was only New Year's Day.

"Are you stuck?" asked a little boy on the sidewalk, peering up at Jack.

"In a manner of speaking," Jack returned. "Would you mind going for help?"

"To my ma?" asked the little boy. "My ma don't know nothing about cars."

"Not to your mother," said Jack. "To the police."

"Ma says for me to leave the police alone."

"In other circumstances," said Jack, "I'd agree with your mother, but these are special circumstances."

The little boy hesitated.

"If I could reach into my pocket, I'd give you a dollar," said Jack, "but I can't move. Miss Bright, do you have a dollar for this little boy?"

Four quarters flew over the smoking hood of the car. The little boy gathered them up and ran off. Jack had no great confidence that the police would come before he either froze, perished from some as yet undetected internal injury, or burned to death in a gasoline blaze (if the automobile turned out to be of the sort that exploded).

"I really am very sorry about this inconvenience," he called out to Susan, who leaned against the locked door of the insurance building with her arms crossed over her breast, both for warmth and to indicate a certain general displeasure with the progress of 1933.

"I really don't believe you are," Susan called back testily. "I really do believe that you and your wife would do just about anything to keep me away from Mr. Dodge. Including trying to crush me against the side of a building with your automobile."

"That's nonsense," said Jack, picking out a large shard of glass that looked as if it were going to come loose from the windshield soon anyway.

"Is it?" said a young woman in a green coat, who had appeared out of nowhere at the side of the wrecked car. "Is it?" she asked again with a wary eye on Jack. "I have seen accidents, in the country and in the city, and this don't look like any accident I have ever seen."

"Nevertheless," Jack said to the woman in green, "it is an accident. I was only attempting to take this young lady home."

"He said," called Susan from the recessed doorway, "that if I saw his friend again, he'd have me killed for good."

"I thought it was something like that," said the young woman in the green coat. "It always is. Are you all right in there?"

"Yes, she's all right," said Jack. "She's perfectly fine, and *no one* tried to kill her. I, on the other hand, have this steering wheel stuck in my stomach, and I am *not* fine. And, Miss Bright, if and when the police arrive, I would appreciate your not trying to maintain that this was a murder attempt."

"If I had a gun," said the young woman in the green coat to Jack, "I'd shoot you right here and now."

"If I had a gun," Susan said, "I'd give it to you."

A small crowd gathered—a few well-dressed drunken revelers on their way to home and hangovers, a few delivery men, a few children whose parents were home abed, a few men and women lucky enough to have work but not lucky enough to have a holiday, a few indigents on their way from one cold stoop to another. The crowd seemed sympathetic to Susan's plight, and indifferent to Jack's. Those who did not look on this accident as an attempted murder were inclined to look on it as a failed seduction. Jack's only ally was a particularly drunken man in a broken top hat who kept calling out, "Marry the girl, and then she'll do whatever you want." Eventually, the police arrived, and tossed the drunken man's cape over the hood of the car to Susan. She wrapped it around her tightly, and thanked the policeman. Soon a truck from a garage arrived. A chain was attached to the already smashed bumper of Jack's car, which was pulled free from the facade of the insurance building.

Four policemen instantly supported Susan away from the recessed doorway, and ignored Jack's cries. When the automobile was pulled free of the building, the front portion of the car dropped heavily to the ground, and the steering wheel jammed even more tightly into Jack's abdomen.

Jack felt one of his ribs crack.

"Ohh—" he started to groan.

Then another one went as well.

"So tell me exactly what you said to her," said Barbara impatiently.

"Said to whom?" moaned Jack. Formerly no bed had been long enough for Jack's legs. Now no bed could be too soft for his ribs. Bandages were wrapped tightly around his chest. He felt he had to struggle for every breath. Beneath his neck was what could be described only as a wide, tender bruise. It was the only thing he wanted to think about.

"To *her*," sighed Barbara. "To that chanteuse. To *Susan...*"

Jack remembered Susan—with no particular fondness. She only made him think of his two broken ribs, the circle of pain that used to be his chest, and oh yes, his viridian roadster. Perhaps his ribs would repair themselves. His automobile wouldn't. "Call Harmon," Jack pleaded.

"Harmon?" echoed Barbara, pacing with a cigarette whose smoke—Jack predicted—was going to make it even more difficult for him to breathe. "Harmon won't say anything about the girl. Pardon me, the *chit*. Harmon knows what I feel about *that sort*."

"No," whispered Jack, deciding that in his life up to this point he had been entirely profligate with his breath. Surely he could get along just as well on only half as many in-and exhalations. "Have him send over some of his good brandy."

"I *hate* brandy!" Barbara fumed. "And what has brandy to do with what you said to that girl?"

"The brandy is for me," said Jack weakly. "It might help to ease the pain."

Barbara looked at Jack as if he were mad. "Pain? You feel pain? Didn't you see the doctor?" Then, knowing very well that Jack *had* seen the doctor, and that his pain must therefore be quite imaginary, Barbara returned to the matter at hand: Susan Bright, and what Jack had said to her. "You were there for over an hour, you said, so you must have had plenty of opportunity to talk to her. You warned her away from Harmon, I hope. You made it very clear that nothing was to come of this infatuation of his, I trust. May I assume that you had the good sense to threaten her a little?"

Jack looked at Barbara for a moment, and then replied, "Yes, I think I can say that Susan felt a little threatened. She was particularly afraid that the car would explode."

"Lincoln LeBarons never explode," retorted Barbara. "Every schoolgirl knows that. I can imagine the entire situation now. You had that girl where you wanted her—

trapped in the entrance of that building—and you might have applied any amount of pressure. But the fact is— Jack, I do know this as if I had been there—she wrapped you around her little finger. I should have handled this." Barbara dropped her cigarette in the ashtray on the bedside table, and then stalked out of the room.

"I wish you had," said Jack sincerely. He spent the next few minutes trying to find a way to reach Barbara's burning cigarette without jarring any portion of his upper body. It proved not to be possible. Finally he gave up, simply reached for the cigarette, stretching every one of the three-hundred-odd muscles that were involved in that mighty piece of work that was the bruise that used to be his chest, screamed a mighty scream, and stabbed out the cigarette with his bare thumb.

Jack was in no condition to return to work. Because Jack did not go to work, Harmon Dodge saw no reason to go to work. As he explained amiably to Jack, sitting on the edge of Jack's bed, and bouncing up and down in a way that made Jack's ribs prod their serrated edges against his lungs, "If a client came in and saw me there, he might ask my advice, and what the hell do I know about bankruptcies?"

"I hope you're not seeing that girl," said Jack dutifully. Barbara had told Jack several dozen times that he was to quiz Harmon *unmercifully*. Jack felt that he had recently attained new understanding of the adverb.

"What girl?" returned Harmon amiably. Then he considered for a moment. "Oh yes, the redhead from the Purple Porcupine Tea Shop. No, certainly not. Haven't seen her for ages. She went back to her boyfriend in Philadelphia. The boyfriend promised to marry her mother, or some such thing. Very romantic, and I was very happy for her."

"No," said Jack suspiciously, "not the girl from the Purple Porcupine, but the girl from Villa Vanity. Susan Bright."

Harmon grinned and smote Jack familiarly on the shoulder. Jack felt as if his internal organs had just undergone some sort of improbable and dangerous rearrangement. "You've had more to do with that one than I, Jackie my boy, Jackie my gentleman. I wasn't the one who put her in certain danger of death just so that I could rescue her. No, Jackie my gentle gentleman, it wasn't I."

"Then you haven't seen her?" Jack persisted, and surreptitiously stuck a finger into his pajamas to see if his bandages were becoming soaked with blood.

"The Villa Vanity is closed," said Harmon.

That wasn't quite the answer that would have satisfied Barbara.

"So you haven't heard her sing," said Jack. "But perhaps you've seen her elsewhere?"

Harmon smiled. "When this damned Depression is over, we're going into criminal law. You'll beat those witnesses down, Jackie, won't you Jock?" Harmon bounced up from the bed, putting Jack's organs into their proper place. Then he wagged a finger at the groaning Jack. "Tell Barbara not to worry about me, Jockie Jack, for I'll be seeing no more of Miss Bright. Miss Bright will cease to exist for me. Miss Bright, I have learned, has vacated her establishment on the Hudson, and it will know her no more. *I* will know her no more. Can I be plainer?"

"No," said Jack, and thought, *Even Barbara would be satisfied with this.* Harmon Dodge didn't think lying worth his trouble. If he said Miss Bright existed for him no more, then there wasn't anything else to it—she didn't exist.

"Well," said Barbara when she returned to the apartment that evening, "something was done right for a change."

"Please don't light a cigarette," said Jack. "And please don't jump up and down on the side of the bed."

"I had no intention of doing either," said Barbara, rolling her head on her neck in a way that made the bones crack loudly enough to be heard across the room.

"And don't make your neck crack like that," said Jack. "It brings back painful memories."

"You're a perfectly wretched invalid," said Barbara.

"As a nurse..." Jack began, but then didn't finish. The best thing that could be said about Barbara Beaumont as a nurse was the best that could be said about certain doctors—they stayed away.

"I've no aptitude for nursing," Barbara conceded. "I'm a Christian Scientist at heart, I suppose. I don't really believe in illness."

"Except when it's your own," said Jack.

"Well, of course I believe in it *then*," she returned, "for I can feel it. Can't I?" She lit a cigarette and studied Jack for a few moments. "You're no good here," she said at last.

"No," he agreed with all the heartiness that a dozen yards of bandages would allow.

"It's quite dreadful sleeping with you," she went on. "That smell of camphor and mending bones never leaves the bed."

"What do mending bones smell like?"

"A little like rancid butter," Barbara replied with an air that suggested she'd thought about an appropriate comparison for some time. "And this apartment really is a little too small for two persons at the best of times, but when one of them is claiming to be ill—"

"Barbara, I broke two ribs—"

"—it is *entirely* too small, and therefore I've decided that we should spend a few weeks in the country with Father."

Jack didn't say anything. Usually when Barbara spent this much time working up to a proposal of some course of action, the idea was harebrained. Jack tended to object to it as a matter of course. But this one sounded pleasant. Jack liked Barbara's father. Jack liked the country, and he liked Barbara's father's mansion. Jack disliked their short, hard bed in New York, and he liked the long, soft bed in their bedroom at the Cliffs. Jack disliked the way that windows rattled in the January wind in New York, and he *hated* the blasting dry heat of New York radiators. He liked the coziness of country winters and the crackling heat of enormous stone fireplaces.

"Harmon will be there," said Barbara, rather as if Jack had objected to yet another of her odious schemes. Harmon had the Dodge mansion, which was called the Quarry, and was situated only a few hundred yards downriver from the Cliffs. "The office will be closed for a few weeks, and we'll all be jolly and cozy, and Daddy will ask why we haven't any children, and you'll make up some excuse the way you always do."

Jack didn't know why he and Barbara didn't have children. It wasn't a bad idea, though as far as the possible offspring were concerned, Jack as a father was probably a slightly more pleasant proposition than Barbara as a mother.

"Yes," said Jack, "that would probably be a very good idea."

CHAPTER FIVE

MARCELLUS RHINELANDER sent the touring car down to New York to fetch his daughter and Jack back to the Cliffs. The Rhinelander driver was a thin, middle-aged man named Richard Grace who was a Communist. Rhinelander kept Grace on, not despite his political beliefs, but precisely because of them. It delighted the old man to throw his capitalistic wealth into Grace's face at every turn. Grace kept the job because he took a kind of grim pleasure in seeing at first hand what terrible ravages unearned wealth made on the character and the social system, and also because the pay was very good. Richard Grace had a wife named Grace, who was cook to Marcellus Rhinelander and had no political beliefs whatever.

Grace (the driver, not the cook) disliked Barbara on account of her being Barbara, and disliked Jack on account of his being yet another of the privileged classes who would be swept away in the coming Socialist revolution.

Grace saw it his duty, in the time before the revolution, to make Jack's life as miserable as possible. This was accomplished amply in the drive from New York to Albany. Grace, who was a very good chauffeur, did not now drive like one, but bumped into every hole, took every possible detour over gravel, made unnecessary and very sudden stops, and accelerated afterward so quickly that Jack yearned for a nation of entirely public transportation.

The trip took seven hours. Jack sweated in a cocoon of four lap blankets, which did nothing to alleviate the suffering of the bumps and batterings. Barbara lounged in the opposite corner, alternately smoking cigarettes (which filled the closed compartment with smoke) and yelling at Grace (who couldn't hear her through the glass partition anyway).

"Are you certain it was only two broken ribs?" Marcellus Rhinelander asked Jack as he staggered up the low steps to the front of the mansion. "You look rather worse. Barbara, are you two children keeping something from me? Some wasting disease, perhaps?" Marcellus Rhinelander was hale and sixty, red in the face, white in the hair, and a vivid blue in the eye.

"I'll be all right," Jack tried to whisper in a seizure of racking cough that was one part cigarette smoke and one part a blast of frigid air that suddenly blew up off the frozen Hudson River especially for him.

"Grace," Jack's father-in-law said with a smile of suppressed glee, "just after you left, you had a visitor here. One of your Communist friends claiming to be your brother. I told him you'd died trying to put together an anarchist bomb."

Grace glowered at his employer. "If I put together a bomb," he said darkly, "*I* won't be the one to die."

"*And*," said Rhinelander with a relish less well disguised, "I took the liberty of telephoning your friend's description to the Federal Bureau of Investigation." Marcellus turned on his heel and roundly thumped Jack on the back with the length of his ebony cane. "That'll show the scarlet scoundrels!"

The Cliffs was a large neo-colonial mansion built in 1893. It had more rooms than any proper colonial mansion, and those rooms had larger dimensions, and higher ceilings, and quainter wallpaper than the originals. The house had a splendid view, from most rooms, of the Hudson—and, on the other side of the Hudson, of half a dozen more neo-colonial mansions. (In this, the reaches of the Hudson just south of Albany were rather like Park Avenue.) The Cliffs got its name not from a promontory over the river, but from an escarpment pitched high above a slate quarry to the south. Jack and Barbara were installed in a suite at the opposite end of the second floor from Marcellus Rhinelander's rooms. The old man played the piano loudly at night with more enthusiasm than precision. As he played, he drunkenly sang tenor arias from the worst of Verdi's operas. To Jack's knowledge, no one had ever mentioned this peculiarity in Marcellus Rhinelander. For all he knew, it might not be the old man at all, but the ghost of an Indian tenor who had been buried on ground the house now occupied.

Outside the windows, the limbs of the trees were slickly black and sheeted with ice. It was a hard winter. Inside, one of the servants had built a fire in Jack's bedroom, and Jack, thinking that nothing could be worse than an ebony cane across his back, pushed one of a pair of green velvet Recamiers before the blaze. The Recamier, Jack discovered, was like a chaise longue with all the comfort taken out of it and replaced with angles that had nothing to do with the human body. Jack wrapped himself in a red velvet smoking jacket and reflected that a layer of velvet over bandages made a very fine cushion indeed, better than half a dozen thick woolen lap robes. Grace Grace brought Jack tea and threw another log onto the fire. She said it was a pleasure to see him and ventured the opinion that perhaps it wasn't going to be such a dull winter after all.

As if on cue, they heard the noise of a fast car pulling up with a sudden stop on the icy gravel directly beneath the windows of the bedroom.

Grace, who was fat and wore a red star on her black uniform to show her husband's sympathy with the Russian workers, went to the window and looked out.

"No!" she cried happily. "Not a dull winter at all. For here's Mr. Harmon and his new wife!"

Jack, fearing and expecting the worst, hopped up from the Recamier and leapt to the window beside Grace Grace. A few seconds before this would have seemed an impossible action. He looked down.

As he was sauntering around the car, Harmon looked up, saw Jack's face in the window, and waved. Jack did not wave back. Harmon opened the door of the snappy yellow roadster. Susan Bright stepped out.

Not Susan Bright, of course.

Susan Dodge.

"Find Barbara," cried Jack, pushing Grace away from the window. Or, rather, putting his arms against her shoulders and making a pushing motion. Grace's bulk and Jack's weakened musculature didn't accomplish much in the way of propulsion. "Tell her to come here and speak to me. For God's sake, don't let her go downstairs before she's spoken to me. Hurry!"

Grace hurried out in search of Barbara.

Barbara was on the staircase landing with the large oval window overlooking the gravel driveway. Jack knew this because of her scream. It was loud, long, and echoing. Before the last echoes had died away, bounding off the walls of the hallways of the first and second floors of the mansion, Barbara had collided with Grace on the way to Jack's suite.

"He told me that Miss Bright no longer existed for him," Jack pleaded.

"Of course Miss Bright no longer existed for him!" Barbara screeched. "He married her! And Miss Bright turned into Mrs. Dodge! This unfortunate union is *your* doing. We owe it to Harmon to see that it's annulled. This will *kill* Father. Father loves Harmon. Father wanted me to marry Harmon. When I married you, it nearly killed Father. When he sees *who* and *what* Harmon married, he'll die for sure."

Barbara flounced out and left Jack to figure out just how much and what part of her last speech had been exaggeration.

Jack oiled and brushed his hair and put on a proper shirt and jacket as introductions were made downstairs. Marcellus Rhinelander already knew of the marriage, it turned out, and had himself invited Harmon and his new wife over. Downstairs, with low frosted windows over-looking the icy brown lawn and the river, was a parlor furnished with chairs and sofas that were deeply cush-ioned and covered with chintz. They were as soft and plush and cold as the interior of an expensive coffin. Here sat Harmon and Susan Dodge on either ends of a small sofa. There sat Barbara across from them, looking both bored and scandalized. Rhinelander at a side table poured real liquor into old cut-glass tumblers.

Jack looked at Susan Bright first, just to make sure it was Susan Bright. It was. Or wasn't. It was Susan Dodge.

He looked at Harmon. Harmon smiled a smile that said *I didn't lie, did I now? And knowing Barbara as we both do, do you blame me, Jackie my boy, for telling the truth in so underhanded a fashion?* Jack didn't blame Harmon. Jack would probably have done the same. But it didn't make life with Barbara any easier.

He looked at Barbara. Barbara frowned at him, then smiled, and the smile was worse than the frown. The smile said, *Whatever happens, I blame you.*

"Jack," said Marcellus, bringing him a tumbler of brandy. Jack knew it was real brandy by the way it sloshed against the clear side of the glass. "You've already met Susan, I understand."

"I wish you happiness," said Jack with a politeness studied and cold, and he raised his glass in a gesture that he hoped was distant and ironical. This was all to appease Barbara, of course. He didn't feel particularly studied, cold, distant, or ironical when he looked at Susan Dodge. He rather pitied her. He could imagine that being married to Harmon Dodge was, in its way, rather like being married to Barbara Rhinelander, though different in details.

"I congratulate you," he said with a little smile of cold mischief to Harmon. The cold mischief was for Barbara, too. Actually, Jack did feel like congratulating Harmon. Possibly Susan could make him happy. She looked like the sort.

"I was just telling Susan that though I'd never met her, I found her face familiar," Marcellus went on. He moved very close to Susan and peered at her.

"I wouldn't be surprised, Father, if her face were familiar," said Barbara in her bland, dangerous voice. "Susan was an entertainer on the variety stage."

"Harmon did say you'd studied music," said Barbara's father in the same tone of voice he might remark to an ax murderer, *I'd heard you'd been employed by a slaughterhouse.*

"Yes," said Barbara, smiling a brilliantly bland, dangerous smile at Susan, "she was known as *Sue Sudan and Her Educated Sheepdogs.*"

Jack choked on his brandy. Marcellus's eyes widened. Susan Dodge sat very still in the corner of the sofa. Her husband smiled a smile that might mean almost anything. "I played Albany only once," Susan said at last.

"Did they wear little outfits?" Barbara persisted. "I've always longed to see a sheepdog *en costume.*"

"They had costumes," said Susan. "Yes."

"Did you sew them yourself?" asked Barbara in that voice of patronizing interest that royalty employs when addressing the lower classes.

"Yes," said Susan.

Barbara leaned forward in her chair as if this were quite the most enthralling thing she'd ever heard in her life. "Perhaps—" Then she paused dramatically. "Perhaps you have some photographs of this most interesting period of your life."

"Not with me," said Susan darkly.

Jack looked at Harmon, who was smiling contentedly and actually seemed to enjoy this sparring. Perhaps sparring was the wrong word, for it was Barbara who delivered all the blows, while Susan only parried and flinched.

Jack looked at his father-in-law, who was staring at Susan as if wondering now what to make of her. Marcellus Rhinelander knew how to handle Communists, Socialists, and anarchists. A former variety artiste appearing now as the wife of his junior partner was an unknown animal.

Grace Grace appeared in the doorway with a bottle of champagne on a silver tray. Jack felt a wave of nausea build beneath his bandages—the fact that nausea had never before manifested itself in the region of his lungs made no difference whatever in its effect. The bottle of champagne reminded Jack of New Year's morning, when he'd first met Susan Bright, and of what happened afterward. Perhaps his internal organs sensed some rope of circumstances that led directly from the bottles of champagne consumed in Harmon's penthouse to the bandages that now constricted them. He felt sick to his stomach.

But he resisted the urge to bolt toward the bathroom when Marcellus Rhinelander popped the champagne cork, and it was with a sickly smile that Jack toasted the bride and groom. He felt a little better when it became apparent that Barbara had finished her bored little tirade against Susan. (And where had she picked up that information about *Sue Sudan and Her Educated Sheepdogs*? Jack had never heard about *that* before.) Perhaps after the champagne, Harmon and Susan would simply drive back to the Quarry, and Barbara would corner her father and tell him five hundred stories about Harmon's new wife, and Jack could return to the velvet jacket, the Recamier, and the fire in the bedroom hearth.

It was not to be.

Barbara invited Harmon and Susan to dinner, and Harmon blithely accepted.

Susan's countenance didn't sink. It brightened. "Oh, good," she said, "that will give us time to renew our old acquaintance."

"Old acquaintance?" echoed Barbara. "We've met only once. At Harmon's. When he was so drunk. Of course, Harmon is always drunk, isn't he? I'd be surprised if he wasn't drunk at the wedding ceremony."

Barbara implied that this was the only state in which Susan might have managed to persuade Harmon to the altar.

"Oh no," said Susan, "that night I met you, I said to myself, 'Barbara's face is very familiar.' And I thought and thought, and finally I realized that we'd known each other in college."

"You went to Radcliffe?" asked Marcellus Rhinelander, startling pleasantly.

"Yes, of course," said Susan with becoming modesty, "as did my mother."

"I did not know you," said Barbara, frowning. "I know I did not know you."

"It was the most droll and amusing thing, really," said Susan, lapsing into a manner of speech that was, Jack had to admit, a droll and amusing parody of his wife's voice. "Did you ever know," said Susan to Jack, "that your wife had been arrested?"

Barbara gasped. Jack spilled champagne down the front of his boiled shirt. Marcellus Rhinelander glanced at his daughter and then wandered back over to the sideboard.

"Arrested for what?" Harmon demanded with a grin.

"Nothing!" cried Barbara. "It was nothing! A college prank!"

"It was assault and battery," said Susan with a gay laugh. "This was when? Oh 'twenty-six or 'twenty-seven— and there was the first talk of repealing Prohibition. And the bishop of Boston—the Episcopal bishop, I mean, of course—had just come out with a stirring statement in favor of sobriety and against repeal. Upset all his parishioners greatly, I can tell you."

Barbara got up and walked over to Jack, holding her glass out to be refilled. "Shut her up," she said quietly.

"You deserve this one," Jack said as he poured his wife's champagne, and then passed on to Harmon, who listened with unqualified delight.

"Get to the assault and battery part," he urged. "Marcellus, did you know Barbara had been arrested in Boston?"

"No," said Marcellus, "I did not."

"Thank you," said Susan as Jack refilled her glass. "*So*," Susan went on with her story, and with her aping of Barbara's mannerisms, "on Easter morning, Barbara and one of her chums—Jean Schmidlapp, I believe it was, wasn't it, Barbara?"

Barbara nodded dourly.

"Barbara and Jean hid in the shrubbery outside the church, and when the service was over, and the bishop of Boston came out with the vice-president, who happened to be in town that week, Barbara and Jean pelted them both with champagne corks."

"Champagne corks?" echoed Jack.

"*Hundreds* of them," said Susan. "Such a gay escapade!" She laughed gaily again. "But, of course, as it was the bishop of Boston and the vice-president of the United States who were attacked, Barbara and Jean were bundled away to the police station."

"How did we know it was the vice-president? Nobody knew what he looked like."

"But how were you involved in all this?" Harmon asked his wife.

"Oh," said Susan as if she'd forgotten this one small detail, "the bishop of Boston was my uncle, and the vice-president was staying with us at the time."

Barbara stared. "You *are* a Boston Bright."

"If you knew I was Sue Sudan, you ought to have known that," returned Susan amiably. "*Well,* I recognized Barbara and Jean right off, though I must say that they were both wearing the *most* unbecoming frocks, left over from the night before, I imagine, and in none the best condition from their having hidden themselves in the shrubbery for an hour or so, but at any rate, having recognized them, I pleaded their case to my uncle and the vice-president, and then my mother provided bail, and my uncle on my mother's side, who's a judge on the Massachusetts Supreme Court, saw to it that the charges were dismissed. So you see," said Susan, turning a bright smile on the dumbstruck Barbara, "if it hadn't been for me, you would have gone to trial for assaulting the second-highest leader in the country—and almost certainly would have been thrown out of Radcliffe."

"I didn't know any of this," said Barbara, shifting uncomfortably in her chair. "I didn't know anything except that we were let go."

"Oh, it wasn't at all important," said Susan with the blandest of bland, dangerous smiles for Barbara. "So long as you learned your lesson: not to attack indiscriminately."

CHAPTER SIX

"WHY DID YOU marry her?" Marcellus Rhinelander bluntly asked Harmon Dodge when the gentlemen had adjourned to the study after a dinner of embalmed chicken and pineapple surprise. He poured brandies for Harmon and Jack, and passed around a cigar case.

"Perfectly obvious," said Harmon. His words were clear, but when he was drunk, Jack knew, he never spoke in complete sentences. "Obvious why I married her. Question is. Why she married me." Harmon fumbled with his cigar cutter and nearly amputated the last joint of the finger on which he now wore a simple gold band.

"Oh ho ho," laughed Marcellus without mirth, "Mrs. Susan Bright Dodge doesn't much look as if rayon stockings and a third-floor back much appealed to her. She'd much rather be in the orchid class and have three or four addresses, I'm sure."

"Thought you. Liked her. Very polite and all that. Seemed as if you. Dinner tonight, I mean. Liked her very much."

"I did," returned Marcellus easily. "I admire beautiful young women exceedingly. It is very easy to be pleasant to them. But I tend to agree with Barbara's judgment—she's a counter jumper. She's the kind of girl you meet in the linen department."

"She *is* a Boston Bright," Jack pointed out.

"Ah, but they crashed very hard. Such falls crack the finish. Then that sort of girl becomes worse than the ones that were born to be behind the counter."

Jack thought that his father-in-law's patronistic opinions had rather hardened since he'd employed the Communist chauffeur.

"Certainly put. The Indian sign. On me," said Harmon with some degree of effort. "And believe me," he added with a lurid grin, "it's not so worse."

Jack didn't like that lurid grin. Even if a man's wife was a gold digger, she didn't deserve to be talked about in that way, in a study filled with drunken men and tobacco smoke.

The doors of the study were flung open, and Barbara marched in. For this little impromptu supper Barbara had worn a full-length Chinese-yellow gown of crushed velvet with extra-long sleeves gathered at the cuff. In the point of accompanying jewelry, Barbara looked as if she'd just made a jump through one of Tiffany's shop windows. Susan's extremely tailored gray silk frock with pointed shoulders and narrow sleeves made her look slim to the point of fragility. Even in the flattering dining room candlelight, Barbara had looked as fragile as a man-of-war. If Barbara had been attempting to upstage Susan, she was as successful as she had been in revealing Susan's history with educated sheepdogs.

"Susan thinks it time she and Harmon were getting home," Barbara announced. "Susan reminds us that she and Harmon are only this afternoon returned from Niagara Falls. Isn't that a charming conceit? A honeymoon in Niagara Falls? I thought only shopgirls did that. Harmon, you and Susan must have had a splendid, riotous time pretending to be a Brooklyn shopgirl and her brand-new twenty-dollar-a-week husband. Were the Falls truly splendid, Harmon, or did Susan's beauty blind you to all else?"

"Blinded me. All else."

"Harmon," said Susan quietly. "Shall we go?"

"No," said Harmon, holding out his brandy glass for a refill. Marcellus was already there with the decanter.

Susan sat down on a chair near the door. She refused a brandy.

Barbara flounced around the room.

Harmon looked at his new wife over the rim of his glass. "No," he said with a repetition of the lurid grin, "let's go. I'm tired. I want to go to bed."

Susan stood immediately.

"*Don't* rush off," said Barbara expansively.

"Must," said Harmon, staggering toward the door.

"Don't drive," said Jack quietly to Harmon. "You're in no condition."

"No," agreed Susan as Harmon slipped on the edge of the rug and pitched forward into his wife's arms, "you're not."

"Am," said Harmon.

Barbara laughed gaily. "Same old Harmon. Marriage hasn't changed you a bit. Still getting drunk every night and falling into the nearest pair of arms."

"Susan," said Marcellus, "you'll drive, won't you?"

"I never learned how," said Susan, trying to prop her husband against the door lintel.

"Couldn't afford lessons, I suppose," said Barbara sympathetically, "or an auto to take them in. Oh, the exigencies of poverty! How they depress me!"

"Actually, we had five autos and two chauffeurs," said Susan, pulling Harmon's handkerchief from his pocket and wiping a drool of expensive brandy from his chin. "It's just that my mother felt that driving was a vulgar occupation for a lady." She smiled sympathetically at Barbara. "Harmon says that you were wrecking cars before he was."

"Jack," said Barbara, "take them home please. Susan looks very tired. Around the eyes, particularly. In fact," she added to Susan in a confidential tone that Grace could hear in the kitchen through three rooms and two closed doors, "your entire body seems in the last stages of droop."

"It has been a trying evening," Susan admitted. "Something seems to have gotten to my head tonight. Either that foul, damp wind off the river or else that perfume you're wearing tonight. It's Miracle, isn't it? Winnie Ruth Judd the ax-murderess wore it to the electric chair, and I'm told it positively *steamed* off her head when they pulled the switch. And yes, Jack, I'd be much obliged if you'd drive Harmon and me home."

Jack glanced warily at his wife to see if she was about to load another bronze-jacketed insult into that gun she called a mouth. But Barbara was silent and only gave a little nod, which was Jack's permission to drag Harmon Dodge out into the frigid night air.

The frigid night air acted as a very large fist to Harmon Dodge's gut, and an indistinguishable mass of brandy, pineapple surprise, embalmed chicken, and champagne churned up over his tie, the gravel of the driveway, the passenger window of the roadster, and Jack's slippered feet. Susan crawled into the backseat from the other side.

The car seemed colder than the night itself, for there is nothing colder than stiff frozen leather at your back. The driveway was dark. The narrow little unpaved road that led from the Cliffs to the Quarry was darker still, overhung with the branches of century-old evergreens. The sign marking the turn to Harmon Dodge's ancestral home (ancestral indicating that it had belonged to Harmon's father for the last six weeks of the old man's life, though he never actually lived in it) had been knocked over by the Communist insurgent who had tried to visit Marcellus Rhinelander's chauffeur earlier that day. Jack drove half an hour trying to find the turnoff. He peered over the steering wheel and wiped away the fog of his breath which instantly turned to patterned ice on the windshield. Harmon snored in the seat next to him, and periodically had to be pushed upright so that he did not fall over into Jack's lap. Susan's teeth chattered in the back.

"Where's the damned turnoff?" demanded Jack.

"You know this place better than I," Susan pointed out. "I was there only once, this afternoon."

"There used to be a sign," said Jack. "And this car reeks to high heaven."

He waited for Susan to say "But it still smells better than your wife's perfume."

But she didn't. Instead, she said, "I'd like to apologize for my behavior. It was wrong of me to insult Barbara in her own home."

"It's her father's home, actually," said Jack.

"Nevertheless, it was very wrong of me. But I was very tired, and also, I suppose, I felt as if I needed to stand up a little for Harmon's sake. I didn't want Mr. Rhinelander to think that his law partner had married someone who had been—merely—a speakeasy chanteuse. Because I will be a good wife to Harmon, you know."

Jack glanced over at his superior, snoring through an open mouth.

"He could use one," Jack admitted. "And—ah—don't worry about Barbara. She's been looking for an equal adversary for a while."

"I have no intention of maintaining constant warfare against your wife."

"Which means you don't intend on seeing us anymore?"

Susan laughed, a gay, pleasant little laugh. Jack tilted his head a little so that he could catch a glimpse of Susan in the rearview mirror. Susan smiled. Jack smiled back.

The roadster ran into a ditch. Harmon pitched forward, cracking his head on the windshield.

"Sorry," said Jack, opening the door. He started to get out.

Susan screamed, "No!"

Jack put one foot outside the door, but it didn't touch ground. It just pushed right on down through the air. The air was very cold, but sweat came out on Jack's high noble brow as if the sun had been beating straight down upon it for hours. He carefully pulled his foot back in and then peered out the open door into blackness.

"It's not a ditch," Susan said, pushing well over against the opposite side of the roadster. "It's evidently some sort of cliff." Quickly, she kicked off her shoes, tossed aside her hat, and crawled out the window.

Jack sat still in his seat, drawing the door carefully closed. The car was tilted forward and toward the left. Jack surmised that the left wheel had gone over the edge of some precipice.

"I can see the river!" Susan shouted from outside the car and somewhere behind. "It's about two hundred feet directly below us." She pulled open the passenger door, and her husband fell out upon the ground.

Inside, Jack felt the car tilt distinctly forward and to the left. The windshield was fogged, but there was nothing outside to see except the two-hundred-foot drop to the Hudson.

Outside, Susan dragged her husband in a direction that was apparently away from the cliff.

"Ah," said Jack diffidently, "can you tell anything more about our situation?"

Susan leaned in the open passenger door. "The car is about to plunge over the cliff, so far as I can make out." She gave Jack a hand, and with a tug that showed more strength than he would have surmised resided in her small and elegant frame, Susan pulled him across the drive stick and nearly out the door.

"Thank you," he said.

"You're not free yet," said Susan, and as if to prove the truth of her assertion, the car began to roll forward. Jack had unwisely dragged the gears into neutral.

Susan jerked him to safety just as the roadster plunged over the cliff.

Jack's feet dangled in cold, insubstantial air. A few seconds later there was a crash, a noise like that of a small iceberg breaking free of a glacier, and then a rude gurgling.

"That roadster was worth twelve hundred dollars," said Susan, dragging Jack from the lip of the cliff and certain death.

"It didn't cost Harmon a penny," Jack pointed out. His trousers had evidently been torn badly, for he could feel cold stones rasping into his flesh. "I have two broken ribs," he said with sudden remembrance. With that remembrance, pain flooded back into that badly bruised area between his neck and his abdomen. He began to wish that he had been inside the roadster when it broke through the frozen waters of this fashionable length of the Hudson River. The novel sensation of drowning in freezing water might have taken his mind off the entirely too familiar discomfort he felt now in his unmended rib cage.

"If you have two broken ribs, then you ought not be driving," said Susan. Harmon was still fast asleep, still snoring on the cold ground. "In particular, you ought not be driving off cliffs," she added with undisguised annoyance in her voice.

Part II

SUSAN

CHAPTER SEVEN

IT WAS COLD. She was sweating, and despite the salt in her perspiration, it froze like tears in a cheap romantic print.

It was dark. Clouds covered the stars and the moon. She could see a single light burning in a house, but that house was maybe a couple of miles away on the other side of the Hudson River.

The road was frozen and hard beneath her feet, and she had stupidly not kicked her shoes out the window of the roadster, but onto the floor of the vehicle. Her shoes were wet and soggy now on the bed of the Hudson River, and did her no good at all.

Harmon was still convinced that he was on Fifty-second Street and kept calling for a taxi. He would have fallen on his face if Susan hadn't kept a firm arm around his shoulder.

Her other arm was around the shoulder of Jack, who had only one slipper, and complained incessantly of the pain in his chest. "It's like breathing knives. Cold steel. I feel like a sword swallower. I used to have a nightmare that I swallowed a razor blade. It felt just like this. Have you ever broken your ribs? Don't."

Susan had no idea that she was headed in the right direction on the narrow, lightless road. But she had chosen downhill, because going uphill, supporting two large men, would have been impossible.

"Can't you shut up for a minute?" she asked Jack. "This is my honeymoon."

"Taxi!" Harmon shouted.

"Do you have any idea where we're going?" the husband of that dreadful woman Barbara wanted to know.

"I don't know *why* I allowed myself to get into a car with you," said Susan. "Considering what our last meeting was. You nearly killed me *again*. And I daresay that if you had figured out a way of sending me over the cliff without involving yourself, you would have availed yourself of it."

"People with broken ribs don't plot murder," he returned. "Only suicide."

"Taxi!" screamed Harmon, and lurched forward. He fell flat on his face. Susan let go of Jack and hurried to help her husband up. Harmon, with the prescience of the habitual drunkard, had dropped directly down on the overturned sign that pointed the way to the Quarry.

Harmon stood in front of the portico of the Quarry and stared up at the neo-Georgian mansion, as if wondering how he had gotten there without benefit of taxi. Susan banged on the door, rousing Audrey, who had come up from New York while Susan and Harmon were in Niagara Falls. The black woman seemed not a bit surprised to find Susan shivering shoeless, Harmon rolling drunk, and Mr. Beaumont complaining of the cold steel cutlery that he had ingested. With Audrey's help, Susan got Jack into one of the bedrooms upstairs. He didn't want to sleep; he wanted to take a hot bath, to melt those icy knives in his breast, and to wash out the muddy pebbles that had been ground into his calves and feet.

"Would you mind calling Barbara and telling her I've had a little accident?" he asked Susan. She replied that it would be a pleasure.

Susan remembered seeing a telephone in Harmon's bedroom—it was hardly hers yet, as she hadn't even slept there once. She wandered along opening doors but couldn't seem to find it again. Presently, however, Harmon appeared, with Audrey pushing him from behind, and fell through one of the doors she hadn't tried yet. While Audrey was pulling off Harmon's clothes, Susan telephoned the Cliffs. Grace Grace answered, and Susan was giving her a message to relay to Barbara and Marcellus Rhinelander, when Barbara herself suddenly jumped into the conversation.

What happened?

"Very little," said Susan, ignoring the rancor in Barbara's voice. "Your husband drove Harm's new car off a cliff."

You weren't in it?

"No," returned Susan. "In fact, it was I who saved the lives of both Harmon and your husband."

Much obliged, I'm sure.

"You're quite welcome. But Mr. Beaumont asked me to let you know he'd be staying the night here, and would much appreciate being picked up here in the morning. He seems to be in considerable pain."

I hope you don't look at this as an opportunity to work your wiles on my husband. You may have sunk your poisoned talons into Harmon's poor unresisting flesh, but I'd advise you to leave Jack quite alone. He has no intention of being unfaithful to me.

Susan stared at the receiver, as if not quite sure what she was hearing. She looked at Audrey, who was pulling off Harmon's trousers. "Audrey," Susan said, speaking distinctly and not too distantly from the telephone, "don't bother putting those drugs into Mr. Beaumont's drink. I won't be seducing him tonight." Then she spoke directly to Barbara again.

"Do join us for breakfast tomorrow, Barbara," Susan said sweetly. "I miss you already."

Then she rang off, and wondered if she should bother keeping Audrey from removing her husband's undershorts. She didn't, reflecting that Audrey wouldn't be doing it now if she hadn't done it many times before.

Susan helped Audrey pull a pair of pajamas onto Harmon, who with the dragging and the lifting and the twisting attendant on this procedure, woke up to the extent that he could call out for a taxi to bring him more brandy.

"There's a taxi strike on, Harm," Susan replied. "Go to sleep. Prohibition ends tomorrow."

With that happy thought, Harmon turned over and snored loudly into a goose-down pillow with a large *D* embroidered on the lace hem.

"Miz Dodge?" said Audrey. "Something I can get you?"

A new life, thought Susan. "Nothing, Audrey. Thank you," she said.

Audrey wandered back to bed.

Susan didn't even know where Audrey's bedroom was in this mansion. It had twenty-three rooms, a detached guesthouse, half a dozen outbuildings, two gazebos, a medium-size swimming pool with a diving tower, an English garden with roses, a French garden with yews, and an American forest garden with rhododendrons and lilacs. She'd been there for only a few hours that afternoon and had wandered about the place, thinking it cold, thinking it depressingly modern, thinking it—most oddly of all—*hers*.

There had been no covers on the furniture, which suggested that Harmon had visited the place frequently.

Once a month, perhaps. Moving in a crowd where your social position was determined by the size of your hangover, Harmon was the first name in the register. So perhaps he had used the place as a cushioned room in which to recover from his heavy debauches. More likely, Susan thought, he had brought young women up here— young women who hadn't required the trip to Niagara Falls before they'd crossed the threshold. That thought made her cringe with shame—not with the thought of how Harmon and the young ladies had passed their time at the Quarry. But at the thought that she, Susan, who *had* required the trip to Niagara Falls, was not more virtuous, but less virtuous than all those others. More conniving, more mercenary, more—

More everything that Barbara Beaumont thought she was.

A gold digger.

Susan lay in the steaming perfumed water in the bathroom that was decorated in gray and aqua, and massaged the soles of her feet. They were tender and cut in several places from the rocks in the unpaved road.

When she felt clean and warm again, she drained the bath and wrapped herself in a quilted silk kimono. She put on furred slippers and wandered through the hallways in the Quarry. Behind three doors she detected snoring— but she had no idea which was Harmon, which was Jack Beaumont, and which was Audrey.

She went down some stairs and pushed open a recalcitrant door. She found herself in a narrow unlighted hallway. She pushed open another sticking door and found herself in a kitchen. Behind a third, gleaming steel door she found a larder with refrigerator. She cut a slice of cheese and poured a glass of milk. She ate the cheese and drank the milk while standing at the corner of the great table in the middle of the kitchen, which was large enough and had the equipment to feed all the guests at the Waldorf-Astoria. When she was done she swept up the crumbs and washed the glass. She wandered out of the kitchen and found the living room. The modern furniture here was better suited for filling in a swamp than for accommodating the human anatomy. She wandered on and found a kind of library with a few books.

God's Little Acre was one of them, and the other was something called *The New Eugenics*, and the plain brown wrapper it had come in was still wadded on the floor. *The New Eugenics* contained advice to married couples on delicate subjects. It had cost $2.98 and had been ordered from the back of a periodical not known for the delicacy of its subject matter.

Susan pulled open the curtains over the French windows. Outside was a black garden. She saw a switch on the wall and flipped it experimentally.

The black garden was suddenly flooded with moonlight. It was a sedate, formal expanse of clipped yews, ivy-colored brick, and gravel paths.

This is a mistake, said Susan, opening the French doors and stepping out into the frigid winter night. She closed the door carefully behind her, and then, folding her arms for warmth across her breast, wandered along the symmetrical garden paths. The yews were clipped and black and solid and looked as if they'd been molded of something that was not twigs and leaves. An owl hooted from somewhere close, and it seemed a sound almost as artificial as the yews and the cold moonlight that flooded the regular gravel paths.

Seven hundred and fifty thousand men were out of work in New York City alone.

There was a civil war in Spain.

Banks had failed, and perfectly honest and hardworking people didn't have enough to eat, and the winds blew hard and dry across the farms of the Midwest, and the red dust covered everything.

Those were the things that Susan should be thinking about. All those *other* unhappy people.

Except she shouldn't be unhappy, should she? Walking in a moonlit garden behind her own mansion that overlooked the Hudson. On the contrary, she should be very happy. For Susan Bright Dodge there'd be no more Sunday-morning shampoos and home-done manicures. No more evenings spent mending runs in silk stockings and rips in shabby gloves. No more cheap little hats and scuffed shoes. No more dollar table d'hôtes in gritty little cafeterias in the west forties. No more leaning on a piano in her only decent dress, singing to the inebriated and the blasé. She'd be a socialite, and she'd live the life of the socialite. Shopping, luncheon, shopping, tea, shopping, cocktail party, dressing, dinner, *fun*. And then she'd go to bed and lie awake till dawn—about twenty minutes—where she'd think about the fact that she didn't love her husband.

Harmon Dodge was charming, handsome, and rich. She was genuinely fond of him, and Susan was determined to pay for her keep. She'd poke Harmon into shape. She'd teach him responsibility. She'd make sure he didn't get drunk *every* night. She'd be much more careful about his money than he was. She wouldn't love him, but she'd act as if she did. If she had gotten security, comfort, freedom from fretfulness, then Harmon Dodge had gotten something that money only rarely buys—a good wife.

She went back inside, turned out the artificial moonlight, and went in search of the doors behind which she could hear snoring. She opened one and found Audrey in her curlers. She opened another and found her husband. She rolled him over, slipped off the kimono, and crawled in beside him. Harmon yelped when he felt her cold flesh against his, but he did not wake up. Susan did not go to sleep.

CHAPTER EIGHT

SHE AND HARMON remained about a week at the Quarry. The mansion was lonely and empty during the day. Harmon tended to sleep late. Breakfast and late afternoon tea were indistinguishable for him. Susan didn't mind. She learned the layout of the house. She walked in the dead gardens, and protected herself better against the cold than on the first night spent at her new country home. She called a garage in Catskill and had the owner send over someone who could give her a few driving lessons. This turned out to be a fourteen-year-old girl whose eyes widened in lust when she saw the four expensive automobiles in the Quarry garages. Susan learned to make a slow circuit of the driveway, and once she even went so far as to the edge of the cliff where she, Harmon, and the idiot Jack had nearly plunged to their deaths. In the evenings, Susan and Harmon drove up to Albany, a place that—owing to the presence of the state legislature—sported as many speakeasies as

Manhattan. Unsurprisingly, Harmon knew every one of them. Susan didn't care to go to speakeasies, no matter how posh. She didn't like to hear the crooners and the songbirds, no matter how splendid their voices or their repertoire. The congealed food, the poisoned liquor, the vile blue smoke, the spurious bonhomie of overweight politicians, and the grating laughter of their young female companions made Susan think of the lonely yew garden bathed in its unnatural moonlight as a place of some genuine charm. Sometimes, when she and Harmon returned to the Quarry as early as four or five in the morning, Susan walked there, and now thought of it as one of the nicer realities of her new life as the wife of Harmon Dodge.

On the night before their return to New York, Susan was glad she had learned to drive. For Harmon got so drunk at a place called the Café d'Esprit that Susan was afraid to ride with him. She drove, very slowly and very carefully, and they didn't get home till seven in the morning, but they got there alive.

Now she'd been in New York City for more than a month, and was getting used to married life in *this* place. In New York, Harmon slept only till one in the afternoon. He was dressed by three, and usually by three-fifteen he'd found a taxi that would take him the two blocks to his offices. There at the office, he'd find out how much money Jack Beaumont had made for him and what sorts of bankrupted merchandise Jack Beaumont had snagged, and would sort through the periodicals and $2.98 books that came to the offices in plain paper wrappers. Then he'd wander off to a club, pour a number of measured draughts of junipered poison down his throat, telephone Susan, and tell her where to meet him for dinner. Invariably, Susan dressed, showed up at the restaurant without any particular hope of finding Harmon there, didn't find him there, instituted a search for him by telephone, eventually found him, picked him up, brought him back to the designated restaurant, consumed a rather bad dinner, resorted afterward to one of the nightclubs she found increasingly depressing, was mumblingly introduced to half a dozen people Harmon called by the wrong names entirely, smiled and looked about, and listened to the singers and imagined what their dreary lives were like.

Just as invariably, Harmon was charming. Full of liveliness, full of compliments, and he seemed genuinely to love her. Not on the same scale as he loved alcohol, nightclubs, and the general tenor of his life—but more than just about anything else. Though there wasn't, Susan had to admit, much more in Harmon's life.

He had plenty of money—rather more than Susan expected, and that made her uneasy. She was a sensible, upright young woman, and it had seemed to her a lesser evil to have married for security than for wealth. Now she was the wife of a man who could be considered rich. He gave her a generous account at the bank, which in turn established accounts at the shops and salons on Fifth Avenue. She shopped and bought smart hats, and smart little suits, and highly polished endearing little shoes. Her old clothes she gave away. But when her wardrobe was filled, she stopped shopping. Harmon gave her a check to replenish her account, and when she informed him that it didn't need replenishing, he looked surprised. "Well, clean out that old money, girl, and make room for some new," he said. So Harmon's girl bought an expensive new piano, and she bought out Schirmer's catalogue of sheet music, and she hired her old nearsighted accompanist to come by every afternoon for a couple of hours so that she could sing. (She frightfully overpaid Mr. Moon, but this was a very real pleasure that Harmon's money brought her. Mr. Moon had a Mrs. Moon and three young Misses Moon, named Miriam, Marjorie, and Marian, all of whom had a predisposition for regular food on the table.) Susan's voice didn't sound right at first, in a room that wasn't filled with tobacco smoke and the fumes of alcohol, but she adjusted. No more tired and blasé faces turned wearily toward her anymore either, just Audrey, sagging over a little straight chair placed in the doorway, and George the elevator man, standing in the open doors of his machine when he wasn't required on other floors.

Susan became a familiar face at the Doubleday bookstore on Fifth Avenue, and she read the books that everybody was reading: *Mutiny on the Bounty*, though she didn't like the sea; *Life Begins at Forty*, even though she was only twenty-seven; *Rip Tide*, though a full novel in verse somehow made her nauseated; Vicki Baum's *And Life Goes On*, though sometimes it seemed it didn't. She even read the advice on delicate matters in Harmon's copy of *The New Eugenics* and discovered that she had already learned from Harmon more than the writer of this book ever knew on the subject.

She had her hair styled at a cost that would have supported her for a week three months ago. Her face was bathed in mud. Her arms were massaged with sliced vegetables. A girl with red hair who was supporting her legless father and three younger brothers made disparaging comments about her cuticles and painted her toenails a pale lavender. All but her head was locked in a box that was filled with steam that could have cooked a lobster.

She engaged a man to teach her to drive. He was twice as old as her first instructor, three times as expensive, and about half as knowledgeable. In her new violet Chevrolet Master DeLuxe Town Sedan—formerly the property of the owner of the largest bakery in Manhattan, sadly bankrupt—Susan drove along the quiet streets of Queens. She saw drawn-faced women on their stoops, men lounging on street corners wearier with inaction than they would have been after ten hours of hard labor, children who seemed either too thin or too fat. When she'd passed her driver's test, she put her car in the garage and made no more journeys across the bridge to Queens.

She had met many of Harmon's acquaintances, but none of their wives visited Susan. Harmon said, "You're in luck, girl, so far as I can make out. I certainly would rather spend the day with Audrey, and George, and Mr. Moon than with that sort of gaggle. Enjoy it now, because it's only a matter of time before they start trooping over here like Franco's boys marching on the Bolshies." Susan knew that no one visited the penthouse in the afternoons because she was perceived as a gold digger who had struck a mother lode in snagging Harmon Dodge. She also knew Harmon was right—it was only a matter of time before she was accepted in the society in which her husband moved. The women would tire of slighting the wife of such a charming man as Harmon, they'd find out somehow or other that she came from a good family and that her father had been a member of Theodore Roosevelt's cabinet, and there would be some other upstart so loathsome Susan would look like royalty next to her. Susan made no efforts toward speeding up this inevitable acceptance, for like the trains in Italy, these things worked on their own schedule. She didn't really care for the women of café society. They were similar to Barbara Beaumont, who was, in her way, a paradigm of the New York debutante. Barbara had come out in 1927 and she hadn't been home since.

So it seemed fitting, in the course of things, that Barbara Beaumont should be Susan's first afternoon visitor. If Barbara Beaumont wasn't the best-dressed woman in the city, she was at least the most dressed. She wore a blue wool overcoat with horizontal stripes in red and yellow, a pillbox hat with a fez attachment, and yellow suede swagger boots. It was the sort of outfit that would have made the pope in full canonicals look drab by comparison. George followed her in, with a kind of box or cage with a brass handle. It shook and rattled and growled in his hand. Whatever was inside was alive, and it wanted to get out. Susan eyed it with some suspicion.

"I am the most loathsome woman in the universe," said Barbara Beaumont. "I woke up in the middle of the night last night—the sun hadn't been up more than an hour or two—and I said to myself, 'Wedding present.' I had no idea what it meant, however, but then I was looking in the hall closet for something and I came across a pair of Harmon's trousers—he left them there on Christmas Eve for some reason—and I remembered that he had gotten married."

She stopped.

"To me," said Susan.

"Yes," said Barbara as if she had just been spared the pain of making that observation. "So here I am to make amends for my neglect of that poor, poor boy. I've brought you Scotty and Zelda."

"Scotty and Zelda?"

"Yes," said Barbara, taking an umbrella from the hall stand and gingerly pushing the catch on the top of the cage George had brought in. "The two most adorable creatures in the universe."

The latch sprang free, and immediately two small, wiry Scottish terriers flew out of the cage. One was white and the other black. The most adorable creatures in the universe immediately began chasing each other around the living room, yapping and snapping at each other, biting the legs of the furniture, relieving themselves on the radio cabinet, and attempting to extract a morsel of fresh meat from Susan's leg.

"They're called Scotty and Zelda because they fight so much," said Barbara. "I'm sure they'll keep this place lively. Jack says Harmon says you're not overburdened with company."

"Not until very recently," returned Susan dryly.

Barbara smiled a bland smile.

"The black one is Scotty, and the white one is Zelda. Or else it's the other way around."

Susan smiled a blander smile than Barbara smiled. "Yes, I'm sure sex could sometimes prove a confusing issue to you, Barbara. And I thank you for the gift. I'm sure Harmon will love these—creatures."

"I agonized, positively agonized over exactly the right gift for you, Susan. Believe me, I did. And with that, I must be on my way. It was lovely to see you again. I love what you've done to the living room."

"I haven't done anything," returned Susan.

"Exactly. I was so afraid you'd bring in something new and dreadful and tasteless."

"New and dreadful and tasteless is definitely passé this year," said Susan. "Shall I show you what I haven't done to the other rooms, or shall I just call for the elevator and a taxi? I'd be happy to make plane reservations, if you're going that far?"

"Please don't put yourself to any trouble. I imagine you'll have your hands full for a little while with Scotty and Zelda." The elevator arrived and Barbara sailed into it. One of the dogs overturned several pots of chrysanthemums in one of the corner conservatories, while a scream from the opposite side of the penthouse announced Audrey's discovery of the other portion of Barbara's wedding gift to Susan Dodge née Bright.

CHAPTER NINE

Harmon DID WHAT he'd never done before. He put down his foot.

He wouldn't have Scotty and Zelda in his home. He suggested that Susan open a window and throw them out and let the winds take care of them. On the whole, Susan agreed that the dogs deserved such treatment, but she found herself arguing with Harmon. She wanted to keep them.

"Why? They're vicious little creatures, and the only reason Barbara gave them to you was that she knew they'd make you miserable."

"That's the first time you've ever admitted you knew how much Barbara disliked me," Susan remarked.

"Well," Harmon said with a little embarrassed cough that was part of every lawyer's stock-in-trade, even a lawyer as unconventional as Harmon, "Barbara would find objection with any woman I married. She's a bit like a jealous sister. You know the type."

"Yes," said Susan. "In any case, I don't want to give Barbara the satisfaction of knowing that I hurled her wedding gifts out a twenty-third-floor window. It's the sort of thing she'd manage somehow to get into Winchell's column. Perhaps I could take them to obedience school."

"They need to be outdoors," said Harmon. Just now the dogs were locked in a dark closet with a number of crates of liquor. "Outdoors where they're in danger of being run over by automobiles, or bitten by poisonous snakes, or trampled underfoot by a parade of the unemployed."

"We could take them up to the country," said Susan.

"Good idea. Lots of dangerous places in the mountains. Bears, cougars. They might accidentally drown while someone was giving them a bath in a cold mountain stream. Or, unthinkingly, someone might hurl them both off a cliff into the river. The difficulty is, we weren't planning on going back to the country till Easter."

"I could go up the Quarry alone," Susan suggested, and didn't know why she'd never suggested it before, for now it seemed a very happy idea, quite apart from the danger the locale possibly presented for Scotty and Zelda.

Harmon looked at Susan strangely for a moment. He even stopped pouring his third cocktail of the hour, so struck did he appear with the notion. "I suppose you could," he said at last.

It was the way he said those words *I suppose you could* that told Susan that her husband did not love her the way she had thought he did. He would be happy to see her go up to Albany on her own, she understood. He would be pleased to remain in the city, temporarily a free man again. In those four simple words, Susan also heard his offhanded resolution to betray their marriage vows.

She was pleased. She didn't have to feel guilty about wanting to get away from Harmon for a bit. As to the probability of his breaking his vows of fidelity to her, she had assumed he had done that little piece of business already. But simply by the way that he took the thought of her going away alone showed her that he hadn't.

So it was arranged in the fifth week of their marriage that Susan would ride up to the country for a few days— merely on account of the loathsome pets with which they'd been saddled. Harmon, of course, would remain in the city, where "urgent business" must be prosecuted.

Susan wasn't certain if Harmon understood how happy she was to get away, but she tried not to make it obvious. He delightfully declared himself utterly miserable just contemplating her departure. "I'll probably get drunk every night, just because you aren't here."

Considering that Harmon got drunk every night, even when she was sitting at the same table in the next chair, Susan didn't doubt the assertion.

Wearing the same thickly lined gloves with which he shoveled coal into the furnace in the basement, George the elevator man reached into the liquor closet and grabbed Scotty and Zelda. The dogs had teeth like sharks and tore into the gloves, George's uniform sleeves, and each other. He thrust them back into the cage, where a two-dollar steak temporarily held their attention as Susan snapped the latch. They went into the backseat of the Chevrolet sedan and Susan took off for Albany, armed (for this first solo journey) with a purseful of roadmaps, an atlas of the entire United States, two hundred dollars in cash, a canister of gasoline, two quarts of oil, and the telephone number of General Motors headquarters in Detroit. None was needed. Susan found her way from the East Side to the West Side by looking at the sun. In the same way, she went north to the tip of Manhattan. There was a bridge there, conveniently, and she crossed over into the Bronx. She didn't take any turns, and found herself on a road north, and on the road north was a sign that read ALBANY—149 MILES. She passed similar signs with diminishing mileage. Once she got in the vicinity of Albany, memory took over—she and Harmon had made the trip to the speakeasies every night of their stay at the Quarry—and Susan found her way to the Quarry without difficulty. In fact, her only difficulty was with Scotty and Zelda. They barked half the way up, and then were utterly silent. From the smell emanating from the cage, they seemed to be suffering from motion sickness and diarrhea simultaneously.

The first thing Susan did on reaching the Quarry was to take the cage out of the backseat and put it on a piece of waste ground behind a stand of rhododendron. Then she unlatched it and opened the top. Black Scotty and white Zelda were green. Together they raised their paws to the top of the cage, rocked in unison, and pushed the cage over. They crawled unsteadily out, snapped and snarled at Susan in a dispirited fashion, and then collapsed in the dirt beside each other.

"All right, you two little heathens," said Susan sharply. "Listen to me now, and listen well, because I'm not going to repeat this."

Zelda made a tiny little snarl, but Scotty laid a black paw on Zelda's neck and she desisted.

"I have explicit instructions to hurl you both off the cliff and into the river, which is very deep and very cold and where there are no two-dollar steaks for miserable little dogs. If I don't throw you off the cliff, then I'm to crush you beneath one of these large boulders. And if I don't do that, then I'm supposed to abandon you in the woods like Hansel and Gretel, and then you'll be the two-dollar steak for the very nasty black bear that is about to wake from his hibernation."

Scotty and Zelda made no sound. They did not move. Silence and stillness were, however, remarkable phenomena for the pair, and Susan understood that her speech had gotten through.

"You two are going to be given another chance. One more opportunity to prove yourselves worthy of a continued existence. I may also remind you that no one has ever been able to provide any proof of a doggy heaven.

Therefore, I'd advise you to pay close attention. You're going to be happy with each other and you're going to be happy with me. When I say frolic, you're going to frolic at my heels. And when I say, 'Be quiet, Scotty and Zelda,' you're going to pretend that you never even heard of a bark, or a growl, or a snarl. And in return, you'll be fed scraps from the table, and you'll get to run around in the woods and frighten the wild-life, and you may even get—I promise nothing, however—a little affection. Have I made myself clear?"

Scotty and Zelda were silent and still.

"Good," said Susan. "I'm glad we've come to this little agreement. So look around for a while, then come to the back door in about an hour, and I'll have a little food for you. When you've proved yourselves worthy, I may even let you sleep in the house."

Susan took her suitcases from the car and went into the house. From the bedroom window upstairs she looked out, and saw Scotty and Zelda lying forlornly on the gravel in the bleak February sunshine.

"Those dogs have promise," said Susan aloud to herself.

The Quarry stood on its own hundred acres or so, and the nearest house was the Rhinelander place a mile away. That first night she spent there alone, Susan heard nothing. And everything. Every twig that snapped, every owl that hooted, every board that swelled or contracted, every glass that rattled of its own accord in the distant kitchen. She could not sleep for the intensity of the silence.

She turned on the lamp by the bed and got up. She turned on the light in the hall and went downstairs. She turned on the lights in the living room, the study, and she turned on the moonlight in the yew garden. She opened the French doors, and she called for Scotty and Zelda.

Scotty and Zelda did not come.

"This isn't a trick," she promised in a loud voice. "I won't kill you!"

Scotty crept out from beneath a black yew, where he'd been quite invisible.

Zelda appeared from behind a white pot that contained the twisted black skeleton of a leafless climbing plant.

"You've been very good," said Susan, "considering that you're probably not used to the country, and not used to the cold, and not used to riding long distances in automobiles. And therefore I'm going to allow you to sleep inside tonight."

Scotty and Zelda remained where they were.

"Come inside then," said Susan. "I promise. No tricks."

Scotty and Zelda slowly crept toward Susan, passing on either side of her and going into the study. She came inside, closed the door, and extinguished the moonlight.

"You've never been in here before, so I'll lead the way," said Susan. Then, turning out the lights as she went, Susan returned to her bedroom. Scotty and Zelda crept in her path so silently that Susan had to turn several times to make certain they were there.

Susan got back into bed. Scotty and Zelda remained just inside the closed door, but looked longingly at the small coal fire that was still burning in the grate.

"All right," said Susan. "You may go over there."

Scotty and Zelda took up positions on either side of the hearth, like the porcelain dogs at either end of the mantel above them.

Susan slept.

Susan wakened to the barking of dogs. She sat up suddenly in bed, pointing an accusing finger at the fireplace. Scotty and Zelda were silent and still, but there was something nervous and uneasy about them. The barking came from outside.

"Sorry," said Susan to Scotty and Zelda.

Susan went to the window and looked out. A large touring car had stopped in front of the house, and two barking dalmatians ran around and around it.

Richard Grace, Marcellus Rhinelander's Communist chauffeur, got slowly out of the car with a broom. He used the broom to fend off the dalmatians as he inched to the front door. Susan was already on her way downstairs when she heard the bell.

She opened the door quickly and jerked the man inside.

"Thank you, Mrs. Dodge," said Richard Grace, leaning the broom into a corner.

"Where did those dogs come from?" Susan wanted to know.

"Oh, they're Mr. Rhinelander's," replied the chauffeur. "He sets them on me, you know."

"No, I didn't."

"It's a war between the upper classes and the workers, according to Mr. Rhinelander," said Richard Grace. "And them two dogs is one of his weapons."

Susan considered this for a moment, and then asked, "May I do something for you?"

"Mr. Rhinelander sent me over with an invitation to dinner tonight, Mrs. Dodge, that's all, and wants to know if it will be convenient for me to fetch you at seven o'clock this evening."

"Tell Mr. Rhinelander that I'd be happy—"

"Mr. Rhinelander ain't just against the workers, Mrs. Dodge," said the chauffeur abruptly, "he's got something against you, too."

"Oh yes?" said Susan uncomfortably. Uncomfortably not because Richard Grace was a chauffeur, but because she didn't like to receive confidences of any sort.

"He don't like you as much as he don't like me," said Richard Grace, "which, as you may notice from the spotted dogs outside, is considerable. He don't like you and his daughter don't like you even more. If I have my way," he added in an undertone, "Miss Barbara will be one of the first what is swept away in the coming social upheaval. But as that time is not yet, my advice to you would be not to come, Mrs. Dodge."

"We don't win wars by running from our enemies," said Susan as the quickest way to end this conversation. "So please tell Mr. Rhinelander that I'll be glad to dine with him this evening, and you needn't trouble yourself to fetch me, Mr. Grace. I'll drive over myself. But thank you for coming."

Mr. Grace, taking his broom, edged back out the door and crept toward the car. The dalmatians raced after the vehicle as it headed back toward the Cliffs.

When Susan turned from watching this spectacle through the lintel windows, she found Scotty and Zelda waiting patiently for her on the bottom step of the stairs.

"You came down to protect me against those other dogs, didn't you?"

Scotty bared his teeth. Zelda produced one genteel bark.

"You are both turning into very good dogs," said Susan, but didn't think it prudent for further praise.

CHAPTER TEN

IT WAS THE SECOND unpleasant dinner she'd had in the Cliffs dining room, a long, high chamber with heavily curtained windows looking out on the black winter night. A massive mahogany table with a cloth that looked like a hallway runner ran across it lengthwise. Marcellus Rhinelander sat at one end of the table, and Susan at the other. Two candelabra and a vase of dried autumn flowers kept Susan from even seeing her host unless she leaned considerably to the right or the left.

The meal was another embalmed chicken, a salad of tinned asparagus and third-pressing olive oil, with a tomato pie for dessert. Susan had never had a tomato pie before, and she understood, after she'd tasted it, why it had never become a national delicacy. The wine was good and plentiful.

Marcellus Rhinelander's conversation was chiefly politics. He deplored the election of Franklin Roosevelt to the presidency, and dreaded the day—only weeks distant—when the man would take office. He deplored the assassination attempt on the President-elect, which had taken place the week before, on two grounds. On the one hand, the Bolsheviks were behind it, as they were behind all the unrest, all the troubles, and all the degeneracy of this country. On the other hand, he was disappointed that Roosevelt hadn't been killed. Mr. Rhinelander almost gleefully anticipated the total disintegration of the noble experiment that was the United States of America, beneath the hand of that turncoat, that blue-blooded scalawag, Franklin Roosevelt. "A man born with every advantage," Marcellus Rhinelander reminded Susan, "who has chosen to throw in his lot with Bolshevik scoundrels, the impoverished and the unwashed, and the—the—"

He faltered for completion of the triumvirate.

"—the badly dressed?" Susan suggested.

"More pie?" Grace Grace inquired, and Susan declined.

Susan hoped she'd be able to leave soon. She didn't like this man. She declined coffee, but Marcellus Rhinelander pressed. "We'll go into the study, if you don't mind, Susan. You don't mind that either, do you, if I call you Susan? Harmon's almost a son to me, you know. Almost a son."

Susan acquiesced politely but with no glad heart. Somehow this house felt lonelier, even with servants, than did the Quarry when she was there with only Scotty and Zelda.

Susan sat in a corner of a wine-red sofa and sipped coffee. Without being asked, Grace brought a rose-colored shawl for her shoulders. When Grace was gone, Marcellus Rhinelander poured himself a glass of port and stood at the fireplace, with one arm stretched along the mantel in lord-of-the-manor style.

"You're very beautiful," he said after a moment.

"Thank you," said Susan. She didn't startle. She'd sung in clubs long enough to have heard this remark from a hundred men, in a hundred different tones of voice, but with a single motive prompting the compliment. Not here though. She wasn't sure what he was getting at. But she did remember the dalmatians that Marcellus Rhinelander had bought for the sole purpose of fretting Richard Grace.

"I can see why Harmon fell in love with you."

Susan made no reply.

"He'd often proposed marriage," Marcellus Rhinelander went on after taking a judicious sip of his port. "But somehow, it never worked out." Marcellus Rhinelander smiled a smile that Susan had seen his daughter smile. "Sometimes Harmon woke up in the morning and couldn't even remember the girl's name. Sometimes the girl found someone who was richer. Sometimes Barbara and Jack were able to...to lend a helping hand against an improvident alliance."

"I should thank them then," said Susan, "for keeping Harmon safe till I came along."

Marcellus Rhinelander looked at her sharply for a moment. "Perhaps you should," he said softly. "I suppose you've heard—somehow or other—that I had always intended for Harmon to marry Barbara? Perhaps even Barbara herself mentioned it to you. Did she?"

"Relentlessly."

"Jack is a very good fellow. An able lawyer, I think. Barbara loves him. I love him. But I think that on the whole, I would have preferred Harmon as a son-in-law."

Susan didn't understand why he was telling her this. Whether or not it was truth, Susan knew he meant it to *sound* like truth. Perhaps he wanted her to be truthful and candid in return. His next question confirmed her suspicion. "Why did you marry Harmon?" he asked with the sort of smile and tilt of his head that was supposed to indicate: *Oh, it's late in the evening, and we've both had a little too much to drink, and I'm a little world-weary tonight, so why don't we unbosom the hearts of our hearts to each other, you and I?* Or something very like that.

"Why did I marry Harmon?" Susan asked, just to give herself that second or two she needed to decide how she should respond.

"Yes," said Marcellus Rhinelander gently, "why did you marry Harmon?"

Susan's decision how to answer the question was not based on how much she'd drunk, her current high level of world-weariness, or the lateness of the evening, but purely on how much she detested Marcellus Rhinelander. She decided, in short, to tell him the honest truth, hoping he'd be so appalled he'd never speak to her again.

"It's quite simple really," Susan said. "I married Harmon because he had a great deal of money and I didn't have any."

Marcellus Rhinelander choked on his port, and he stared at her over the rim of his glass as he took more as soon as he could.

"I can go into it in more detail if you wish," Susan said.

"Please do."

"I was tired of having no money for anything beyond shelter and the dress I wore when I was leaning against a piano singing. My only meal was the food I ate in the club where I sang. I was born in a family that was richer than Harmon is now, that was probably richer than you are now. And eventually—when all that money melted away—I learned to get by on two dollars a week. When I didn't have two dollars, I still got by. And when I had three dollars, I sent one of them to my sister, who's in school in Massachusetts, and I still got by on two dollars a week."

Susan paused, to give Marcellus Rhinelander the opportunity to speak.

"Go on," was all he said.

"I might have found a man to...to keep me—isn't that the way the French talk about it? I don't think the moral question would have bothered me very much. I'm afraid that wickedness and moral turpitude mean less to me than that two-dollar-a-week business. But having a gentleman—whether married or single—provide for you is not a permanent solution to the problem. It's the sort of arrangement that could end at any moment, and when it does end, it always ends suddenly and inconveniently, and you're older and not as beautiful as you were, and then you might as well put a gun into your mouth. I've always worried about the future—it's a real fault, I think—but marriage seemed to me the only solution to my problem."

Susan paused.

Marcellus Rhinelander still stared.

"Might I have a drop of that port?" Susan asked.

He went around and poured her a glass. He refilled his. He didn't return to the fireplace. He sat down in a deep chair and turned away the shade of the lamp next to him.

Susan took his place at the mantel.

"Should I go on, or am I boring you?"

"Not at all," he replied quickly. "Please do. Please do go on."

"I was singing in cafés. One after another. Pretty dreary business, being part of a floor show. First comes the Spanish dancer with the wobbly knees and the petti-coats that haven't been laundered in three months. Then the crooner, who has a crooner's voice and a crooner's mannerisms, and wants to be carried back to old Virginny, and everybody in the audience is all for it. Then comes the colored man who's painted his face *really* black and tells jokes about washerwomen and their alligator-bait offspring, and when he goes off to change his clothes— because he's going to be sweeping up the place when everybody goes home—that's when I come on, and I sing about love, and cigarettes in the dark, and I sing about crying when I'm happy, and I sing about laughing even though I'm sad, and I look out at the audience, and I see Harmon Dodge, who's handsome and charming and rich, and just like all the boys who used to take me out and beg me to marry them, only I didn't because I didn't love them, and I didn't need to marry them because I had money myself. Only now I didn't have any money, and I thought maybe I could get Harmon to ask me, because if he did, then I'd accept."

"And Harmon did ask..." said Marcellus Rhinelander.

"And I accepted," said Susan. "I told you it was simple."

Marcellus Rhinelander leaned forward out of the shadows of the wing chair, reaching for the humidor. "Do you mind if I smoke?"

"Certainly not," said Susan.

She was silent as he did his business with picking the cigar, cutting the end, igniting the long wooden match, twirling the cigar so that it lighted evenly. He leaned back into the shadows.

"Why are you telling me this?" he said at last.

"You asked me," Susan replied. "I assumed, perhaps wrongly, that you wanted the truth."

"I'm not certain I got the truth," said Marcellus Rhinelander.

"You got what you thought you'd hear if I did tell the truth," said Susan. "You think I'm a gold digger. You think I seduced the man you wanted for a son-in-law. Though I think it only just to point out that Barbara spoiled that little plan first, by marrying Mr. Beaumont of the interminable legs. You think that I have connived, and subterfuged—is there such a word?—and played wanton, played virgin, played coquette, played whatever role was necessary to marry a man who hasn't seen a sober sunset or a sober sunrise in ten years."

Marcellus Rhinelander didn't answer. Obviously, it was what he thought.

"It's what your daughter thinks of me, too," said Susan.

"But it's not all the truth, is it?" said Marcellus Rhinelander. Susan liked him for that. A little, anyway.

"No, of course it isn't all the truth. I'm very fond of Harmon. How could anyone not be? Harmon is very fond of me. I'm already a good wife to him, insofar as I'm the kind of wife that least disturbs his peace of mind. I don't try to stop his drinking. I don't tell him to work harder or to bring home more money. I don't try to make him take me out more—if anything, there are many evenings I'd rather stay home. I don't ask where he's been, what he's been doing, or who he's been doing it with. I try to appear as beautiful, and as happy, and as in love with him as I can. Certainly, if you're afraid that I'm spending all his money, you needn't concern yourself. I don't accept half what he tries to give me. I didn't want to be rich—I've been that. I just didn't want my entire life to revolve around that damned two dollars a week. I think Harmon loves me as much as he could love any woman who hangs around more than six weeks or so, and I think I love Harmon as much as I could love any man I married for his money." Susan swallowed off the last of the port in her glass. "That's still not all the truth," she concluded, "but it's most of it, I think."

"I believe you," said Marcellus Rhinelander. "Now the question is, why are you telling it to me?"

"Because I want you to believe the worst of me, that is, what you've believed all along, so that I'll never be invited back to another of these dreadful dinners."

"Not a chance," returned Marcellus Rhinelander, blowing out a blue cloud of smoke from his cigar. "We're having dinner again tomorrow night. Now that I've heard the truth, or most of it, I've come to the conclusion that you are the best possible wife for Harmon Dodge. And beyond that, I've decided I like you."

"I don't like you," returned Susan. "Not one little bit."

"Quite beside the point, really."

He called the next day and Susan said that she didn't want to return to the Cliffs for dinner.

The Bolshie will pick you up at seven.

"He might not be a Bolshie if you treated him decently," said Susan.

The man's paid better than any chauffeur on the Hudson. I built a house for him and his wife, and it's bigger than the house I grew up in.

"What about the dalmatians?"

A warning, so that he doesn't try to assassinate me.

"In any case," said Susan, "don't bother sending him over. Because I don't want to have dinner with you tonight."

I promised Harmon I'd take care of you while you were staying at the Quarry. In fact, you have no business being there alone. When the Bolshie picks you up, I'll send one of the extra maids over. I'll send Louise. She can cook and she knows how to handle a gun. Killed a thief over here once; only took her five shots.

"No, Mr. Rhinelander. Don't send Mr. Grace, don't send Louise. I'll tell Harmon that you've done everything possible to make me happy. And if you leave me alone, you'll be doing just that."

She rang off.

The Bolshie showed up at seven. Susan came out with a broom, in case the dalmatians mistook her political leanings, and told Richard Grace to go back to the Cliffs. Before Richard Grace could reply, the door opposite the driver opened and a young woman with a fierce expression stepped out. She was carrying a suitcase in one hand and a large revolver in the other.

"I'm Louise," she said. "I know the place and can find a room on my own." Before Susan could reply, Louise marched up the steps and into the house.

The back door of the touring car opened and Marcellus Rhinelander himself stepped out.

"I told you," said Susan, "I'm not going to the Cliffs tonight."

"I knew you wouldn't," said Marcellus Rhinelander. "You're just that sort of person, aren't you? So that's why our Socialist friend here is going to return to the Cliffs and bring back Grace and our dinner. Your husband's cellar is a trivial thing, Mrs. Dodge, so I've taken the liberty of bringing a few bottles that aren't entirely unpotable. Comrade Grace," he said, turning to the chauffeur, "if you aren't too occupied with your plans for a Socialist utopia, could you please bring in that small crate?"

Louise served the dinner, which was an embalmed duck with a bullion aspic, tinned asparagus again but crowned tonight with limp pimento rings, and for dessert an overly generous portion of frozen prune whip. Susan wondered edgily where Louise kept her revolver.

The evening was pleasanter than Susan could have predicted. Scotty and Zelda sat quietly on either side of Susan's chair, and even when Marcellus Rhinelander called them with scraps of the embalmed duck, dripping with aspic, they wouldn't go till Susan said, "All right." Having told Marcellus Rhinelander so much truth the night before, Susan wasn't able to retreat into politeness and avoidances with the man.

"Don't talk about politics," she pleaded with him.

"You find them boring? Most women do."

"I don't find them boring. I just think you're entirely wrong. I find your opinions either wrong-headed, reprehensible, or simply bizarre."

"Of course they are," he laughed. "What sort of pompous old fool would I be without them? I'm all alone, my dear Mrs. Dodge. My wife is dead, though I never particularly cared for her, and she certainly never cared for me. My daughter has married and moved away, though one hundred and fifty miles seems rather too short a distance where Barbara is concerned. The few friends I made in my youth are either indicted for crimes, members of the national legislature, or dead—and some of them are all three. What fills my life? Newspapers, and begging letters from relatives I never knew I had, and a law practice that takes a couple of hours of a couple of afternoons every other week. You must never, never tell him, my dear Mrs. Dodge, but I would positively shrivel up and die if Richard Grace ever left my employ. I'll tell you something else I suspect: If the revolution came, I think I'd see Richard Grace at the door, defending my person and my possessions with his life."

Susan didn't honestly believe this last to be the case, but she didn't think badly of Marcellus Rhinelander for deceiving himself on this little point. The man's honestly disarmed her, and she increasingly liked him, even though Barbara Beaumont's father was not the sort of man you gave your trust to with a whole heart and head. When the man has been trained as a lawyer, you have to be doubly careful. Susan's mother, who was daughter, sister, and wife to lawyers, had always stressed this maxim. But tonight was tonight, and there wasn't much that he could do to her in her own home, so she smiled at him and she laughed at his moribund philosophy, and when he asked her, "Is there anything that you regret from your two-dollar-a-week existence, Mrs. Dodge?" Susan once more told the truth.

"I miss an audience."

"Ah, your singing."

"Yes."

"Sing for me. I'll be your audience."

Susan didn't demurely demur. "I'd love to," she said. "May I invite Louise and the Graces to listen?"

"Only if you tell them that I vehemently protested against their presence."

"They wouldn't believe me if I told them otherwise," said Susan.

Louise sat by the door as if guarding against the intrusion of persons who did not have a ticket. The Graces sat on an ugly little love seat covered in silk. Marcellus Rhinelander sat opposite, where he could glower at the servants to greatest effect. Though he did offer his chauffeur a glass of his best port, he remarked, "The stuff is almost undrinkable anyway" as he handed it over.

Susan accompanied herself with simple chords and didn't bother bringing down the sheaf of music she'd brought with her from Manhattan. She sang the old songs she knew from before the Villa Vanity. Songs she had sung in duet with her mother back in Boston. Simple songs by Mr. Work and Mr. Foster. Her audience knew the songs and they joined in on the chorus. It even turned out that Marcellus Rhinelander had a rich tenor, and Richard Grace had not a bad bass. Grace was tone deaf, but Louise could do harmony, though she sang everything rather as if she were standing behind one of her husband's revolutionary barricades.

Susan, as she sang and urged the others to sing with her, thought about what Marcellus Rhinelander had said earlier about his wife, his daughter, and his friends—and told her to what his life had been reduced. Susan felt the same, as if her own life had been reduced to this. This cold room in this large house between the Catskills and the river, singing the old songs to three servants and a man she probably ought not to like at all.

She felt reduced, but she didn't feel very bad about it.

CHAPTER ELEVEN

HARMON CALLED HER every day from the office to tell her how desperately unhappy he was in her absence. Susan replied that it was very lonely in the country, that her heart was breaking without him, but that the dogs still needed considerable training before they'd be fit to take up a residence in the penthouse.

Is Marcellus taking care of you?

"Oh yes," said Susan vaguely. "He's even lent me one of his maids."

Is it the one with the pistol?

"Yes. Louise."

So you're not too lonely?

"Except for you, of course. But I rub along."

As do I. I'm going out with Barbara and Jack tonight to some dreadful O'Neill thing. It should be over by Saturday or so, I suppose, and as they're driving up, perhaps I'll come along.

"Oh do," said Susan, wishing he wouldn't. In just a few weeks she'd grown accustomed to life at the Quarry. Despite what she'd told her husband, Susan hardly felt alone. Scotty and Zelda frolicked at her heels, Louise was always in the kitchen, making sandwiches or polishing her revolver, dinner was always with Marcellus, alternating evenings at the Quarry and at the Cliffs. And, at either place, music afterward. Marcellus, Susan discovered, was a fair accompanist himself, and sometimes he'd even sing one of the Verdi arias he usually reserved for the last wee, drunken hours of the nightwatch. Though he was her husband, and though the Quarry was his home, Harmon's coming seemed very much an intrusion to Mrs. Dodge.

Marcellus Rhinelander felt the same, and he didn't hesitate to tell Susan as much.

"Why doesn't the man leave you alone?"

"He's my husband," Susan pointed out. "And he probably wouldn't have thought of coming at all if Barbara and Jack weren't driving up for the weekend."

"Barbara never spends Easter in New York. She's deathly afraid she'll come across someone who's more outlandishly dressed than she, I think."

"I can't imagine she'd be afraid of *that*," remarked Susan. "In any case, I have rather missed Harmon. He's always in good spirits, and he's someone who does exactly what he wants to do in life, and I have always found that a delightful quality in anyone." Susan found herself in the uncomfortable position of defending a desire to see her husband of only two months.

"What about our dinners? Our diversions at the piano? Your husband is going to cause considerable disruption in our lives. You've told me how Harmon feels about those two pets of yours. And I certainly know how Barbara feels about you. Most important, when Harmon goes back, I'm certain that he's going to want you to return to Manhattan with him. That may make you happy, but it certainly won't do anything to improve *my* humor," he added with a little of his old testiness.

Susan didn't know what to say, so she said nothing.

Harmon told her they'd be in by noon on Saturday, so Susan didn't bother to look out for them till five. They got there at six. Barbara Beaumont climbed languidly out of the backseat of Jack's new car. A bright green beret was perched over her right ear, and a leopard jacket was flung negligently over her shoulders.

"Oh!" she exclaimed in a tone that managed to suggest both surprise and boredom in equal parts. "You're here. When Harmon didn't appear with you today, I just assumed he'd forgotten and left you behind in the city. Jack," she said languidly to her husband as he climbed awkwardly out of the car—those legs! "Jack, you remember Susan, don't you?" Barbara managed to suggest that Susan was the sort of person you forgot unless you were daily reminded of her existence and shown photographs of her face.

"Hello, Jack," said Susan coolly as she leaned in the passenger window and kissed her husband.

"Hello," said Jack. Then, turning to his wife, he said, "Of course I remember her, Barbara."

Harmon kissed Susan, drew back, and smiled at her, and then kissed her again. "Get in the back, Susan," he said. "We'll go on up to the Cliffs with Jack and Barbara. Marcellus is bound to have something decent to drink. It's these last days before the repeal that are getting me down. Do you think we'll live to see that damned thing out of our lives?" Then he leaned over and called to Jack. "We're all going up with you!" He stretched in the narrow seat, thrusting one arm out the window and behind Susan's back. He drew her in closer and kissed her again. "Those damned dogs dead yet?" he asked.

Without having conferred on the matter, Susan and Marcellus Rhinelander made no mention of their recent friendship.

Barbara, thinking it a barb, had even made the comment, "I'd no idea that Susan was up here, Father. The houses being so close, I hope you two have seen a great deal of each other."

"Now and again," said Marcellus, glancing at Susan. "Harmon asked me to look after her."

"Your father sent Louise over," said Susan, as if that had been the extent of his protection.

"Has she murdered anyone yet?" Barbara asked in a tone that suggested her disappointment that Louise hadn't yet turned her revolver on her new mistress.

It was a strange evening. Susan and Marcellus were distant. Though Susan knew—or thought she knew—that his coldness was a sham, she couldn't help but be pained by it. Too, Harmon seemed a stranger. Not a disagreeable stranger, and he still was handsome and charming, but it was *very* odd to think that she was actually married to him. Barbara was her usual thorny self, but Susan no longer felt the need to match barb for barb against this florid hothouse rose. Jack seemed out of sorts, distracted, and even clumsier than usual.

She didn't think she disliked Jack Beaumont any longer. Not after her experience with Marcellus Rhinelander, who had turned out to be someone quite nice. Certainly, to be married to Barbara was, in itself, a kind of penance for any minor faults the man might have. He was handsome, too, when you forgot that he was a lawyer, and if you tried to imagine him without his wife.

Barbara tried to make Susan and Harmon stay after dinner. Probably because none of her nicks had drawn blood, Susan thought. Harmon said, "I haven't said hello to my wife properly," and he produced a grin that was one part drunkenness and three parts embarrassing lasciviousness. Susan wasn't wont to blush, but did so. Jack Beaumont blushed harder. Susan liked him for that, too.

Richard Grace drove them home in the touring car. As she and Harmon were getting out, the chauffeur said quietly, "I missed our music tonight, Mrs. Dodge."

"So did I," said Susan evenly. She wanted to say it quietly, so that Harmon wouldn't hear, but her sense of fair play to Grace wouldn't allow that. She didn't want the chauffeur to imagine, even for a moment, that she might be ashamed of him before her husband.

Harmon had heard his remark anyway. As she was opening the front door, Harmon said, "Been serenading the help?"

Susan was displeased. "Not only did Marcellus lend me an armed domestic, he accompanied me several times at the Cliffs. I wanted to keep my voice in practice. Mr. and Mrs. Grace listened."

"Ah," said Harmon, squeezing her, "thought you might have grown tired of me. Me absent. Him there. All that sort of thing."

Susan was good at interpreting Harmon Dodge, even though she had been married to him for only a short time, and most of that time they had spent apart. This series of remarks told her quite plainly that he had not been faithful to her in New York. She was glad of it. If he hadn't betrayed her, she would have felt more of an obligation to feel more for him than she felt now.

He sat in a low, deep, deeply upholstered chair and watched her undress. Scotty and Zelda were relegated to the bedroom next to theirs. Harmon drank off a large glass of what he called unpotable brandy, and he told Susan once more how much he missed her.

"I missed you," said Susan, thinking, *I missed certain things about you.* If Harmon was invariably charming at cocktails, the most amusing possible companion at a dinner table, the very midnight sun of the gathering afterward, then he was also an accomplished gentleman when the lights went out. Susan really had missed that part of the marriage, and if Harmon had consoled his loneliness during Susan's absence from New York, he was a most agreeable liar in the way that he now showed her how much he had missed her.

On Easter Sunday they all went to church, and Barbara's outfit was considerably more astonishing to the congregation than was the rolling away of the stone on the sacred tomb. The minister, who was very high church, was duly introduced to Susan. Afterward, Susan saw, Barbara took the gentleman aside and whispered a few chosen words in his ear. Probably he heard the bit about Sue Sudan and Her Educated Sheepdogs, and the assertion that in order to get him to the altar, Harmon had been drugged, bound, and threatened with the Shanghai death. Susan didn't care. The Brights had been Unitarian anyway, and had been taught to consider High Church Episcopal as but one ill-disguised step from the worst sort of Neapolitan idolatry.

That night, the two couples went to the Café d'Esprit in Albany. Barbara made frequent allusion to Susan's career as a "crooness" in similar places, and at one point, when Harmon had wandered away in search of a place to relieve himself, Barbara wondered aloud what would happen when the laws against liquor were repealed. "There'll be ten times as many places, and each one will have a dreary crooness with a voice that is passable only because it's midnight and we're all drunk and all she wants anyway is a rich husband, or just someone—anyone—to pay her rent and provide her a decent wardrobe."

"Barbara," said Jack Beaumont, "I'm tired of hearing it."

Susan liked him for that, too.

"Of hearing what?" Barbara asked innocently.

"Of hearing you make remarks about Susan." He glanced at Susan directly as he said it. In a way, that was a compliment. He wasn't treating her with that cold politeness in the mode of Barbara's class. "She married Harmon, and I suppose she loves him."

"I do," said Susan simply. Barbara wasn't the sort of person you trusted with the simple truth.

"And I know he loves her," said Mr. Beaumont, who wasn't sounding at all like a lawyer. "For he's told me so. We will be seeing one another all the time in New York, and here in the country, since there's hardly anyone else we know. I'm not asking you two to make a truce, but the constant barrage of artillery makes my head ache."

Barbara stared at him. "I don't believe you said that. I don't believe you can accuse me of disliking Susan when she has married the man that I love like a brother. A favorite brother." She turned to Susan. "I have nothing whatever against you."

"Then perhaps you should act that way," said Susan.

"I intend to. I always have. We're to be bosom friends, it was meant to be. It was written in the book of our fates."

"I've always felt exactly the same," returned Susan.

"We must go shopping together when you come back to New York tomorrow. I'll show you where you can find some clothes that will flatter your figure. Your coloring is almost unique—I am abysmally jealous of the paleness of your skin and the unmatched ebony of your hair—and you must be very careful what shades you select."

"Barbara..." said Jack warningly.

"I'll be glad of any help you can give me," said Susan. She smiled, but she was troubled. Not by Barbara's inference that nothing she wore now or had ever worn was in the least becoming to her, but rather by Barbara's offhanded assertion that she would be returning to Manhattan with Harmon.

Susan didn't want to leave the Quarry.

They got home at three in the morning. Harmon drank more of the unpotable brandy. He watched Susan undress once more. They saw the sun rise. When Harmon was just about to turn over and fall asleep, Susan asked, "Would you be horribly disappointed if I didn't return to the city with you today?"

He didn't turn over. He faced away from her. She thought he might already be asleep. Finally, he asked, "Why would you want to stay here?"

"I thought I might get the garden in order," she replied carefully. "It's been badly neglected. If it's not done now, it will be too late. We'd have to wait till next year."

"I hardly see how I can do without you any longer," he said. He was still turned away from her.

"It would be dreadful," she conceded. "I've missed you so much, and this has been such a splendid two days."

There was another pause.

"Jack told me we're to be horribly busy this coming week," said Harmon after a moment. He turned over on his back. He looked at her, propped on her elbows. "Ever so many bankrupts. And it's particularly difficult when they've committed suicide. Widows are dreadful to deal with. If you came back, we might have very little time together anyway..."

If the firm had taken on the bankruptcies of Morgan Guaranty Trust, the United Fruit Company, and General Motors on the same day, Harmon wouldn't have spent more than an hour in the office each afternoon. In short, Harmon was allowing her to stay. Better than that, by his lie he indicated he *wanted* her to stay. Susan was pleased— because she got to remain at the Quarry. But she was also saddened—because they'd so early come to this mutual understanding that the marriage was in name only. He'd miss her, but he liked the consolations he procured for his loneliness. She'd miss him, but she now preferred what she had in his absence.

They were a very modern couple. It was chic, but it was melancholy, too.

When she'd had money, Susan had hoped for romance and love. When she hadn't money, she'd looked for security—and she'd daydreamed that romance and love might come with it. It hadn't, but that wasn't Harmon's fault. He was still likeable, charming, affectionate, courtly, and generous. They both had a pleasurable life. He wasn't begrudging her that, at least, and for that she was grateful.

She kissed him tenderly. He smiled.

"Every moment without you will be misery," he said gallantly.

"Perfect misery," she echoed. "I don't know what I'll do..."

Barbara and Jack picked up Harmon at the Quarry on Monday afternoon. Barbara smiled knowingly when Susan said she wouldn't be coming along. She made a smart remark about lovebirds that pecked each other to death, but Susan affected not to hear it. Barbara Beaumont could think what she pleased. Susan was, however, disturbed by the look of curiosity on Jack's face, when Harmon remarked, "I think Susan must be in love with a gardener, or the postman, or someone of that brawny ilk, and that of course is the reason why she's not coming back to Manhattan. As for me, why, I intend on making violent love to Audrey as soon as I can get home. As the months go by, I find I've become deeply attracted to her asthmatics."

"Good-bye, darling," said Susan, kissing Harmon.

"Utter misery," he replied easily. "Utter, utter, utter."

She walked a few dozen yards down the driveway, waving to them. When the automobile disappeared behind a stand of birch, just showing the first hint of spring green, Susan turned back toward the house. Suddenly she heard the sound of another car behind her.

The Rhinelander touring car pulled up beside her, and Marcellus stepped out. He waved his chauffeur on. "Are you relieved?" he asked Susan, taking her arm and guiding her across the lawn. For the first time, the ground felt soft beneath her feet and no longer frozen.

"Yes," Susan admitted. "I must admit that I am. It's going to be spring here soon. I told Harmon I wanted to work on the gardens here. I do, in fact."

"It's very modern of you," Marcellus Rhinelander remarked.

"Gardening? I should have thought that would be considered fairly old-fashioned."

"No, not that. Allowing Harmon to return to New York and his paramour."

"His what?"

"Your husband is"—he sought for a delicate way of putting this indelicate matter—"is occupying himself with another woman."

Susan stopped short and stared at Marcellus Rhinelander. This might just be one step too far, even though Susan had every suspicion, no, every confidence that what he said was true.

"You look surprised," said Marcellus Rhinelander with a broad smile and a twinkle in his eye.

"I'm a little surprised to hear you say it to me with such apparent satisfaction, and with such—"

"With such what?" Marcellus Rhinelander asked with a broader smile and a brighter twinkle in that eye.

"With such certainty, I suppose."

"I am perfectly certain of it," said Marcellus Rhinelander. "The detective I hired is entirely trustworthy in such matters."

Previous astonishment had already stopped Susan. Now greater astonishment propelled her onward again. "You hired a detective? Why?"

"To obtain proof of Harmon's infidelity to you."

"Why on earth would I want that?"

"You want it so you can get a divorce."

"Why on earth would I want that?" Susan repeated.

Marcellus Rhinelander laughed heartily at her apparent obtuseness. "Why, so you can marry me, of course!"

Part III

JACK AGAIN

CHAPTER TWELVE

HARMON ALMOST immediately fell asleep in the backseat. He snored. Barbara complained about life in the country with the same intensity as she complained about life in the city. Jack kept his eyes on the road, the mileage gauge, and his watch, but he might as well have been in one of those infinitely frustrating dreams in which the road never led anywhere, the mileage gauge went backward, and time stood still. New York seemed never to come closer.

"Susan looked very pale, didn't you think?" said Barbara. That was how Barbara initiated a conversation about any other woman. She remarked the other woman had looked pale. If she had wanted to talk about Hottentot Venus, Barbara would have started off remarking, "She looked very pale, didn't you think?"

Jack hadn't thought so. "No more pale than usual," he said. He didn't need to glance over into the backseat to see if Harmon was listening. The man was snoring loudly. He wouldn't hear anything Barbara said about his wife, though Jack still didn't want Barbara to say it.

"Let's talk about Susan later," said Jack quietly.

Barbara looked at him sharply. "There's something to talk about?"

"Yes," he admitted reluctantly.

"Hmmm…" said Barbara, and was quiet for a while.

They let Harmon off at his building. Harmon stood on the sidewalk, looking about vaguely in the twilight, as if wondering in what city on what continent he now found himself. Jack pulled Harmon's bags out of the back and placed them beside the front door. "This is New York," said Jack. Harmon stared at Jack as if he weren't quite sure who Jack was that he should be telling him this. "And this is where you live," Jack added, pointing at the wide double doors of the building. "And here comes George to take up your bags. Hello, George," said Jack carefully, in case Harmon had forgotten the elevator man's name, too. "I'll see you tomorrow," said Jack slowly to Harmon. "At the office."

"Oh yes, of course," said Harmon as if he'd just remembered who he was, who Jack was, what they did for a living, and why this black man in a red uniform should be carrying bags into a building with the numbers 128 over the doors. It all came together at once for him.

"Harmon really is a little peculiar," Jack sighed when he got back in the car.

"A little? Anyone who would marry that pale-faced simpering hypocritical gold digger is a candidate for the lunatic asylum so far as I'm concerned."

"She is pale-faced," Jack conceded. "But she certainly doesn't simper, and I don't see that she's particularly hypocritical."

"She most certainly is. She obviously hates me because I see right through her," said Barbara hotly. "And yet she's always so polite."

"That's not so much hypocrisy as good manners, I think."

"You can't deny she's a gold digger though, can you? She married Harmon for his money. She obviously doesn't love him. If she loved him, she wouldn't be spending all her time in the country. Leaving Harmon alone here to fend for himself."

"That's the strange thing about it," said Jack.

"What is?"

"I thought, too, that she was a gold digger. But most women like that, when they've married good money, the *last* thing they want to do is hide themselves away in the country. They stay in the city, they run up bills in the shops, they go out every night to expensive restaurants, they sail along in new cars with new furs and new dogs and new jeweled bracelets. I've heard Harmon complain that Susan doesn't spend *enough* money."

"You see? She *is* a hypocrite. She's a gold digger but she won't act like one. There's perfidy for you," said Barbara complacently.

It was obvious Barbara wasn't to be convinced. But Jack didn't know what to think. He wondered what was going on in that marriage. The two when together seemed romantic and happy, but they were also content to live apart. Harmon said three times a day how desperately he missed his wife, but so far as Jack knew, he had never asked her to return to New York, and she had never begged Harmon to come to the country. But every marriage was a mystery, and the happy ones more enigmatic than the unhappy ones.

Barbara and Jack went out to dinner that night. Barbara chose El Morocco, which is where they always went when Barbara wanted to talk about something.

Tonight Barbara didn't want to talk about anything.

She pushed bits of meat about on her plate. She sipped at a glass of water. She smoked a cigarette and dropped the ashes on the zebra-striped fabric of their banquette.

She tugged at the fronds of the silly cellophane palm trees on the dark blue walls.

"Harmon was making a joke," said Barbara at last. "But do you think he was right?"

So they were going to talk about Harmon and Susan after all. But there was something different here. Barbara very rarely asked Jack's opinion.

"What joke are you talking about? Harmon never says anything seriously."

"The joke he made to Susan when we first got to the Quarry. He accused her of having an affair with the gardener. Do you think that's why she stays up there?"

Jack stared. "No, I don't think that at all. I think that's ludicrous. Harmon doesn't even keep a gardener up there."

"Then with someone else. She could be having an affair with anybody. It doesn't have to be the gardener, per se. But someone with muscles beneath his shirt and sweat on his brow. Someone who doesn't use proper grammar. Susan's the type to die for the type."

"How do you know that?"

"The way she talks to the servants. You can tell. Maybe she's seeing Richard Grace. I don't think I'd doubt it for a minute. A chauffeur is the next best thing to a gardener when you're starved for love."

"I wasn't aware," said Jack. "But I don't think the reason Susan is staying at the Quarry has anything to do with her being, as you put it, starved for love. In fact, I think it much more likely that Harmon is occupying himself with the equivalent to your gardener-chauffeur. A girl in the hat check, or one of these"—he nodded to the gowned young woman with silver hair in the style of Harlow who sidled between tables with a tray of cigarettes and cigars around her neck—"would be very much to Harmon's taste."

"Probably you're right," said Barbara dismissively. "Luckys," she said to the gowned girl with the tray around her neck. When she'd ripped the foil from the pack, and

Jack had lighted her cigarette, Barbara went on. "But if Susan *were* having an affair, and she were discovered—"

"How?"

"It doesn't matter how. But if she were discovered, then it would be grounds for divorce, wouldn't it?"

"Yes," said Jack. "But husbands don't generally file. Only wives file."

"But husbands *can* file?"

"Yes, of course. But it looks bad."

Barbara shrugged. "It looks worse to keep a wife like that."

"Why are you so concerned with this?"

"I'm not a bit concerned," said Barbara. "Do I look concerned?"

She didn't. She looked bored, but then, Barbara always looked bored.

"But Father's concerned," said Barbara. "He thinks that Harmon made a terrible mistake. He'd like to see Harmon freed of that dreadful crooness. Do you know any detectives?"

Jack blinked. "Why do you ask?"

"A detective could get evidence that Susan is sharing her bed with Father's chauffeur. Do you know any?"

"Yes," answered Jack reluctantly.

"Hire him then."

"No," said Jack.

"Why not?"

"Because it's none of our business."

"It's very much our business. Harmon is our best friend. He's your employer. He's Father's favorite person in the world next to me. We owe it to him."

"We owe it to Harmon not to interfere with his marriage. If it's the wrong marriage for him, then he'll get out of it of his own accord, in his own good time. I won't hire a detective."

"All right," said Barbara. "Then give me his name, and I'll hire him, and I won't even tell you I've done it."

"No," said Jack.

"I'm tired," said Barbara, stabbing out her cigarette in Jack's butter. "Let's go home."

They went home, and Barbara said not another word about Harmon, about Susan, or about the detective.

"Mr. Rhinelander is on the line," Miss Clairville said next morning as Jack walked into the office.

Jack took off his coat and dropped his brief case into a chair. He sat down behind his desk and picked up the telephone. Before he spoke to his father-in-law, he called out for the secretary to close the door. She did so. Jack listened till he had heard her hang up in the other office. Miss Clairville was fat and efficient and curious, and Jack had an intuition that this call was not about the normal business of the firm of Rhinelander, Rhinelander, and Dodge.

I don't suppose Harmon is there.

Jack nearly laughed aloud. The only time Harmon could be found in the office at nine A.M. was when he'd passed out on the reception sofa the night before. "He's not quite in yet," said Jack.

Good. I want you to do something for me. I want you to come to Albany today. Don't tell Harmon you're coming. And don't tell Barbara either.

This was one to handle carefully. Jack could tell that already.

"Is this about Susan, by any chance?"

It has nothing to do with her.

Jack knew Marcellus Rhinelander was lying, but he also knew that that was not something he could say.

"We're very busy here," Jack temporized.

It doesn't matter. Come anyway. You'll be back in New York by ten tonight. Harmon probably won't even notice you've gone, and if Barbara asks, just tell her you were on Long Island.

Barbara hates Long Island so much, she'll never question you further.

There was nothing for Jack to do.

"I'm on my way," he said.

"It's about Susan" was the first thing Marcellus Rhinelander said as he opened the door.

"I suspected," said Jack. "You want me to hire a detective."

"No," said Marcellus, "I've taken care of that myself."

Grace Grace took care of Jack's coat.

"You have?" asked Jack in surprise.

"A man named MacIsaac."

"He's worked for us before. A scoundrel."

"Yes," said Marcellus complacently. "He's in the study now. And he brought photographs."

Jack's eyes widened. He stared at the closed double doors of Marcellus's study. "You mean—"

Marcellus Rhinelander smiled. "Yes, exactly. Proof of infidelity. There won't be any problem with a divorce. And that's why you're here. I'd like you to handle it."

Jack sighed. It was the sort of thing he'd feared, only he hadn't expected the business to have proceeded so far, so quickly. But he wasn't as surprised at that as he was to learn that Susan Dodge actually was carrying on with the gardener or the chauffeur or some other ungrammatical but muscular and sweaty gentleman.

The study doors were opened from within by Malcolm MacIsaac. He was short and thin with shiny black hair and a shiny black suit. He had shiny black eyes and shiny white teeth and a bright red tongue which darted between his thin parched lips.

"Good afternoon, Mr. Beaumont," said Mr. MacIsaac in a voice that was parched and thin and the least shiny thing about him. "You mustn't call me a scoundrel. I only track scoundrels. I expose scoundrels. I turn scoundrels over like mossy wet rocks and I peer at the little horrors that have bred beneath their fat scoundrelly bellies. But no, I am not a scoundrel myself."

"If I called you a scoundrel, and you are not, in fact, a scoundrel, then I apologize for it," said Jack. This was as far as he could go as an apology with Malcolm MacIsaac.

"No offense taken, of course," said the detective. "We have worked together before, Mr. Beaumont. We shall work together again. In the meantime, I have brought you a few scoundrelly photographs to peruse."

He stepped aside with a bright flourish of his shiny-suited arms. Marcellus pushed Jack inside the study.

Most surprising of all was what Jack found in the study.

Or rather, whom Jack found in the study.

Susan Bright Dodge.

She sat on the leather sofa, soberly leafing through a sheaf of photographs. From the way they stuck together, they were probably damply fresh from the darkroom.

CHAPTER THIRTEEN

SHE LOOKED UP at him from the sofa accusingly.

Jack blushed violently. He turned right around and pulled Marcellus back out into the hallway. He slammed the doors shut, nearly crushing the shiny bright toe of Mr. MacIsaac's bright new leathers.

"This is very cruel," said Jack to Marcellus, offended. "To show her those photographs."

"The infidelity had to be proved," said Marcellus, smiling like a villain.

"But to bring her here and show her photographs of herself and—and—and who was it? It wasn't your chauffeur, was it? This is very cruel, Marcellus, and I'm ashamed to be here as if I were part of it."

Marcellus Rhinelander stared at Jack. Then he laughed. "Are you playing the simpleton, Jack? Or do you really not understand?"

"Understand what?"

"Those are certainly not photographs of Susan and Richard Grace—" He laughed loud and heartily at the idea, and Jack blushed again to think that the poor woman in the study could hear that laughter in the hallway. "Those are photographs of Harmon with another woman."

Jack blinked. "It's *Harmon's* infidelity?"

"Of course. Is it such a surprise?"

"Yes," Jack had to admit. "But why was MacIsaac following Harmon? Last night Barbara wanted me to find a detective to prove *Susan's* infidelity. She said you felt Harmon had made a disastrous match."

"Harmon is the luckiest man in the world. It was Susan who made the disastrous match. It's that error I intend to rectify—with those photographs."

"I don't understand," said Jack. "You're right about that much at least."

"It's very simple," said Marcellus, employing the tone of voice with which he addressed children and Communists. "Proof of Harmon's infidelity will allow Susan to file for divorce. And when she has obtained her freedom, I will marry her."

Jack stared. "This is a very elaborate practical joke," he said at last. "Very elaborate, and so far as I can determine, pointless. It is certainly in bad taste."

Marcellus's villainous smile faded. "Don't annoy me," he said in a low voice. "This is not a practical joke. I want you to go in there, look at the photographs, and then talk to Susan about the divorce. We can do the entire business quietly, or we can do it loudly. I would suggest for Harmon's sake that it be done quietly. But it will be done, and if not by you, then by another."

Jack said nothing for a moment. Then he asked, "Do you know how Barbara will take this?"

"I've an inkling," said Marcellus. "And if she prefers to call Susan 'Susan' rather than 'Mother,' I'll understand."

Jack felt that the matter would neither begin nor end there so far as Barbara was concerned.

"May I speak to Susan alone?" Jack asked at last.

"Of course. She's your client now," said Marcellus. "I'll take Mr. MacIsaac out to the kennels. Perhaps he'll be bitten. He's quite useful, but on the whole I agree with you, he is a scoundrel."

"I didn't expect to see you again so soon," said Susan as she handed Jack the photographs.

She smiled faintly.

"Ah, yes…" said Jack.

The first photograph made him blush.

It was of George, holding open the door of the apartment building for Harmon and a young blond woman in a tight cloth coat.

The second photograph made him wonder why he'd blushed at the first.

It was of Harmon kissing the same young blond woman in a corner booth of a restaurant that looked vaguely familiar to Jack.

The third photograph was a relief. Merely a series of identical brownstones on an anonymous side street. Probably in the west forties, Jack thought. An X in purple ink was marked across a set of windows on the third floor of one of the brownstones.

The fourth photograph made Jack turn pale and tremble. He had no doubt they were inside the room behind the windows marked with the purple X. The room was furnished the way he'd always imagined rooms on the upper floors of anonymous brownstones in the west forties would be furnished. A couple of mismatched chairs, a scuffed dresser, faded prints behind dusty glass—and, hardly surprisingly, one of those beds that was not quite wide enough for two. Despite that narrowness, two persons occupied that bed. The young blond woman's lipstick was smeared. Harmon hadn't removed his socks and garters.

"She worked at the Villa Vanity," said Susan. "In the cloak check room. Her name is Dorothy. Her father lost his leg in the War, and her mother was once arrested in a suffragette march."

Jack laid the photographs facedown on the sofa. He hardened his heart.

"This is very distasteful," he said at last.

"I agree," said Susan.

"What Harmon did is reprehensible," Jack went on, "but I cannot refrain from saying that I think what you're doing is worse."

Susan looked surprised. Or at any rate, Jack decided, she feigned surprise.

"Go on," she said with interest. Or at any rate, feigned interest.

"Barbara—"

"Ah," said Susan. "Barbara."

"Barbara has always felt you were a gold digger. Perhaps I thought so, too, at first. One is bound to think so, in these times, whenever a poor girl marries a rich man. But I had come to think Barbara wrong in her assessment."

"Oh yes?" said Susan placidly. "What altered your opinion in my favor?"

"Your failure to spend Harmon's money. Harmon's failure to complain about you, or your behavior, in any fashion. Your marked and proper attention to him in public. Your apparent desire to make a home of the Quarry. All these things suggested that you had married Harmon primarily for love."

"It's always interesting," Susan remarked, "to see ourselves as others see us."

"You've been cleverer than I could have given you credit for."

"Oh yes?" She took up the proof of her husband's infidelity and aligned the photographs neatly. "In what way did I exceed your expectations in the matter of cleverness?"

"You saw Harmon, and you snared him, but once you'd met Marcellus, you realized there was a bigger fish to fry. So you lured him, and snared him, and now you're throwing Harmon back, and you're reeling in Marcellus. You'll get a settlement out of the smaller fish at the same time you're landing the bigger one."

"Extended metaphors are very boring," Susan remarked languidly, sounding very much like Barbara. "Especially extended piscatory metaphors."

"I may as well tell you now," said Jack. "I don't intend to involve myself in this sordid affair. You can procure a divorce, I'm sure, with the aid of these photographs, but you won't procure it by my assistance."

"What makes you think I want a divorce?" Susan asked, smiling.

"You can't marry my father-in-law without one," responded Jack.

"What makes you think I want to marry Marcellus?"

"Marcellus is very rich. Much richer than Harmon. And he's evidently so bewitched by you that he's willing to go through with such a preposterous proceeding."

"He may be," said Susan. "But I'm not."

She picked up the photographs again and, without looking at them, ripped them into quarters.

"I have no intention of divorcing Harmon."

"But what about the cloak check girl? What was her name?"

"Dorothy. Dorothy Rudge. I must say I was surprised to see the photograph of Dorothy in bed with Harmon. I can't imagine what Dorothy's girlfriend, Henrietta, would say if *she* saw it. Henrietta is very jealous of Dorothy. Henrietta once threatened to slit my throat if I made any advances on Dorothy."

"I don't understand."

"Obviously you don't," returned Susan. "You're a lawyer. Lawyers know nothing about life. They know nothing of what poor girls will do, and what they won't do, and what they want, and what they don't want. I'm not a poor girl anymore, but I remember what it was like. What I don't want is to be married to Marcellus Rhinelander, and what I do want is to remain married to Harmon Dodge."

"But you don't love him!"

"You don't know that. Though, in truth, I don't. Or rather, I love Harmon as much as Harmon loves me. Harmon is a convenience for me. He provides me money, and security, a splendid house, and he's a handsome, charming companion on public occasions. I'd like to point out, however, that he gets just as much in return. He's no longer badgered by mothers of your set who are desperate for a provident match for their impecunious, buck-toothed daughters. He's nearly thirty, and a bachelor of that age is suspect, I think you know what I mean. That's no longer a concern for him. If he needs me to be at his side at a dinner of state, or when he makes a speech, or at a regatta, or some such nonsense, I will act the decorative, affectionate article. These cloakroom girls and these dimestore honeys no longer badger him for marriage. They'll now have to do with new gowns and new flats and dinners in the sorts of restaurants where married people never go—at least not with each other. Harmon has what he wants. I have what I want. Why should either of us desire a divorce?"

It was a more complicated matter than Jack had thought. But it all made a kind of melancholy sense. In its way, he supposed, it was no worse than the arrangements he'd made with Barbara.

"But what about Marcellus?"

"I like him very much. He's not as dreadful as you probably think he is. It was very foolish of him to fall in love with me. It was even more foolish of me not to realize that he was doing it. I did not ask him to hire Mr. MacIsaac, and it will be very embarrassing and inconvenient for me to have to acknowledge Harmon's infidelities. I'm afraid my heart really isn't broken in the least, and I'm going to be hard put to produce tears and hysterical recriminations at the proper time."

Jack didn't know what to say.

"I don't know what to say," he said.

"You might say," Susan suggested, "that you don't think it would be a very good idea to tell Barbara what has happened. This is already a situation of some difficulty to a number of people, and I'm not sure that Barbara would be of material assistance in making these rough places plain."

"I think that's probably true," said Jack. "But what about Marcellus?"

"I'm going to tell him that Mr. MacIsaac should be paid and dismissed. I will tell him that I'm not going to marry him, but that our friendship will continue exactly as before. And I hope that I will be able to tell him that you will remain absolutely discreet on this subject. May I tell him that?"

"Yes," said Jack fervently.

"Good," said Susan.

"I'm glad I was wrong about you," he said, initiating an entirely new round of blushes.

"But you weren't wrong," said Susan. "You were right from the beginning, and so was Barbara, for that matter. I am a gold digger, and I married Harmon for his money."

To that, there was nothing a very uncomfortable Jack could reply.

"How did you get into that apartment when they were in bed together?" Jack asked Mr. MacIsaac in the hallway.

"Professional secret," replied the detective with a wink of his shiny black eye.

"Destroy the negatives," said Jack.

"Sure I will," said Mr. MacIsaac and Jack somehow knew that he wouldn't.

"If you haven't yet been paid, then I'll be happy—"

"I'm as free and clear as that lovely young lady in there soon will be."

"Yes," said Jack, thinking it not appropriate to divulge anything at all to Mr. MacIsaac. "Good day, then."

"If you need me," said Mr. MacIsaac with a shiny smile, "I've my old number, and my old office, but my camera and my caution is spanking new for you and for whoever else, Mr. Beaumont."

"Thank you," said Jack.

Mr. MacIsaac slipped out the front door and was gone. Jack could hear the voices of Susan and Marcellus in the study. His quick and distressed, hers low and soothing. Jack went into the dining room and looked at the prints on the wall. Steel engravings of Roman excesses—gladiatorial combats between Christian children and Ethiopian warriors, a patrician family suffocated by an avalanche of rose petals, infants hurled from the city ramparts and caught on the spears of invading Visigoths. It was no wonder his digestion was so poor in this house.

The study doors were flung open, and Susan Dodge hurried out. She threw him one glance, and then was out the front door.

"Stop her!" cried Marcellus, hurrying after.

Jack didn't know what he should do or say. But he felt that he should be stopping not Susan but his father-in-law. "Ah, Marcellus," he said, then realized it was the first time he had ever called the man by his Christian name.

"You idiot," said Marcellus, turning on Jack in a fury. "What nonsense did you talk to her?"

"I didn't talk nonsense!"

"You convinced her not to marry me!"

"I didn't have to," Jack protested.

"I love her."

"She doesn't love you," said Jack, blushing. It wasn't the sort of conversation one usually had with one's father-in-law or, for that matter, with the senior partner of the law firm that employed you.

"Are you saying she loves that drunk? That moral toad? That inexcusable excuse for a husband?"

"No, I'm not saying that," said Jack with reluctant truth. "I think what she's saying is—"

"I don't care what she said to you!" cried Marcellus. "Anybody would say anything to you. You're an idiot!"

"I don't think—"

"Nobody but an idiot would have married Barbara," snapped Barbara's father, and flung himself out the door.

Jack sighed. He wished he'd remained in New York, not lied to Harmon and said he was in court, not lied to Barbara and said he was visiting a client in Montauk. He wished he'd done anything but take that tedious drive up the Hudson, look at embarrassing photographs, listen to uncomfortable truths about private matters, and be called an idiot by his father-in-law. Probably he wouldn't even get dinner. Or worse, Grace Grace would serve up one of her embalmed fowl.

He heard car engines outside. He stepped out the front door onto the porch. Susan's car was halfway down the driveway. It disappeared round a curve.

Richard Grace, in his weekday uniform, stood beside the open door of the touring car. Marcellus Rhinelander swiped the keys from the chauffeur's hand, jumped behind the wheel, and slammed the door. A moment later the touring car revved into life and lurched off with a spray of gravel onto the greening lawn.

Richard Grace kicked his way through the gravel toward Jack. "He hasn't driven in ten years. The old idiot. He wants to marry her. Only decent idea he's ever had. I hope he drives off a cliff."

"I'd better go after them," said Jack.

"I suppose you'd better," said Richard Grace. "The old idiot."

The situation, already complicated, was now in danger of becoming even more difficult. Susan would be returning to the Quarry. Marcellus would follow her there and try to convince her to divorce Harmon and marry him. If Barbara was upset about having Susan the wife of their best friend, Jack could only imagine how she would take the news that Susan was to divorce her best friend in order to marry her father. He contemplated the battle of Argonne.

Jack sighed. He climbed into his Ford sedan, the utterly ordinary automobile that had replaced the splendid vehicle he had wrecked on New Year's Day. He reached into his pocket for the key. He couldn't reach it, owing to the Ford's dimensions and the length of his legs. He got out of the Ford and pulled the key from his pocket. He got back into the Ford and started the engine. He set off in pursuit of his best friend's wife and his father-in-law.

He found only Susan.

Her car was parked against a wall of slate that had been exposed when the road was cut along the side of the mountain. Susan herself stood at the lip of the cliff overlooking the Hudson. A low fence of weathered poles had been broken through there. Jack pulled up behind her car and got out.

"He was following me," Susan said as Jack crossed the road toward her. "He was driving fast, trying to catch up. I saw him in the mirror. He crashed through the railing. So I stopped and backed up."

Jack held on to the broken railing and peered over the edge of the cliff. Two hundred feet below, there was no sign of the touring car or its driver.

Nothing but the dark blue water that flowed on toward the less fashionable side of Manhattan Island.

"There's no chance that he"—she faltered; Jack had never heard her falter before—"no chance he survived, is there?"

"Absolutely not," said Jack. And he knew neither what to think, or do, or say.

CHAPTER FOURTEEN

They WALKED SILENTLY down the narrow road to the Quarry, and from there, Jack telephoned the police. "There's been an accident," he said, feeling rather lame. It was the sort of thing stupid people in tedious films said ten minutes before Warner Oland showed up to say *This was no accident.*

Susan drove Jack back up to the Cliffs. She went slowly, and they looked carefully on both sides of the road all the way, as if in hope they'd simply overlooked Marcellus Rhinelander's automobile—but on one side was the sheer rise of hewn slate, and on the other side was the sheer drop to the Hudson River. There was nowhere, certainly, for a large car to have been overlooked, even supposing it to have been hidden on purpose.

"You've been very good," said Susan in a tone she might have used with a child.

"Thank you. This is a very difficult situation."

"Not you," she said. "Scotty and Zelda." She indicated over her shoulder. The two terriers sat at either end of the rear seat. Jack hadn't even known they were there.

"Harmon told me they'd died," said Jack, thinking they were so quiet and still that perhaps they *had* died and been stuffed. They didn't even make a move to get out of the automobile when both doors were opened. Only when Susan said, "All right now. But be very quiet. This is a house of mourning," did the dogs soberly climb down from the seat and walk sedately across the gravel path at Susan's heels. This surprised Jack, as he'd remembered Barbara's call to the kennel, asking for the most ill-behaved, rambunctious, *impossible* pair of canines on the premises.

Richard Grace and his wife stood on the steps of the Cliffs, waiting for them. Louise had telephoned them with the news already, it appeared. Both servants were weeping.

"He was a vicious old capitalist," sobbed Richard Grace, "and as such he ought not to have been out driving alone, he ought to have had me to take him, and I would have, and he couldn't have beaten me away from my duty to him."

"He thought a lot of you," said Susan, "and told me he would have tripled your pay rather than let you go." This seemed peculiar to Jack, but somehow he didn't doubt Susan's consolation to the bereaved Bolshevik.

"Oh, he *was* vicious, wasn't he?" moaned Richard Grace. "And what are we to do without him? Until the revolution, of course," he added, with lip-service loyalty to the cause.

Inside, Jack said to Susan, "It's not the sort of news I ought to break to Barbara over the phone."

"No," Susan agreed. "You go on to New York. I'll speak to the police, and make what arrangements I can before you return."

"Thank you," said Jack, and he meant it.

It was not a pleasant drive from Albany to Manhattan, and not just because it poured rain all the way and made the trip slower than it was usually. What made the journey miserable was thinking of how Barbara loved her father. *Had* loved her father. Barbara went into hysterics when she chipped a nail. How would she react to this melancholy, unexpected news?

"He's dead?" she asked quietly. Afterward, her lips didn't quite close. Barbara always closed her lips when she finished speaking. Still, by any stretch, this didn't qualify as hysterics.

"He went over the cliff—on the road from the house down to Harmon and Susan's place."

Barbara looked at him. She still hadn't closed her lips, and she hadn't said anything else.

"Grace wasn't driving. Your father was. He must simply have lost control."

"Did he drown?" asked Barbara curiously. As if she might have asked, *Did he have eggs for breakfast?*

"Ah, I'm not sure," said Jack. "I came straight down here as soon as—" He broke off, not knowing how to continue. "When I left, the police hadn't even come, and they hadn't recovered the—ah—they hadn't pulled the car out or—"

"Then you're not even sure he's dead."

"Great Christ in heaven, Barbara! Susan saw the car go through the railing and over the cliff. The water is two hundred feet down. I don't know if he'd drowned, or if he died when the car hit the water, or if he died of fright halfway down—but let me assure you, your father is very definitely dead."

"Call and make sure," said Barbara. *Numbly.* That was the word for it, Jack decided. She was numb. And she was right. He really ought to have made sure Marcellus was dead before he'd come down to Manhattan with the news. It just had never occurred to him that—

He went into the next room and telephoned the Cliffs. Grace Grace answered and put Susan on the line. "He is dead, isn't he?"

That's a very peculiar question.

"Barbara just wanted to make sure. When I left we didn't actually know. We just assumed—"

They pulled the car from the water. Marcellus is dead. Please tell Barbara I'm very sorry. I talked to the police, told them what I knew. Well, some of what I knew. Evidently, it was fairly general knowledge around here that Marcellus spent a good deal of time down at the Quarry, which surprised me, but it also meant they didn't even ask why he was going down there. And they regard it simply as an accident.

"What else would it be?" asked Jack, wondering. He felt like looking over his shoulder for a portly Swedish actor made up to look Oriental, to say, *It might be murder, Mr. Beaumont. In fact, it* was *murder.*

But Susan said nothing to what else it might have been.

He was taken to Albany, and they're waiting for Barbara's advice on further arrangements. Bromer Brothers. The number in Albany is Circle 5022. And if I can do anything for you here…

"No, no, no, I'm sure we'll be coming right up," said Jack. "Have you called Harmon?"

I couldn't find him, but I left messages with both Audrey and Miss Rudge.

Jack suddenly remembered, hotly, the blonde, in the bedroom in the west forties, and he said quickly, "Let me see if I can find him."

Thank you.

"Thank you, Susan. I should probably get back to—"

I understand. Barbara. Good-bye, Jack.

Jack hung up the telephone. The door of the closet he was privileged to call his study opened and Barbara stood there, all in black.

"Do I keep it on or do I take it off?" she asked.

"Keep it on," said Jack.

The trip north again was no less mysterious so far as Jack's understanding of his wife's feelings went. Barbara didn't ask questions, she didn't lament, she didn't weep. She carefully removed her hat, leaned her head back against the seat, and slept or pretended to sleep.

It wasn't raining, and that was a blessing, but it was night. The sky was black. His yellow headlights picked out a hundred and fifty miles of narrow black road, and once in a while another pair of yellow headlamps blinded him temporarily. Barbara's breath was slow and regular beside him. Twice she sighed, long sighs. But Barbara always sighed in her dreams, and perhaps she was dreaming now. Jack wondered if he ought to tell her why her father had been driving without benefit of chauffeur.

He was angry and upset, Barbara.

Why was he upset?

Susan said something that distressed him.

What did she say?

No.

No what?

No, Susan said to your father, I won't divorce Harmon and marry you and become Barbara's stepmother.

On the whole, Jack decided, it would be best if that particular dialogue could be avoided in the difficult days that were ahead of them.

It was dawn when they arrived at the Cliffs. The sun was rising over the hills on the opposite shore of the Hudson. "Barbara..." Jack said softly.

"I'm awake," she said, her eyes open and lucidly staring at the two black wreaths on the doors of the Cliffs.

Jack slept a few hours. He wakened to the sound of soft voices downstairs. He knew somehow that they had been speaking for some time. He showered quickly, climbed into a soft black wool suit, and unsteadily went downstairs. Sudden death, long drives through the rain and the night, uncomfortable sleeps at unfamiliar times, can make one unsteady. Especially sudden death.

Barbara was sturdily receiving visitors in the great hallway. She wore a different black dress from the one she'd worn in the car on the way up. This one was smarter, more becoming. She wore a half-veil, her eyes wide and black behind it, as if encircled with kohl. Beneath the veil her lips were the shade of red that rose fanciers are pleased to call black. As Jack came further down the stairs, he caught sight—through the double doors of the sitting room—of a corner of dark wood raised upon a trestle.

He came down and stood beside Barbara. "I've taken care of everything," she said. "Father is in the sitting room. I'm afraid it wasn't possible to keep the casket open."

Jack shook hands with a cadaverous man in a blue suit who Jack knew in his soul was a shyster lawyer, and tried to make sense of the soft words the shyster lawyer's wife was saying to him in condolence.

Jack shook other hands, listened to other mumbled words, and finally made his way into the sitting room. The coffin was placed in the embrasure of a wide window that looked out over the Hudson and was surrounded by wicker baskets of flowers that stank of refrigeration.

"Those baskets are so peculiar," said Susan, standing suddenly beside him. "Why does a basket that's six feet high need a handle?"

"For the evil giant's young daughters, of course," said Harmon, appearing on his other side. "That's obviously whom these baskets were made for. Old Jackie, I really am very sorry."

"I couldn't find you in New York," said Jack.

"Susan's messages found me," said Harmon, "and I took the first train up. Didn't trust myself to drive, even though I never heard anything that shoved me so quick to sobriety. Poor old Marcellus," he said, glancing at the coffin and shaking his head. "Missed seeing Repeal by a matter of days."

"Barbara seems to be bearing up," said Susan, on the other side of Jack again.

Jack looked at her sharply, fearing irony or sarcasm in her voice. She returned his gaze steadily. "I'm glad," she said. "Barbara, for all her faults, is a strong woman, and I was certain she'd come through at a time like this."

"Barbara is strong," Jack agreed, and smiled a smile of thanks.

He startled when the telephone rang on the small table beside him. Everyone in the room turned and looked at Jack as if he'd just done something to precipitate this mundane intrusion. While Jack hesitated, trying to break down the blush that seemed an admission of that accusation, Harmon answered the phone quietly. He spoke a moment, then handed the receiver to Jack.

"It's for you. Someone named MacIsaac."

Susan glanced at Jack worriedly as he took the receiver.

"MacIsaac," Jack said, "I can't talk to you now." He listened, though, for a couple of minutes. His face paled. Harmon and Susan moved politely away. At the end of the conversation Jack said, "Thank you, MacIsaac," and hung up.

"Didn't we once hire a fellow named MacIsaac?" Harmon asked. "Toady sort of fellow? Made you think you could get warts just to look at him?" He took a glass of sherry from a tray Grace Grace was taking about the room.

Jack nodded. He looked at Susan. "He called to say that the police had examined Marcellus's car. Someone had tampered with the brakes. Marcellus didn't die acci-dentally, he was murdered."

Though Jack had spoken softly, Grace Grace had evidently heard him. For she dropped the tray, the glasses shattered, and the odor of the fine sherry mingled with that of the refrigerated blooms in the giant's baskets.

CHAPTER FIFTEEN

EVENTUALLY, THOSE WHO had come to pay their condolences departed with mumbled words, and slightly bowed heads, and airs of *something's not quite right here*. Jack had said nothing, and neither had Susan or Harmon. Maybe it was just the way Grace Grace had dropped a tray with seven sherry glasses on it, and what everyone had heard of Marcellus's commerce with Harmon's new young wife, or just the brooding irregularity of a closed coffin. But however all these respectful guests divined it, they all left with the impression that there was something untoward in the circumstances of Marcellus Rhinelander's accident.

"It wasn't an accident," you could almost hear Mr. Chan saying, bowing slightly and smiling to these curious mourners as they departed, "it was murder."

Grace Grace closed the doors of the dining room to muffle the noise of the clearing away of the funeral meats.

Her embalmed fowl had never been more appropriate than on this afternoon.

Jack drew the doors of the drawing room closed with a final uneasy glance at his father-in-law's coffin.

Harmon and Susan were the last to take their leaves. Susan had fetched Scotty and Zelda from the kitchen, where they'd remained invisible and unheard the entire afternoon. She now carried them tenderly in her arms. The dogs looked with wary eyes at Harmon Dodge, and Harmon Dodge looked back at them in a way that suggested their wariness was justified.

"Barbara," said Susan, "I really am—"

"I know you are," returned Barbara with a smile that, for her, was positively fiery with warmth. "And you two, please, I'd beg you on my knees, if my knees bent after standing about so long like this in these positively déclassé pumps, please don't leave Jack and me alone. Stay with us for dinner."

"Of course," said Harmon. "Let me just run down to the cellar right now and see what Marcellus left in the way of potables."

"Susan," said Jack, "could I talk to Barbara alone for a few moments?"

"Certainly," said Susan, already stepping away, but Barbara stopped her.

"Oh Jack, what could you possibly have to say to me that you couldn't say in front of Susan? After all, she's family. Someone or other keeps pointing that out to me. Especially after today, I suppose one might say. *Stay,*" she added to Susan with a repetition of that furnacy smile.

Susan put down the dogs and pointed to the corner by a Chinese umbrella stand. The dogs crept behind it, out of sight.

"The police called—" Jack began awkwardly. Barbara's hand was on Susan's wrist, not letting her go.

"And?" Barbara prompted.

"It appears that your father's death might not have been accidental."

"They found something, then?" Barbara asked, not looking surprised.

"You knew they were looking?" asked Susan.

"I asked them to," said Barbara innocently. "Just in case. Father had enemies—all lawyers have. Father even had a few friends who were worse than enemies to him. All rich men have."

"Someone tampered with the brakes," Jack said.

"But how could anyone know that Marcellus would be driving that car himself?" Susan asked.

"Probably they didn't," suggested Harmon, appearing suddenly with an armful of dusty bottles. "Probably they intended to murder Marcellus and do away with the Bacillus of Bolshevism at the same time. A pair of avians brought down with but a single pebble. And speaking of two animals that want killing..." He looked around for Scotty and Zelda, and Jack now understood why the terriers were hiding behind a large and heavy vase.

"But do you have *any* idea who might have wanted to kill Marcellus?" Susan asked Barbara.

"The police asked me that very question earlier today," said Barbara with a smile for Susan that was positively hellish in its warmth and intensity. "I suggested you."

"Ah," suggested Jack, "could we pursue this conversation in another...another venue? This hall's a bit drafty." It was also very easy to be overheard here, by any one—or more likely, all—of the servants.

"Anywhere there's a corkscrew," said Harmon cheerfully. "Help me with these, would you please, Jackie my boy." The dusty bottles in his arms were rolling and clanking about, in fair danger of smashing themselves on the marble flooring. "The news that my wife has just been accused of murder is rattling my equilibrium. Generally, you know, on occasions when my spouse *hasn't* just been accused of a capital crime, I can juggle any number of bottles of fine wine. Perhaps we should adjourn into the dining room if Grace has finished clearing."

"I'd prefer the drawing room," said Susan, still trying to release her hand from the taloned grasp of the woman who'd just accused her of murder.

"The coffin's in there," said Jack in a low, miserable voice. He somehow felt he'd just fallen into a very deep pit.

"Unmasking a murderer—or murderess—could hardly be construed as disrespectful to the corpse of the victim," said Barbara, pulling wide the double doors. She stood aside with a ravishing smile for Susan to enter. "Don't worry, dear. The coffin is closed. If Father's corpse starts to bleed in the presence of his murderer, no one will notice."

"Barbara!"

Barbara smiled a terrible smile and retreated into the hallway again while the others entered the drawing room.

"Jack," said Susan, falling into a corner of the sofa, "please don't bother defending me to Barbara. I didn't murder Marcellus. You know that. Harmon knows that. The police would know that. Barbara is very upset right now, and I have no intention of taking offense at anything she might say."

"Well, just in case you do feel a little threatened," said Barbara, who had evidently heard at least the last of this little speech, "I've brought you a couple of defenders." Barbara brought in Scotty and Zelda—holding them at arm's length, with a jeweled hand clasped around each gasping throat, very much the way cops on the beat push delinquent children along the sidewalk. She dropped the dogs onto the sofa next to Susan. "*They'll* love you no matter what you've done."

"Yes," said Susan, picking up Scotty and smiling quietly at him in reassurance that she did not intend to continue the throttling, "dogs do have several charming qualities. They're loyal and trusting, for one thing. For another thing," she said, putting Scotty down and picking up Zelda, "I have never run into a bitch who was overdressed for every occasion. So, say on, Barbara. Now that the police have told us *how* I killed Marcellus, do we have any idea *why* I might have done this terrible thing?"

"Should I open this Gevrey Chambertin?" asked Harmon.

"You murdered my father for his money, silly," laughed Barbara gaily.

"Is there any whiskey?" asked Jack, heading for the sideboard.

That stopped Harmon in the act of twisting the corkscrew into the cork of the Gevrey Chambertin. Jack fumbled the stopper of the decanter and sloshed the finest pre-Prohibition whiskey on his soft wool jacket.

"Barbara," said Susan after a few moments, "that makes no sense whatsoever. *I'm* not to inherit his money, *you* are."

"Do I look it?" cried Barbara to her husband.

"Like an heiress?" Jack returned, wondering.

"No! Like a babe in the woods. Because that is what you obviously all take me for. A babe in the woods, crawling under the leaves to keep warm and freezing to death anyway. Well, let me tell you all something, I am not a babe in the woods."

"I never supposed it for a minute," remarked Harmon. He had joined Jack at the sideboard.

"Let me tell you two subtle, sophisticated lawyers a thing or five. Let me tell you about my father, and about this hard-boiled babe sitting here so neat and pretty in the corner of the couch as if she were the canary who had just swallowed the mouse."

"Ought I to defend you manfully?" Harmon asked his wife as he slid down easily beside her on the sofa. "Give her a smart slap to bring her to her senses? With Jack's permission, of course."

"Thank you," said Susan. "I'd like to reserve that option for myself. But for now, I, the canary who has just swallowed the mouse, would like to hear what Barbara has to say."

"I'm not sure I would," said Jack, dropping into a chair as clumsily as Harmon had suavely dropped onto the sofa. This time Jack spilled the finest pre-Prohibition whiskey on his soft wool trousers.

Barbara swept dramatically out of her chair and placed herself next to her father's casket, framed herself against a six-foot basket of white carnations, and grasped a silver handle of the ebony coffin with a hand that crackled with diamonds. As she raised her black veil, she looked like the apotheosis of grief—Medea in some dreadful modernistic Russian production.

"Harmon," Barbara said, "it *kills* me to tell you this. Jack, it *breaks my heart* to admit something like this aloud." They waited for the thunderbolt.

Barbara took a deep breath. "Father was senile."

Jack, Harmon, and Susan blinked.

"Senile?" Jack echoed.

"He must have been," said Barbara. "Otherwise, why would he have succumbed to the wiles of *that viperess*?" She pointed at Susan as if there might have been a dozen other viperesses in the drawing room and she wanted to make sure Jack and Harmon understood exactly which reptile was guilty.

Susan shook her head and sighed. "Jack," she said, getting up, "I hope you didn't spill *all* of that whiskey on your suit."

"There's a little left, I think," Jack said.

"What wiles?" asked Harmon curiously when Susan returned to the sofa.

Susan stared at her husband. "Harmon," she said quietly, "you know very well you should not feel that you have to ask me that question."

"Hmm," said Harmon, which could probably not be construed as an apology. "Well, if I can't ask you, I'll ask Barbara. What wiles, Barbara?"

"Well, I don't know exactly, having never resorted to a wile in my life," said Barbara, turning around suddenly from where she'd buried her face in a mound of yellow chrysanthemums. She brushed petals from her bosom and went on. "But whatever wiles she used, they obviously worked, because otherwise why would Father have asked Susan to marry him?"

Jack spilled the remainder of his whiskey on the arm of the chair, and in attempting to wipe it up with his sleeve, knocked his glass to the floor. It rolled over to Barbara's feet. She kicked it smartly away.

"Marcellus asked you to marry him?" Harmon asked his wife in wide-eyed astonishment. Jack didn't think he had ever seen Harmon Dodge either wide-eyed or genuinely astonished at anything before.

"Don't deny it!" cried Barbara.

"I wasn't going to deny it," said Susan.

"He did?" said Harmon, still astonished. "He actually asked you to marry him?"

Susan nodded.

"Did you point out to him that you were already married, and that, in fact, he was acquainted with your husband, and that your husband was his partner in law?"

"I didn't have to point it out," returned Susan rather coldly. "Marcellus was already acquainted with the facts."

"But it wasn't going to be a problem," Barbara interjected, "because Susan was going to get a divorce."

"I see," said Harmon. "On any particular grounds? Inconvenience, perhaps? Incompatible china patterns?"

"Infidelity," said Barbara smugly. "Yours, Harmon."

"Mine?"

"Father, in his senility, hired some dreadful man by the name of MacIsaac—Jack knows him intimately—"

"I do not!"

"—and this dreadful man fabricated some photographs that purport to show you in the embrace of some Ninth Avenue sloozy."

"What is a sloozy?" Jack inquired, and immediately wondered why, of all the important questions that occurred to him just now, he chose to propound this one.

"A sloozy is something between a slut and a floozy," said Barbara. "These fabricated photographs would have proved your infidelity, and Susan could have gotten a divorce. She would have gotten a very fair settlement from you, and then she would have gotten even more money from Father when she married him."

"How do you know all this?" Jack asked his wife. "About MacIsaac and the photographs, I mean." Barbara smiled a secret smile and shredded a white carnation.

"So," said Harmon to his wife as he gently eased one leg over another and swiped at one of the dogs which had come an inch or two closer to him on the sofa, "when Marcellus asked you to divorce me, and marry him, what answer did you give him?"

Susan blinked twice, very slowly. "I find that question insulting."

"She said no," said Jack. "And, I might add, I think that she acted very properly throughout the whole affair."

"Oh yes?" said Harmon, putting aside his drink. Jack had never seen him do that either. "So you knew about this little business as well? I suppose Richard Grace and Grace Grace and Louise of the Firing Range knew about it, too. Everyone knew but me."

"I saw the photographs MacIsaac obtained," said Jack quietly. "They didn't look manufactured. It appeared to me that Susan had quite legitimate grounds for a divorce. In fact, Marcellus asked me to arrange the entire thing. I would have turned it down in any case, but it didn't come to that. Susan herself declined his proposal, with just and proper indignation."

Harmon seemed unmoved by Jack's defense of his wife. "Where are the photographs now?"

"I destroyed them," said Susan.

"Did you think they were real?"

"Of course not!" cried Barbara. "She's the one who paid MacIsaac to fake them! She sold a fur coat to a Jew on Hester Street and paid MacIsaac with the proceeds."

Susan stared at Barbara in amazement.

"I made that part up for effect," Barbara admitted. "But everything else is true."

"Did you believe the photographs were real?" Harmon asked Susan as if this were a matter of no consequence. At the same time, he pulled at Scotty's ear till the dog whimpered in pain.

"Whether I did or didn't doesn't matter," returned Susan in quiet dignity. "I tore them up because I didn't want you to be embarrassed. I didn't want a divorce from you. I certainly didn't want to marry Marcellus."

"She didn't need to anymore," Barbara cried, flinging her arms wide. One of her diamonds scraped across the top of her father's coffin, gouging out a little ditch in the ebony.

"I didn't need to?" Susan echoed.

"Because you'd already got what you wanted," said Barbara, slowly advancing toward the sofa.

"What was that?" Susan asked curiously.

Barbara reached deep into her bosom and pulled out several sheets of paper folded in thirds. She dropped it into Harmon's lap.

"Father changed his will. He left everything he had to you."

"Oh no..." said Susan, clapping a hand to her mouth. She looked at Jack in wide-eyed astonishment. Jack was perfectly certain that his own eyes were wide in astonishment, and he had a pretty good idea that he was blushing as well.

Harmon was quickly reading through the pages. Susan reached for them. He turned smoothly out of her way.

"Well, Barbara," Harmon remarked, "it's a good thing you have a trust fund, because you certainly won't get anything out of this little document."

He turned over to the last page. "Oh, what an extraordinary coincidence. It's dated the day before yesterday. The day before yesterday Marcellus made his will, leaving everything to Susan, my wife. Yesterday he made a proposal of marriage to Susan, my wife. Today he's in his coffin, being decorously mourned by Susan, my wife. Who would have thought the world could move along so quickly?"

Harmon handed the will out for Jack to take, but Susan was quicker. She reached across the sofa and grabbed the papers out of her husband's hands.

"Everything you wanted," sighed Barbara, leaning over the back of the sofa and idly trying to poke out Zelda's eye with the stem of a chrysanthemum. "I suppose it's what you'd call a happy ending."

Susan looked up into Barbara's face. She was silent a moment. Jack wondered what she'd say. Something nasty, and then to spit in Barbara's eye seemed an appropriate response.

"Say thank you" is all she said, however.

"'Thank you'? For what, pray tell?"

"For this," said Susan, and with that she ripped the will in half.

Then in quarters.

Then Jack recovered from the surprise of the thing and leapt up from his chair to grab at the document.

Susan ripped the will up into eighths and flung the bits into Barbara's face.

"Thank you," said Barbara, brushing the foolscap fragments from her dress. "Well, Jack, it appears that I'm an heiress again."

"You shouldn't have done that," Jack said miserably to Susan.

"No," said Harmon, "you certainly shouldn't have, Susan. Because when *I* file for divorce on grounds of adultery, you may end up with nothing at all."

Yes, definitely Jack had fallen into a very deep pit. Now, there at the bottom, he thought he heard the hiss of snakes.

CHAPTER SIXTEEN

BARBARA FLUNG DIRT onto the top of her father's coffin with a silver trowel.

"It really is the most unfortunate thing," grumbled Harmon Dodge as they turned away from the grave leaving five burly men to finish what Barbara had only begun.

"What?" Barbara asked. "Death?"

"No. This bank moratorium. The papers say the banks will be closed for two weeks at the least—which means a month—which means that I've got to live on what I've got in my pocket, which is about twenty dollars, I think."

"There are more important things to think about just now," said Jack quietly, nodding to the clergymen who had performed the burial service for his father-in-law.

"There certainly are," said Barbara vehemently, "such as the fact that Harmon's soon-to-be-ex wife and murderer of my father is standing right there in plain sight of every-body here, in the company of a Communist chauffeur and an incompetent cook, holding two extremely ugly dogs with crudely clever names." Barbara pointed vehemently off to the side, where Susan and the Graces were standing in the shade of an overgrown yew. "The *audacity*!"

"She hasn't been convicted of the murder," said Jack, glancing uneasily in Susan's direction and noting that all three of that small party were quietly weeping. Barbara seemingly hadn't wept since learning of Marcellus's death. And she certainly wasn't quiet.

"The *gall*! I'm certain it's only a matter of time before she's arrested, and if I were she, I wouldn't be flaunting myself at the graveside of my victim waiting for a pair of handcuffs to be slapped on my wrists. Harmon, it was bad enough for you to fall for a gold digger, but I don't think I can ever forgive you for making me go out to dinner continually with the woman who has made me a homeless orphan."

"Oh, you've forgiven me worse," shrugged Harmon, and climbed into the back of the limousine. Then he remembered his manners, got out, and let Barbara precede him in. "Besides," he pointed out, "you're hardly home-less, with the Cliffs, the apartment in New York, and that fourteen-room cabin in Maine."

"I hate that place in Maine," said Barbara as she climbed in. "You know how I feel about trees."

While this little bit of business was being transacted, Jack looked over to Susan and wondered.

She returned his gaze steadily, and he knew she knew what he was wondering, and he blushed and got into the limousine.

He was wondering whether she had in fact murdered his father-in-law for his money.

"If she did murder him for his money," Jack remarked in the back of the limousine, "then why did she tear up the will?"

"Once it was established that Father had been murdered, the will became the evidence of her motive," said Barbara, sounding more and more like Mr. Chan of the Honolulu police. "You simpleton," she added just to mar the resemblance, "she *had* to tear the damned thing up."

"You'll handle the divorce for me, won't you, Jackie my boy?" said Harmon easily. "I don't think I have the heart for it, funerals and bank holidays and all."

Jack didn't answer Harmon. He didn't want to handle the case. On the other hand, he didn't want to let this one get into the hands of anyone else. Anyone else would doubtless make it more sensational than it already was if such an increment were possible. With a tiny jolt of surprise Jack realized he was more concerned here with Susan than with Harmon.

"Of course Jack will handle everything. Harmon will take me back to the city," said Barbara. "You stay on and deal with the viper."

"Give her enough money to keep her quiet and send her to Nevada to get Reno-vated," said Harmon. "Get rid of Louise. I can't stand servants with guns, never could. Then close up the Quarry and kill the dogs."

"Don't you think you might wait just a little while?" asked Jack. "Just till there's some sort of proof—"

"*Proof!*" shrieked Barbara. "Why are you defending her? She murdered my father, for God's sake. The only reason she took all those driving lessons was so she could learn how to tamper with the brakes. That seems perfectly obvious to me. And the *will*, Jack, you saw the will. She got half his fortune, and she didn't even have to marry him. Let the damn dogs live, kill *her!*"

Jack was silent under this barrage. Barbara leaned forward over the seat and peered into the rearview mirror to rearrange her hat, which had come askew in her tirade.

"Besides," she added quietly, "the people we know don't get divorces because one or another of them is a murderer. You divorce them because their hair is the wrong color, or they pack their luggage improperly, or something. Better to divorce the reptile now than wait till they're strapping on the electrodes."

Jack still said nothing.

Harmon's eyes were closed and he looked asleep, slumped in the corner against the door. But he wasn't asleep. "You'll take care of everything then?" he asked quietly.

"Yes," said Jack. "Of course."

Jack dreaded the meeting with Susan. She would think that he suspected her of murder. He didn't at all. He knew that Susan Dodge would no more have set out to kill Marcellus Rhinelander for his money than Jack himself would have followed Harmon's instructions to do away with Scotty and Zelda. But circumstances pointed toward Susan's at least having a motive, and the issue was confused.

He put the meeting off a night.

He learned from Richard Grace that Susan had returned to the Quarry. The chauffeur turned away, halted, came back, stammered, and finally said he hoped that Jack did not believe that *he* had murdered his employer "on account of any little difference we might have had on certain political questions, none of them of any real importance, of course."

"No," said Jack gently. "Neither I, nor the police, nor anyone else I venture to say, could believe that you would destroy the brakes of the automobile that *you* drove every day."

"Have you ever thought," said Grace Grace, sidling up out of the darkness of the dining room, "that Richard might be the object of a plot on the part of the new administration to do away with Socialist domestics?"

"Mr. Roosevelt's been in office for only a few weeks," Jack pointed out, "and there's hardly been time to set such a plot into motion."

"He closed the banks quick enough," Grace pointed out. "And where am I to get my fowl, I want to know!"

Jack had often wondered where Grace got her fowl. A medical research facility providing small animals for classes in dissection seemed more likely a source than a poulterer's.

"And who are you to serve your fowl to?" sighed Richard Grace mournfully, and trudged away into the darkness of the masterless house.

❀ ❀ ❀

Jack put it off the next morning, too.

He visited the police in Albany instead, and inquired into the progress of the investigation.

There was no progress. The wires on the brakes had been cut. That was all that was known, and all that was likely to be known.

Jack shifted uncomfortably in an uncomfortable straight chair and tried to look the detective in the eye. He couldn't, and looked instead into the eyes of Franklin Roosevelt, whose patrician smiling likeness now hung on the wall.

"You haven't seen the will?" the detective asked. He was balding and fat and probably not as bright as he thought he appeared—just the sort of detective who picked the obvious suspect.

"Ah, no, not really," said Jack. "I haven't seen my father-in-law's will." It was the absolute truth, in that he hadn't actually seen Marcellus Rhinelander's final will, because Susan had torn it up before he had had the chance to look it over. Jack may have spoken the absolute truth, but it wasn't quite the real truth.

"Everything's left to your wife, which is right and proper," said the detective. Jack thought he should probably be relieved, but he couldn't manage it. The chair was too uncomfortable, perhaps, for that.

"Except for one very strange bequest. A legacy for Mr. Richard Grace, his chauffeur," said the detective, consulting notes. "Mr. Grace may take any amount of money from the estate from one dollar to fifty thousand dollars, with the proviso that an equal amount be sent to Generalissimo Franco in Spain to help in his war against the Communists."

This time Jack was genuinely relieved.

No peculiar bequests involving Susan Dodge, nor himself for that matter.

"What do you think of that?" the detective asked.

"I think that last wills and testaments are no place for practical jokes," said Jack in a huffy, lawyerly manner.

He couldn't put it off any longer.

It was Grace Grace's last embalmed chicken from the larder. Who knew when there'd be cash in the country again and she could buy more?

"I couldn't," said Jack with truth both absolute and real. "Please, you and Richard have it. To yourselves. Please. I must see Mrs. Dodge down at the Quarry."

"I'll telephone and tell her you're on your way," said Richard Grace, and added with little enthusiasm, "unless of course you'd like me to drive you—"

"Oh no," said Jack. "Stay. Enjoy the chicken."

He hurried out and into his car.

Susan awaited him at the door of the Quarry, flanked by Scotty and Zelda.

She was quiet, sober, but not unfriendly.

"Have you eaten?"

"No," he admitted.

"You're welcome to share what we have," she said, leading him inside. Scotty and Zelda retreated, as if expecting a kick. He smiled at the dogs. The terriers still didn't come any nearer him.

They didn't sit at either end of the long table. Susan set places for herself and Jack directly across from each other, and even moved the centerpiece entirely away. "I'll take care of everything, Louise," she said to the servant, invisible in the kitchen. "You go out and practice." She came back into the dining room with a tray of food, but called out as an afterthought, "Leave the dogs here with me."

"Her aim is better all the time," Susan confided to Jack in a low voice, "but I'd rather not take chances. If Mr. Beaumont says it's all right, you may come in," she said to Scotty and Zelda, sitting on their haunches beside each other in the doorway.

"Of course," said Jack. The dogs trotted in.

"Zelda," said Susan, "you keep Mr. Beaumont company, and Scotty, you can stay with me today." The dogs took up their positions.

This was getting more and more difficult for Jack. Since Susan didn't ask why he'd come, he put it off a bit longer. The lunch was the best he'd had in a long while. A simple casserole of meat and vegetables, exactly the way it was served in Parisian brasseries. A salad of watercress and romaine, and then to finish, Camembert and apples. Simple, elegant, and more continental a repast than was ever provided by the most expensive of New York restaurants sporting French names.

"Did you spend time in France?" he asked as she was bringing in coffee.

"Yes," she replied without elaborating, "but now it's time for you to tell me why you're here."

Jack hesitated. He thought he'd delay till he'd at least tasted the coffee. He was certain it would be good. He spilled it on the tablecloth, his tie, and his shirt, and shrieked with the scalding.

Susan sighed, and shook her head. "We have to talk about it sometime."

Jack plucked at his shirt, pulling it away from his skin. "Talk about what?'

"Oh please," said Susan, closing her eyes in pain. "Don't you know how difficult this is for *me* as well? I like you, Jack, I like you very much."

"You do?" He looked up in surprise and overturned what was left of the scalding coffee in his cup. It poured down on top of Zelda, who yelped once and then at once dropped down on her belly, all four legs outspread in submission.

"It wasn't a punishment, darling," said Susan to the quavering dog. "You didn't do anything wrong. It was just a stupid clumsy accident on Mr. Beaumont's part and it won't happen again. I hope." She threw a napkin down on the stained cloth and poured Jack another cup of coffee. "I don't mind about the linen, but I would appreciate it if you wouldn't maim the pets. I've grown fond of them, even if it was Barbara who gave them to me. Sorry. I didn't mean to say that."

"This is difficult for me, too."

Susan smiled a sad smile. "You don't believe I killed Marcellus, do you?"

"No, I don't. But how did you know I don't?"

"If you did think I'd killed your father-in-law, you wouldn't have sat through lunch and eaten absolutely everything I put in front of you, and you certainly wouldn't be so eager to spare my feelings that you spilled your coffee *twice*."

"I don't think you'll be charged," said Jack. "There's no record of the last will—the one you tore up—so as far as the police are concerned, you have no motive. The only evidence remains the brake cables that were cut."

Susan laughed.

"What's funny?"

"You may not have believed I killed Marcellus, but you did believe that I was worried I'd be arrested, and tried, and convicted, and hanged."

"Electrocuted, actually, in this state. Yes, I suppose I did believe you were afraid."

Susan shook her head. "I've been mourning, that's all. I was quite fond of Marcellus, and I'm very very sorry that he's dead, and it's quite terrible to think that I had *anything* to do with his death. If I hadn't run out of the Cliffs, and he hadn't followed me..."

"Oh, you shouldn't think *that!*" cried Jack, actually in anguish that she should be so troubled. Especially when Barbara took her father's death so much in stride and seemed to want Susan convicted of the crime less because Susan might be guilty than because Susan was Susan. "After all, if it was murder, then it certainly *wasn't* your fault, and if he hadn't died that way, then the real murderer would have gotten him in another way."

"You're beginning to sound like Charlie Chan," said Susan.

CHAPTER SEVENTEEN

JACK COULDN'T put it off any longer.

"I came to talk to you about the divorce," he said.

Crack.

Jack startled and hadn't recovered before there was another, even louder *crack.*

"It's Louise," said Susan. "And you needn't worry. She never fires toward the house."

"Ah—" Jack said, forgetting where he was.

"Of course you came about the divorce," said Susan, taking it up for him. "I expected you yesterday."

Jack blushed. "I tried to put it off for as long as possible. I hate this."

"The divorce isn't necessary, you know," she remarked, but added quickly, "though of course you understand I have no intention of protesting. If Harmon doesn't want to be married to me, then I'm not going to force my continued presence on him. Of course, if he truly believes I'm a murderer..." she mused.

Even though the reason for his visit had been broached and acknowledged, Jack was no more comfortable. If anything, this was rather worse, having to take Harmon's side when he was very much on Susan's and considered that Harmon was a pickled idiot.

"I don't know if you can believe this," said Jack, "but I really am interested in making this as painless as possible for you."

"I do believe it," said Susan. "I told you, I like you. And I don't like people I don't trust. I do trust you. Harmon is your employer and I don't see very well how you can have refused to handle this for him."

"I think Harmon is making a very bad mistake."

"That's Harmon's business, not yours. I suppose you want to talk about terms."

"Ah—yes."

Susan looked around at the dining room. She sighed. She grimaced. "I'd love to ask for this place, but it wouldn't be right. I couldn't afford to keep it up anyway, and I've never enjoyed spoils. I don't want anything from Harmon. Except, of course, Scotty and Zelda."

Jack stared. "That's very foolish."

"Of course it is. It was very foolish of me to tear up a will that would have made me a very rich woman, independently of Harmon. But I do very foolish things sometimes. If I didn't, I wouldn't be able to live with myself. I don't want any of Harmon's money."

"But you told me—" began Jack uncomfortably.

"Oh, I know, I told you I married Harmon for his money, and I did. But I also gave him value for that money. I was a good wife—not in the general manner of the way wives are good, probably, but a good wife for Harmon. But if we're not married, then I don't deserve his money. That's all. If he wants to think himself very generous, then he can let me take a few things from the wardrobe he paid for."

"I don't like this," said Jack.

"I thought I was making your job easy," said Susan with a small smile.

Crack.

"Susan, if you don't get a settlement from Harmon, you won't have anything more than what you had before you married him."

"I know," she said, and shrugged. "In fact, I'll have less, with two new dependents." She reached down and lifted Scotty into her lap. Zelda made a small whine of jealousy, and Susan motioned her over. Zelda leapt into Susan's lap beside Scotty. "For three years I lived on birthday cake and caviar—that was what was usually left at the end of the evening at the Villa Vanity. I suppose I can do that again."

"I'm not going to Harmon and tell him you don't want anything—"

Susan considered for a moment. "He can pay the expenses of the divorce. I can't really afford that. I suppose he wants me to go to Nevada. That's very fashionable."

"Probably best," sighed Jack. "Six weeks' residency requirement."

"Oh, I don't mind." Susan shrugged. "In fact, I'm rather looking forward to it. Didn't I ever tell you? I'm a major landowner in Nevada."

"I beg your pardon?"

"I own several thousand acres of land in Nevada, about thirty miles outside of Reno. Some wild-eyed uncle of mine bought it in the nineties, during the gold boom. Of course he was very careful to purchase land on which there was no gold at all. No silver either. Or water, or anything else, so far as I know. The land was all that was left of the Bright fortune after twenty-nine."

"Why didn't you sell it? Why don't you sell it now?"

"Great God! Why didn't I ever think of that? Then I wouldn't have had to marry Harmon, and I could have waited till I came across a man I actually loved." She looked at Jack, giving him not too long or lingering a look, but one that made him blush harder than he had since he'd arrived at the Quarry.

Then she laughed. "You find me a buyer, and I'll sell that land in a minute. I'll go down as low as twenty cents an acre." She shook her head sadly. "No one wants that land. I've tried to sell. Besides, my cousin Blossom lives there now. She was knocked out in twenty-nine, too, and went out there and fixed up an abandoned ranch, makes a living by taking in fat women who want to get divorced."

"Fat women who want to get divorced?"

"She drives them like slaves, I understand. After six weeks they're twenty pounds and a husband lighter. I'd stay with her, but I don't think I need to lose the weight."

Jack shook his head admiringly. "You're perfect now."

"Oh, thank you, Mr. Beaumont. But flattery won't get me to lower my demands in this case. I still get to keep Scotty and Zelda."

Crack.

Jack glanced around. He'd remembered something else.

"Harmon wanted me to let Louise go."

"I think you'd best let me tell her," said Susan.

Crack. Crack.

"Possibly that would be best," said Jack, relieved.

Jack drove Susan to New York. She took with her only one bag, and Jack was certain it contained only clothing that Susan owned before her marriage. He was both sad for her and proud of the dignified way in which she was handling this dreadful business. He decided Harmon had never deserved her.

He took her to her apartment, first making sure by telephoning Audrey that Harmon was out. Packing didn't take Susan long. In fact, she appeared again with only one, much smaller bag. "Scotty and Zelda are inside, and they promised to be very quiet so that I could get them into my compartment. Otherwise, they'll have to ride in the baggage car." She smiled a little smile of self-deprecation that broke Jack's heart. "It's a long ride to Reno, and I think I may want their company."

She hugged Audrey. "Harmon is bound to propose to you," Susan warned. "Think twice before you say yes."

"Get that divorce," said Audrey. "Marry another rich man. Then send for me."

"If I was rich," said George, holding open the door of the elevator for Susan, "I'd marry you."

"If you were rich, I'd make you marry Audrey, and then you'd send for *me* to work for *you*."

Jack drove Susan to the train station. He procured her tickets, and then led her to the first-class car.

"No," she said. "I made reservations for third class—" Jack blushed.

"I changed them," he said. "Ah—because of the dogs. They're much less likely to be discovered in first class. Of course, until the divorce they're Harmon's joint property, so he'll be happy to bear the increased expense."

Susan laughed. "Thank you, Mr. Beaumont, for taking such care of Scotty and Zelda."

The conductor took her bags and escorted her to her compartment.

"Oh, please don't wait with me," she said to Jack, leaning out the window and speaking to him on the platform.

"I've an appointment in the neighborhood in half an hour—I'd just as soon wait here. Oh, just a moment, there's something I have to do. You get settled and I'll be right back." He hurried off, ducked out of sight against the side of the train, and then climbed onto the first-class coach.

"Yes sir?" said the conductor.

"Take care of Mrs. Dodge for me, will you?" said Jack, and slipped the conductor two worn ten-dollar bills.

"Yes sir..."

It was the last of his cash, except for some small change, and the banks might not open for another month, but Jack didn't fret about that twenty dollars. It was well placed so far as he was concerned.

He slipped surreptitiously from the coach and sauntered back to Susan's window. He started to knock on it, but she was waiting for him.

"Had to make a quick phone call to confirm—"

"You *always* blush when you lie," laughed Susan. "Again, thank you...for whatever it was you just did for me."

She disappeared for a moment, and then came back to the window. She quickly held up Scotty and Zelda, and then the two dogs disappeared again.

"They say good-bye," she said.

"I'll miss them very much. Never can remember when I found myself so much liking a—a...ah—"

Susan's smile faded. She looked suddenly so very much troubled that Jack broke off.

"Please," he cried earnestly. "You'll be all right. I'll make sure of that. Don't trouble yourself. Enjoy Nevada. Visit your cousin Blossom and give her my best."

Susan looked even more troubled. She wouldn't take her eyes from his face.

"Please," he pleaded. "Harmon Dodge isn't worth it." He blushed. "I'll take care of you."

"I'm not worried about myself," she said in a low voice. "I'm worried about you."

"About me?" he asked in surprise.

"Be careful," she said.

"Careful about what?"

"About Barbara."

Jack frowned.

Susan shook her head. "No. Don't misunderstand me. This is quite apart from anything Barbara has ever said or done to me. This is not about her and me. This is about her and you. Please be careful."

"In what way?"

She didn't answer. Drawing back inside the cabin, she called, "Good-bye, Jack!" Then the curtains across the window were drawn.

Jack waited on the platform for another ten minutes. But the curtains did not open again, and Jack did not venture inside the coach. If Susan wanted to talk to him, she would open the curtains. He would not force himself on her or demand her confidence.

Finally, the conductor called "All aboard," saluted Jack with a grateful grin, and said, "Don't worry, I'll take care of her. And in six weeks, Colonel, she'll be a free woman, and I'll bring her back to you."

Jack started to protest that that wasn't the situation between them at all, but the train took off then, with a squeal and a growling and a grumble and a flash of electric sparks. His denial was lost.

The curtains opened then, and Susan waved good-bye.

CHAPTER EIGHTEEN

"THANK YOU, JACKIE my boy," said Harmon, clapping him on the back in such a way to make Jack remember that he had broken several ribs a few months back. "John my man, I am in your debt."

"You certainly are," said Jack. "It was a very unpleasant business."

"Can't argue with you there. As the old ladies say, I sat down in the wrong pew with that young lady. In fact, if Barbara were here, she'd probably say that I got drunk and wandered into the wrong church entirely."

"On the contrary," said Jack, who had always disliked the way Harmon perched on the edge of his desk and tore little scraps off the corners of important documents, "I think that you made an excellent choice of a wife. God protects drunks, they say."

Harmon drew back in apparent alarm. "Harsh words those, Jackson my savior. But I can't argue with you there—about Susan, I mean. How long do you suppose I would have survived before *my* car was run off a cliff into the river?"

"You don't really mean to tell me you believe Susan killed Marcellus."

"Barbara believes so."

"Barbara is deranged on other topics as well," said Jack.

"Harsh words for everyone this morning," Harmon noted. "Forget those little chocolate tablets last night?"

"No. My harsh words are in response to what I feel is some fairly callous treatment of a woman who deserves nothing but consideration."

Harmon was silent a moment, and then grinned. "She is beautiful, isn't she?"

Jack blushed, and despised himself for blushing.

"A piece of advice, Jackie my innocent, Susan's got beauty that'll melt your heart. And Susan's got a heart that'll freeze your balls. Barbara always knew it, and I found it out. Take my word, it's not something you want to learn from experience. And take my word on something else, too—don't talk about Susan to Barbara the way you've just talked about Susan to me."

Jack looked at Harmon long and hard. He liked him less and less.

"She has done everything to make this as easy as possible for you, Harmon. She hasn't asked for a dime, she left for Reno within two days of your announcing your intention of divorcing her, and she's agreed to file for divorce on grounds of mutual incompatibility. Rather than your adultery."

"Or her murderousness," Harmon pointed out.

"You're an idiot if you believe she's guilty."

"If you think she's innocent, Jackie, then you should prove it."

"How do you mean?"

"Go up to Albany. See what the police are doing. Look around on your own. See if you can find who the murderer really is. If it isn't Susan, then it's someone else. Relieve your mind. Disperse the clouds of suspicion that now hover over that poor unfortunate chanteuse with the heart of ice."

"I think that may be a good idea," said Jack.

"On the contrary," said Harmon, smiling a cool smile, "it's probably a very bad idea. For if you found incriminating evidence or meddled too much in the investigation—if there is one—it might appear that I had sent you to *prove* the charge against the woman who is divorcing me."

"I'll do my best to keep your reputation for straight-forwardness and generosity intact," said Jack dryly.

"And take Barbara with you, would you please? When you're away, she does hang on me."

"And gets in the way, I suppose?"

"In the way of what?" echoed Harmon, as if he had no idea what Jack meant.

Barbara was, as Jack suspected she would be, incredulous.

"You're going *where*?"

"Albany."

"To do *what*?"

"To see what I can do to clear Susan's name."

"The only clearing that vampire's name needs is to get rid of the Dodge at the end of it."

Jack was silent.

Barbara looked at him steadily from the other end of the couch. She wore a robe of beige velvet, a gold turban, and embroidered slippers with curved toes that ended in tinkling silver bells. It was one of her most annoying at-home ensembles.

She tapped a foot impatiently. The tiny little silver bell clanged, as if announcing a fire in a mouse hole.

"May I remind you," she said—and whenever she said that, Jack knew that she was going to bring up something that she had made perfectly clear a hundred times before—"may I recall to your failing memory the fact that Father was murdered, and that his murderer goes yet unpunished. In fact, Father's murderer is probably at this very minute turning her pale skin up to the beautiful sun of the great American West. Suntans are going to be fashionable this year, I'm told."

Jack blinked. "I really am not sure what you're trying to say to me, Barbara."

"I'm saying that I think it is in terribly bad taste for you to be assisting a murderess to set herself up as a fashion plate, when you should instead be trying to put a noose around her neck. I think that anyone—even someone like me, who never had a suspicious thought in her life—*anyone* would begin to imagine that there was only one reason you were doing it..."

She stared at him.

The tiny bell clanged again, and this time the conflagration seemed to be somewhere behind Jack's brilliant cheeks.

"What would that reason be?" asked Jack in a strangled voice.

Barbara paused a moment before answering. "*Anyone* would think that you had paid the woman to do the deed in order to get at the inheritance through me. And that you had to make certain she wasn't arrested, so that you wouldn't be implicated. After all, I'm a very rich young woman now, and rich young women are a good deal rarer in 1933 than they were in 1923. You paid Susan Dodge to murder my father—that's what even an *un*suspicious mind might think."

A suspicious mind, thought Jack, might think that he was doing it merely because he was falling in love with Susan Bright Dodge.

"In any case," said Jack, "I'm going up to Albany and look around for a few days. And I'd like you to come with me."

"I'll stay here and look after Harmon."

"I'm not sure Harmon needs looking after."

"Of course he does, and I'm the one to do it."

Jack started to protest, and then he realized he wouldn't mind if all Harmon's pleasures throughout the rest of eternity were stymied, canceled, punished, or turned into bitter ashes by Barbara's "looking after" him. In fact, he hoped that she managed to make his life quite miserable. Harmon deserved it.

"I think that's probably a good idea," said Jack. "For you to stay here and look after Harmon."

The bell on Barbara's slipper abruptly stopped its annoying peal.

"I don't like it when you say that," said Barbara suspiciously. "It means you're up to something."

"I am. I need to borrow a few dollars from you for gasoline."

"Absolutely not. I'm not going to stop you from making a fool of yourself. But I'm not going to pay you to do it either."

"Barbara, the banks aren't going to open again till Monday at the earliest. I don't have a penny—no, actually I have four pennies, but that's all—and all I need is two dollars to get to Albany."

"Beg for it," said Barbara, getting up.

"Barbara," said Jack, ashen with anger. "I will not beg you for anything. That is not what marriage is about."

"Oh, I didn't mean for you to beg me," she said, going out of the room. "I meant beg on the street."

The chiming bells of her slippers muted as she walked toward the bedroom, and when she slammed the door, they were silent altogether.

Jack looked around the room for something to destroy.

He saw Barbara's pocketbook—flat and fashioned of the skin of an infant alligator, whose reptilian head was pushed beneath a kind of miniature croquet hook for a clasp.

Jack opened Barbara's purse and went through it. He found over a hundred and forty dollars in cash. That was more legal tender than Rockefeller himself probably had at that moment. Jack started to count off five one-dollar bills, but then he decided against taking the money.

Instead, Jack took the two tickets to the opera that he and Barbara were to have attended that evening. It was *La Forza del Destino*. That seemed appropriate.

He had already packed a bag, and he left without saying good-bye to Barbara. He drove over to York Avenue, to the gasoline station where the attendant— Jack had remembered—was always whistling Verdi. In exchange for the orchestra circle tickets Jack got a full tank of gasoline, an extra two cans for the trunk just in case, and a sparkling windshield. The thrilled attendant wanted both to kiss Jack and give him a new tire, but Jack said that he already had a spare.

He drove to Albany, and was at the Cliffs by evening.

Grace Grace met him at the door. "Miss Barbara called," said Grace, "and said that if I was to let you inside, she'd fire me and Richard both."

Jack grinned. "She found out about *The Force of Destiny*..."

"Miss Barbara has known about *that* sort of thing a great long while," remarked Grace, and she wasn't wrong either. "But she has another thing coming if she thinks I am turning *you* away, Mr. Beaumont. In fact, as soon as I knew you were coming, I put a chicken in the pot."

Jack took a deep breath. "Perhaps I should just stay down at the Quarry," said Jack. "I'd hate to get you and Richard in trouble with Barbara. After all, the house is hers now, and she's paying your salaries."

"Quarry's shut up, Mr. Beaumont," said Grace. "Now that poor Mrs. Dodge is gone and Louise was let go." She took a confidential step forward. "Richard and me brought Louise back here," she said in a low voice. "No jobs to be had these days. Not for those willing to work, not for those needing to work, not for those who'll die without work even..."

"I know," said Jack.

"Mrs. Dodge telephoned long distance this morning," said Grace suddenly.

"Oh yes?" said Jack.

"She is in Reno now, and wanted us to know she got there safe. She gave me her address and the number of the telephone there just in case—"

"Just in case what?"

"Just in case anybody was to ask," she said with a grin.

Jack blushed.

So as to avoid trouble for the Graces, and more particularly to avoid another dose of embalmed chicken, Jack didn't stay at the Cliffs. He didn't stay at the Quarry because it was closed up, and more particularly because he knew the place would remind him entirely too much of Susan.

Charging the expense to his firm, Jack spent the night in a hotel in Albany, frequented principally by the mistresses of state legislators. He could tell this by the number of politicians who came in alone, tipped the staff, and waltzed alone up familiar stairs, and by the number of beautiful women who ate in cozy pairs and trios in the dining room.

Next day he visited the detective who had been attached to the Marcellus Rhinelander murder case.

"A great deal, everything possible," was what was being done in the case.

"Nothing, nothing at all" was what was new in the investigation.

"No one, no one at all" was who was suspected of the murder.

Jack stayed two more days in Albany, not because there was anything for him to do there, but because he knew that he would be returning to the Cliffs for the sole purpose of getting Susan's address from Grace. If he went the next day, he knew how deep would be his blush when he stammered out his request.

So he spent a full day wandering the streets of Albany, falling asleep in the visitors' gallery of the state senate after only twenty minutes of a speech on the dangers of Bolshevism under the new Socialist leadership in the country, staring into shop windows and dangerously thinking of gifts to buy not his wife but a dark-haired woman whose pale skin was reddening under the Nevada sun, eating alone in the hotel dining room and trying to overhear the conversation of the mistresses of the state legislators.

The next day he went back to the Cliffs, and Richard Grace appeared.

"Just wanted you to know that I was on my way back to the city," said Jack lamely.

"I wouldn't have kept you out of here either," said Richard Grace, who still looked as mournful as on the day his employer died.

"I know that," said Jack.

There followed an embarrassed silence.

It was made more embarrassing for Jack by the fact that he gradually turned beet-red in its duration.

"Are you all right, Mr. Beaumont?" Richard Grace said finally.

"Do you have Mrs. Dodge's address?" Jack blurted out.

Richard Grace looked astonished for a moment. "Yes," he answered after a pause.

"Well, could I have it?"

Richard Grace blinked at him.

The beets in Jack's cheeks looked as if they'd just been thrown into boiling water. They got redder than you'd have believed possible a moment before. They turned a kind of cheap religious purple.

Finally, even Jack thought he might have some sort of attack if he did not bring this business to a close.

"Please, Richard, give me Susan Dodge's address in Reno! So I can write her! So I can help her in any way I can! Because I probably love her!"

Oh God, he thought. *What have I just said?*

Richard Grace stared.

"You have it already," he said at last.

"What?"

"Mr. MacIsaac came by yesterday and said you'd sent him to get Mrs. Dodge's address. So Grace gave it to him. The telephone number, too."

"Mr. MacIsaac?"

"The private detective, I believe, who was here the day Mr. Rhinelander was killed."

"I didn't send him," said Jack.

"Then perhaps Grace shouldn't have—"

"It doesn't matter," said Jack. "Just give it to me now."

"Of course," said Richard. "I'll be right back."

He brought the address a moment later, written on a sheet of Marcellus's personal stationery.

"Thank you," said Jack. "About what I said earlier—"

Richard shook his head. "Mr. Beaumont, you'd be a fool not to love that woman."

Jack laughed, and didn't blush for once. "No, I'm not a fool."

"However," Richard pointed out, "you did marry Miss Barbara..."

On the drive back from Albany to the city, Jack wondered about Malcolm MacIsaac and why he should want Susan's address in Nevada. Not for his own sake, of course; he must have been hired by someone.

By Harmon? Because of the divorce proceedings, perhaps.

By Barbara? Because Barbara wanted to stir up trouble about her father's murder, perhaps.

By the murderer? Who wanted to make sure he didn't lose sight of a possible lamb to sacrifice on the altar of justice, if more evidence were ever discovered in the case, perhaps.

But maybe MacIsaac *did* want the address for himself.

Because, perhaps, MacIsaac himself was the murderer.

Jack ran over some small animal that had hurtled itself out into the road. Then, looking behind him to see what life he had snuffed out, Jack nearly rammed into the automobile coming toward him. Then, swerving to avoid that, he narrowly missed flipping the car over in a ditch. Finally, he struck another small animal—possibly the anguished mate of the first.

At last, however, Jack regained control of the Ford. But during that brief excitement of two animal deaths framing two very near automobile crashes, Jack had become utterly convinced that Malcolm MacIsaac was the murderer of Marcellus Rhinelander. The detective was at the Cliffs that day. He had parked his automobile next to the touring car. He must have had ample opportunity to make the simple cuts in the brake cables. He was a wily, conniving, scurrilous, slimy scoundrel, and wouldn't have given a second thought to the moral question behind a planned murder, and wouldn't have suffered a moment's regret over the fact that he had done it.

The only difficulty, of course, was that Jack knew of no reason why Malcolm MacIsaac should want Marcellus

Rhinelander dead so much that he'd risk the electric chair for getting him out of the way.

In the scheme of things, this seemed a secondary question.

The primary question was Susan Bright Dodge, and whether she was in any danger from the real murderer.

It wouldn't do to take chances. In his head Jack composed a telegram:

IMPERATIVE THAT YOU IMMEDIATELY SEE THE BLOSSOMS IN THE NEVADA DESERT STOP LEAVE NO FORWARDING ADDRESS STOP TELL NO ONE STOP TRUST ME STOP DESTROY THIS STOP

JAB

She'd be safe at her cousin's, and even if Blossom's last name were not Bright, Jack would find her somehow. But he did not want Susan to remain anyplace where Malcolm MacIsaac could find her.

Feverishly, he parked the car and ran inside the apartment building. He didn't wait for the elevator, but raced up the stairs. He fumbled with the key in the lock, calling all the while, "Barbara! Barbara!"

He couldn't get the key to turn in the lock, but it didn't matter. Barbara threw open the door. She was stunningly dressed and made up, wearing a yellow crepe suit with a shined bosom and a yellow hat with a wide black brim.

"Barbara," Jack said breathlessly, "I know who murdered your father."

"I do, too," she said. "I'll say hello when I see her."

"What?"

"I said, quite plainly, I believe, that I will give Susan your regards when I see her. *Fondest* and *most loving* regards are the words I think I may use."

"When you see her where?" said Jack, forgetting to protest that Susan *wasn't* the murderer he had been talking about or to wonder much about the meaning behind *fondest* and *most loving*.

"When I see her in Reno."

"Why are you going to Reno?" asked Jack, mystified.

"Why does anyone go to Reno?" Barbara replied, picking up a small suitcase Jack hadn't noticed before.

He stared at the suitcase. He stared at Barbara.

"I'm getting a divorce."

Part IV

SUSAN ONCE MORE

CHAPTER NINETEEN

RENO IS THE Biggest Little City in the World.

Even if it isn't, everyone believes so because of the relentlessness with which everyone in Reno makes the claim.

Certainly, for a city its size—about twelve thousand permanent residents—it has the biggest courthouse in the world. Reno's courthouse would probably do for all five boroughs of New York.

For a city its size, Reno has the greatest number of gambling casinos and other places of doubtful resort. More than would do for any five sovereign nations of Europe you could pick at random.

For a city its size, Reno has the greatest number of temporary residents at any one time—two or three times its stable population—than any other place in the world except perhaps Mecca. But whereas the streets of Mecca are generally filled with righteous Islamic men come to worship at the holiest shrine of Allah, Reno's streets are filled with the unhappy, the disappointed, or the treacherous wives of America.

Consequently, Reno is a city with three principal components—a massive courthouse whose principal business is that of record-keeping for cases of divorce; a web of gambling casinos and nightclubs whose clientele is an amalgam of the rich and unhappy of every American city, town, and village; and street after dusty street after depressing street of rooming houses whose tenants never stay more or less than six weeks by the court calendar.

Susan took a room in a boardinghouse belonging to Mrs. Bertha Pocket, a large woman in middle middle age with a thick waist and a pickled countenance. She had come to Nevada for the six weeks' residence necessary for a divorcement of marriage certificate, and had so far fulfilled sixteen years of that brief requirement. Her ex-husband had married again, and again unhappily, and had sent his second wife to Mrs. Pocket's boardinghouse with his recommendation. That lady had stayed on in Reno as well, and now owned a small nightclub of her own, and was splendid friends with the first Mrs. Pocket.

The boardinghouse was a vast, rambling, old Victorian house, with peeling paint on the outside, and on the inside, dusty walls, dusty rugs, dusty furniture, and enough dusty knickknacks to fill a hundred curiosity shops and make them all seem uncommonly dusty. From her dusty room Susan could look through a dusty window and see the courthouse where she established her residency in Nevada. In anticipation of six weeks spent in that large, empty, dry state, she filled out a petition of divorce against Mr. Harmon Squire Dodge, of Albany, New York, and New York, New York.

After two days Susan decided Reno must be the most boring and expensive place in the world. The rent for her room in

Mrs. Pocket's boardinghouse was triple the rent for her flat in New York, and it was every bit as inconvenient, small, and unpleasant. It was, moreover, a great deal dustier.

The boardinghouse was filled with women in her straits. Susan hoped she didn't flatter herself when she considered that the similarity ended there.

The other women, rich and supercilious, deplored the exigencies of the system that condemned them to the mercy of Mrs. Pocket and her ilk. Or they were loud and determined to run up as large a bill as possible for their ex-husbands to struggle to pay. On one side of Susan was a woman from Pennsylvania, suicidally depressive over the prospect of losing her husband, the only man she'd ever seen with his shirt off. On the other side of her was a woman who knew every nightclub in Reno, and the maître d's by name, and whose own bed hadn't been turned down since she'd arrived four days before Susan.

It was this young woman, Esther Ladd, who tried to persuade Susan to go out to a nightclub her first night in Reno. According to Mrs. Pocket, Esther Ladd's husband was a notorious criminal in Pasadena. Esther Ladd not only looked the type who would marry a notorious criminal, but would marry another one once she'd divorced the first. She was what was known as a bottle blonde, because that's where the color came from.

"Thank you," said Susan, "but I'm very tired."

"You're not tired," said Esther boldly, "you're miserable. You're depressed. You're pale blue from the bottom up. You can't get him out of your mind."

"Him?" said Susan, wondering how Esther Ladd, who was from Pasadena, knew about Jack Beaumont.

"Your husband."

"Oh, *him*. No, I can't," Susan lied, "but despite that fact, I'm very tired, and I really don't want to go out."

So she stayed in, and shared a little supper with Mrs. Pocket, who told her more than she wanted to know about all the women who were currently in residence. Then she walked Scotty and Zelda around several blocks, and was depressed by the number of boardinghouses just like Mrs. Pocket's. Each, she was sure, was jammed to the rafters with women either wanting or being forced into a divorce.

After breakfast she lingered about the parlor till it was nine o'clock and the only bookstore in town opened. She walked over to it, bought a novel, brought it back to the boardinghouse, started it, stopped in the middle to have lunch with Mrs. Pocket, who told her more than she wanted to know about the last set of women who'd stayed with her, walked Scotty and Zelda again, but took a different route and found even *more* boardinghouses, came back, finished the novel, checked her watch, and discovered it was too late to go back and buy another book. Thus, on her second night in town, Susan visited the Owl Club, owned by the second Mrs. Pocket, Olita.

The Owl Club was just like the clubs in New York and Albany—too small, too crowded, too loud, too expensive, and totally insufficient as a means to acquire either pleasure or mere forgetfulness. Susan sat at a tiny table between Esther Ladd and the suicidal lady in the room next to hers.

"I'm sorry!" Susan shouted above the din of the music, the hysterical laughter, and the other shouted conversations, "but I don't think I ever heard your name!"

"Oh, don't bother," said the suicidal lady, "my divorce comes through tomorrow and I'm leaving on the four o'clock train for Mexico City."

"Why Mexico City?" shouted Esther.

"Why not?" shouted the suicidal lady.

Susan saw women she remembered from New York. She had sung for some at the Villa Vanity. Others she'd been introduced to by Harmon. Still others had studiously and pointedly *avoided* being introduced to her by Harmon.

Here in Reno, however, they were all her best friends.

They saw her from across the room. They smiled and caught her eye. They waved and raised their eyebrows.

You, too, I see. They waded over through the crowd. They leaned down closely and confidentially between Susan and the suicidal lady bound for Mexico City.

"So surprised to see *you* here," they all said in a tone that belied all surprise. "But it happens to the best of us."

Many of them added, "Are you here to sing?"

"No," replied Susan invariably.

One who had always avoided being introduced to Susan went to Olita Pocket and informed her that a well-known café chanteuse from New York was in the house, and if called upon, would probably be more than happy to favor the crowd with a song or two.

Susan was prevailed upon.

Susan refused politely.

The dreadful woman from New York smiled a simpering smile of entreaty. It was not surprising to Susan that this woman had once professed undying admiration for Barbara Beaumont's hats.

Olita Pocket pressed, saying that Susan owed it to Mr. Pocket's first wife, Bertha, because not everyone in Reno would take in a woman with even one pet, much less two.

Esther Ladd pressed, maybe not because she wanted to hear Susan sing, but because if Susan went up before the microphone, there was a very handsome dark-haired man who had indicated by certain movements of his eyes that he would take Susan's place at the tiny table.

Susan wouldn't be persuaded.

Then the suicidal lady leaned over and whispered, "Do you know that song—'Don't Ever Leave Me'?"

"Yes," said Susan with misgiving.

"Please," said the suicidal lady, "please sing it for me."

Susan took a deep breath. She couldn't refuse. She got up. Her identity had been spread around the room already, and her reputation for any number of things inflated as dangerously as Roosevelt was going to inflate the economy. She conferred with the leader of the orchestra. She was introduced by Olita in such a way as to suggest that she was a combination of Fanny Brice, Eva Le Gallienne, and Mahatma Gandhi. Susan smiled and gave the bow of an amateur, not a professional. The lights dimmed, and Susan began to sing.

> Don't ever leave me, now that you're here
> Here is where you belong.
> Everything seems so right when you're near,
> When you're away, it's all wrong.

The suicidal woman began to weep, but not alone.

> I'm so dependent when I need comfort,
> I always run to you,
> Don't ever leave me! 'Cause if you do,
> I'll have no one to run to.

The applause, if such a thing is possible, was both ecstatic and dismal.

That very night Olita Pocket telephoned Bertha Pocket and told her to tell Susan that she had a job at the Owl Club for the next six weeks, or longer, if she cared to stay in Reno.

Susan said she'd give her answer tomorrow.

Left alone, Susan hugged Scotty and Zelda tightly to her. She wondered if she would turn into Bertha Pocket, or Olita Pocket, or any other drunken, lurid, impecunious old woman who'd come to Reno for six weeks and stayed one hundred times that long.

She half feared she might, but took the job at the Owl Club. It occupied the dusty evenings of Reno. If she was singing on the tiny stage, or sitting with her eyes closed in the dressing room (Scotty and Zelda collapsed across her feet like warm slippers), then she didn't have to talk to all those dreadful women who'd come to Reno for the same reason she had. Too, it gave her money, and with that money she'd pay Bertha Pocket her weekly rent. She didn't want to be beholden to Harmon Dodge even for the expenses of the divorce he'd insisted on.

He was a dream already, after only three days in Reno.

Of course, so was Jack Beaumont. But a different sort of dream altogether.

Harmon Dodge was a curious dream of the miserable past.

Jack Beaumont was a lush dream of the impossible future.

As it turned out, she liked singing in the Owl Club. Every song, whether happy or sad, or comic or sentimental, seemed to mean something to someone in the packed room. Derisive laughter or uncontrolled sobbing sometimes greeted the same line of the same verse. Susan, after so little time spent in this place, where the unit of temporal measurement was forty-two days, had already begun to feel at home.

This is what she had done before Harmon Dodge (and Jack Beaumont) had come along, and this is what she was doing now that Harmon Dodge (and Jack Beaumont) had gone away.

She didn't have long to lull in this poppied oblivion, however. On the third night of her tenure at the Owl Club, the noxious little boy in the tight red jacket with all the brass buttons stood at the lip of the stage and screamed out at the end of her applause: "Unknown gentleman paging Mrs. Barbara Beaumont! Mrs. Barbara Beaumont!"

CHAPTER TWENTY

SUSAN HAD SEVERAL immediate thoughts.

First, that the unknown gentleman was paging some other Mrs. Barbara Beaumont. But Susan knew enough about the forces of destiny to know that this was the Barbara Beaumont whose intention in life was evidently to make Susan's as miserable as possible, and who seemed to be succeeding.

Second, came a happier thought. It wasn't like Barbara to go so far out of her way—Manhattan to Reno—simply in order to torment Susan. That would have accorded Susan an importance in Barbara's life that Barbara would have committed ritual suicide rather than admit.

The only other reason for Barbara Beaumont to be in Reno was to get a divorce from Jack Beaumont.

Susan decided that she would tie herself to Barbara Beaumont with a three-foot rope for six weeks if that meant that Jack Beaumont would be a free man. So it was with a vast and genuine smile that Susan came down from the stage and looked all around the smoky confines of the Owl Club until she spotted Barbara Beaumont in the farthest corner, seated at a minuscule table with another woman.

Barbara looked ravishing. Strategically placed beneath a flattering rose light, she wore a salmon-colored gown of shimmering ciré satin. Thrown loosely over her shoulders was a little capelet of Russian ermine that probably cost as much as the entire separation settlements of half the women in the Owl Club that night.

"Barbara? Barbara, is that you?" cried Susan in affected surprise but unaffected delight.

Barbara looked up in apparent shock at hearing her name called.

"It *isn't*," said Barbara. "It isn't *you*, is it? Oh, it *is* you. I can hardly believe it."

Susan sighed a theatrical sigh. "It happens to the best of us, Barbara..." In Reno, on first meeting old friends or old enemies, you didn't say the D word aloud.

"And to the worst of us as well," replied Barbara.

"An unknown gentleman was paging you a moment ago," said Susan. "Perhaps you didn't hear."

"I don't respond to unknown gentlemen," said Barbara.

Susan realized then that Barbara had initiated the page herself as a means of alerting Susan to her presence in the Owl Club. There was no unknown gentleman at all.

Barbara didn't ask Susan to sit.

"May I sit?" asked Susan, and without waiting for a reply signaled for one of the waiters—half of whom were already riotously in love with her (the other half being in love with those in love with Susan)—to bring over a chair.

"I'm singing here now," said Susan, "and it's ever so much more fun than in New York." She spoke in the tone a member of the New York deb crowd used when she explained why she'd just taken a job as a fitter on the fifth floor of Macy's. It was never for the money, of course, only for the novelty and daring of the thing.

"I thought I heard your voice," said Barbara, "but I didn't trust my ears. 'It couldn't actually be Susan,' I said to myself." Barbara evidently spoke to herself in a fairly loud voice, because as she reproduced the monologue now, it could be heard three tables over. "'Barbara,' I said to myself, 'it can't be Susan. To parade herself in a night-club in the middle of the desert would reflect so *very* badly on Harmon, and I can't believe that after all she's done to him, she would now do *that* as well.'"

"I'm not very interested any longer on how anything reflects on Harmon," said Susan.

"Introduce me, Sugar," said Barbara's companion at the table in liquid accents and a baritone voice. She was thirty perhaps, but it appeared that she had crammed every day with the very sorts of experiences that lend your face character. She looked the way Judith Anderson would have liked to look when she played Hamlet. She had short, thick brown hair that might easily have been cut in thirty seconds by someone using a bowl and a pair of hedge clip-pers. She wore a little black dress, a single string of pearls, and a Daché hat that appeared to have been beaten onto her skull with a mallet. She peered at Susan over the top of a pair of slanting spectacles with blue lenses that probably belonged to a Japanese aviator.

"Susan, this is the Princess Vinogradov-Kommisar-shevskaya."

"Call me Vinnie," said the princess. "I will call you Sugar, because I call everybody Sugar. I narrowly escaped the bullets of the Red Army, but my mother and father were thrown down a well on our estate, and my poor sisters— I had six of them—were taken to the Winter Palace and forced to polish the boots of the soldiers, and all my clever cousins and aunts and uncles and the charming czar and czarina were shot, and I've nothing now but my memories and this ring…"

She showed Susan a rather cheap-looking silver band with some scratches on it.

"Now I am getting a divorce from Eizo Susumu, the famous Japanese aviator, who flew from Tokyo to Melbourne in nine hours and thirty-five minutes and beat me."

"How long did it take you?" Susan asked sweetly.

"No," cried the princess, "he *beat* me. With a whip!"

"I see," said Susan.

"Now I have only three more days, and I will be free to marry again. I will marry Chiao-Yao. You know Chiao-Yao, of course?"

"Chiao-Yao?" asked Susan. "I don't believe so."

"He is the famous Chinese long-distance swimmer who swam from Chungking to Shanghai in five days, four hours, and twenty-two minutes. He loves me desperately, and he promises me that on our honeymoon we will travel to Moscow and he will shoot Lenin for me."

"Very romantic," said Susan.

"Tonight I am here to keep Sugar company," said the princess, laying her ringed hand atop Barbara's, "so that she does not get lonely and depressed and put a gun into her mouth because of what that terrible man did to her." The princess smiled at Susan, and Susan saw her face reflected in the blue lenses of the Japanese aviator's glasses. "If I meet him, I will scratch out his heart with my fingers, and I will tread upon it, and I will feed it to my cats. And if I meet the woman who stole him away from my sweetest Sugar here, and assassinated Sugar's poor father, I will tear her apart with my bare hands, and there will be nothing left for my cats."

Barbara smiled sweetly at Susan.

"I didn't tell her your name," Barbara whispered loudly.

"This is she?!" screamed the princess, rising so precipitously that she knocked over the tiny little table, which fell against another tiny table and spilled as many as a dozen glasses of liquor into the lap of a young divorcée from Atlanta, who jumped up, screaming in hysterics.

"I didn't murder Barbara's father," Susan remarked to the Russian princess, who was staring at her as if Susan might have been the Red Army soldier who murdered her parents.

Carefully, Susan had not denied that she had stolen the love of Barbara's husband. Susan hadn't dared believe it before, but she liked the thought of it very much. Even if Barbara had only made it up for effect.

In the meantime, the miserable Georgia woman had rushed from the Owl Room into the desert night, leaving a trail of wonder in her wake. Everyone looked over into that corner, and what they saw was the Russian princess, in a simple black dress and pearls and blue glasses, standing over the club singer in a very threatening manner.

"Murderess!" screamed the princess. Now, with the entire attention of the Owl Club, she pointed down at Susan. "She seduced Sugar's father!" She pointed at Barbara, in explanation of who Sugar was. "Then she seduced Sugar's husband, and then she murdered Sugar's father, and now she is here, singing songs about love, while Sugar is an orphan and a widow!"

"Grass widow," said Susan with a smile of correction to Barbara. "I didn't murder Jack. I just stole him away from you."

"*I will kill you!*" shrieked Princess Vinogradov-Kommisarshevskaya, and leapt on Susan, so that her chair fell backward onto the floor. The princess's fingers were embedded deep into Susan's throat, and Susan felt royal nails puncture her skin.

"*I will strangle this songbird!*"

A half-dozen waiters flew to Susan's rescue and dragged off the Romanoffs' cousin. The princess shrieked in frustration.

"*Die!* She must die for the sake of Sugar!"

Barbara, who hadn't moved during all of this, opened her purse and gave a five-dollar bill to one of the waiters not engaged in holding back enraged royalty. "Call the princess a taxi, if you would. We're staying at the Waverly."

The shrieking princess was dragged to the door. Susan was helped up from the floor, and Olita Pocket came over and examined her neck.

"I'm sorry for this disturbance," said Susan, determined, as she had never been before determined in her life, not to allow Barbara Beaumont to get the better of her.

"Don't worry," said Olita. "It's good for business. Tomorrow night we'll be turning 'em away at the door." Olita smiled at Barbara. "You and your friend come back tomorrow night—drinks free." This embarrassed Barbara as nothing else could have, with her vengeance turned into a carnival act.

Susan sat down again, in the chair vacated by the princess. Everyone in the room was still looking at Susan and Barbara.

"Everything's all right," Susan announced, "and after I've had a little chat with my dear friend Barbara Beaumont here, I'll be ready to sing for you all again if the princess hasn't done permanent damage to my throat..." She laughed a gay little laugh, and everyone else in the Owl Club laughed, and then applauded, and then went back to their business.

"You have nerve," said Barbara, "I'll give you that."

"You're divorcing Jack?" said Susan.

"I certainly didn't come to Reno to see you," returned Barbara.

"I didn't seduce Jack, you know. Any more than I murdered Marcellus."

"It still makes me ill to hear you call my father by his first name," Barbara remarked parenthetically. Then she said, "But you don't deny that you're in love with my husband, or that he has somehow been so stupid, so blind, and so pathetically idiotic that he imagines that he's in love with you."

"I am in love with him," said Susan, "but if he knows it, he didn't hear it from me. And though I'd very much like to think he's in love with me, he's never told me he is. And most of all, I'd like to think that when I'm divorced from Harmon, and Jack's divorced from you, he and I will—"

"I don't think that will happen," said Barbara.

Susan only smiled.

"There won't be time," said Barbara.

"No?"

"You'll be in jail by then."

"These accusations are boring, Barbara. You know very well I didn't kill your father."

"Evidence says you did," said Barbara smugly.

"What evidence?"

"A pair of wire cutters found in your bedroom at the Quarry. And a page torn from the car manual—the page showing the location of the brake cables. Oh, they were well hidden, but the police were very thorough. For once."

Susan blinked and stared at Barbara.

"The police are searching for you right now," said Barbara. "And of course, my civic duty impels me to telephone them instantly and tell them where they can find you. Have you a nickel I can borrow for the phone?"

Susan said nothing, only stared.

"No nickel? Oh well, I'll reverse the charges." She rose.

Susan remained seated. "Someone put those things there—the wire cutters and the page from the book. I didn't—"

"These denials are very boring, Susan. I'm glad I won't be forced to listen to them much longer." Barbara sailed out of the Owl Club in her satin and ermine.

Susan went to Olita and said that she didn't think she could sing again that evening after all. Her throat was sore. But she promised she'd return the following night.

She gathered up Scotty and Zelda and returned to the boardinghouse.

Bertha Pocket stopped her at the door and gave her a telegram. Susan hurried up to her room and ripped it open. The telegram read:

> IMPERATIVE THAT YOU IMMEDIATELY SEE THE BLOSSOMS IN THE NEVADA DESERT STOP LEAVE NO FORWARDING ADDRESS STOP TELL NO ONE STOP TRUST ME STOP DESTROY THIS STOP
>
> JAB

Susan trusted Jack.

She tore the telegram to shreds and placed the fragments in her pocketbook. She packed her bags and changed her clothes. She put on an old tweed skirt and a sweater that was much too large for her. She picked out a hat with a wide brim and put it on top of her suitcase. Then she turned out the lights in her room, seated herself on the edge of the bed, and waited.

The house grew quiet. Now and then she'd hear a door slam, or footsteps on the stairs, or the ringing of the telephone in the parlor, or some broken shrill laughter. But finally, about three o'clock, there was only silence.

Susan waited another half-hour. Then, leaving the rest of the week's rent in cash on her bed, she took her bags and crept downstairs. Scotty and Zelda followed in meek and careful silence.

Susan walked to the bus station and sat in the all-night coffee shop for two hours, her face turned away from the window beside her, staring down into a cup of coffee that had long grown cold.

At six-thirty she took the first bus that was going north.

Since receiving Jack's telegram, she had neither seen nor spoken to anyone.

CHAPTER TWENTY-ONE

THE BUS TOOK Susan as far as Black Springs, a town so small and empty and desolate, she began to think that perhaps Reno wasn't the most boring place in the world.

She walked out of the bus station and stood on the dusty, hot street. She asked an old man climbing into the cab of a truck whose doors were hung on with baling wire if he would take her to Pyramid, about twenty miles away, for two dollars.

He stared at her.

"Three dollars," Susan said.

"Who do I have to kill when we get there?" he asked.

Three dollars in Black Springs was evidently a greater sum than it was either in Manhattan or Reno.

The ride was bumpy and hot, and Susan was reluctant to answer the old man's questions about her identity, her past, or her purpose. He finally concluded, "Well, maybe *you're* going to Pyramid to murder somebody."

"Please don't say that," she sighed.

Scotty and Zelda ran around in the back of the truck until the heat of the sun exhausted them, and then they burrowed their way into a loose bale of hay there. An hour later the old man pulled the truck up to a small general store in Pyramid—this seemed to be the principal building in the entire place. For a few moments Susan was frantic, thinking the dogs had spilled out of the back. But when she called, they burrowed their way out of the hay again, and hung their heads as if they'd done something terribly wrong.

"Best-trained dogs I *ever* saw," said the old man. Then he turned to Susan. "Sure you don't need me to take you any farther?"

Susan declined. He was the curious type, and Susan didn't want to disclose her destination.

He drove off. Susan and her two dogs were alone in Pyramid, a town so small and empty and desolate it made Black Springs look as exciting as Reno. It was on the shore of Pyramid Lake, a large body of salty water that looked as if it had no business being in the middle of the desert, and, in compensation for its geographical effrontery, had made itself as unappealing as a lake can be. The water had a faint but distinctly noxious odor, the surface looked black and oily, and no matter where you looked on its surface, something dead and rotted suddenly bobbed to the surface.

Leaving Scotty and Zelda on the shore of the lake, with strict instructions neither to go into the water nor to eat anything they came across, Susan went into the general store.

It was one of those places that carried everything you'd need if you were being hunted down for a murder you didn't commit and anticipated spending eighteen months in a mountainous desert wilderness.

But Susan hadn't come to that point quite yet.

All she needed now was someone to drive her on to her cousin Blossom's ranch, five miles away.

Someone could indeed take her there, Susan learned, for ten dollars.

She started to protest, then realized that the alternative to this abject bilking was to walk the distance. She made a feeble objection to the price, however, just because she imagined everyone did, and she did not want to be remembered by any eccentricity of behavior.

She had to wait two hours for the woman's son to come back with the truck. The vehicle had no doors, and no seat beside the driver's, so Susan was forced to jounce around in the rusty, filthy truck bed with Scotty and Zelda. She and the dogs coughed in the dust and exhaust fumes.

Being a fugitive had very little to recommend it, Susan decided. In fact, the only thing that could be said in favor of her flight was that it fortuitously coincided with her residency requirement for a divorce from Harmon.

The thought suddenly occurred to Susan's sun-baked brain that she might well be riding through land that she herself owned, and she looked around with more interest. This desert was drier, hotter, emptier, and less inviting than she had ever imagined, even when told it couldn't be sold for the price of the negligible taxes on it. Just the sort of land that she *would* own, she decided.

Finally the truck neared the ranch, which was nestled in a flat stretch of land between two jagged spurs of a desolate-looking mountain. It looked, actually, as if a conscious act of God had been required to prevent the Excelsior Ranch from being buried beneath a landslide of rock from above. It was noon, but every building in the ranch was in deep shadow. Cooler, perhaps, than what she'd just been driven through, but rather like a sickroom in the tropics with all the shades drawn. Not exactly a cheerful shadiness.

The Indian let Susan off at the gate, and she had hardly gotten her bags off the back, and gathered up Scotty and Zelda, before he drove off again. She had wanted him to wait until she had at least made certain that Blossom was still running the ranch, and this idea seemed the pinnacle of prudence a moment later, when a woman ran screeching out of the largest building on the property, screaming, "You criminal!" and firing off both barrels of a shotgun by way of exclamation points.

Susan's heart sank, thinking that she'd been discovered here and would be arrested even before she'd had the chance to wash the dust from her face.

But then it became clear—when the woman with the shotgun fired not at Susan or her dogs, but at the fast-retreating truck—that the opprobrium of criminal had been delivered not to her but to the Indian in the doorless vehicle.

"How much did those thieving McAlpines charge you?" she demanded suddenly of Susan.

"Ten dollars."

"I've shot both doors off that Indian's truck. Next time I'll get him, and when I've done that, I'm going to pick off his mother."

"Are you Blossom?" said Susan, who'd never met her cousin.

"I am. Blossom Mayback. And you should have let me pick you up in Reno. I go in twice a week, at the least. I wasn't expecting you till tomorrow."

Susan realized Blossom assumed she was one of the divorcées who'd made reservations on the ranch.

"No, you weren't expecting me at all," said Susan.

Blossom was a tall, thin, angular woman, about forty. She wore men's jeans, boots, and a patched blue shirt. There was a family resemblance, and on the whole, Blossom Mayback looked about like what Susan had always imagined her brother would look like if she'd had one.

"Well, there's always room for one more," said Blossom, and scooped up both Scotty and Zelda, and rubbed their noses against her cheeks.

"I'm Susan," said Susan. "Susan Bright. Your cousin."

Blossom stopped and stared at Susan. Pressed against Blossom's cheeks, the dogs were absolutely still and silent, as if they feared that this peculiar maneuver might yet turn into a new sort of punishment.

"Then I don't have to welcome you," said Blossom with something strange in her voice—repressed anger, disappointment, fear. "Since you own this place."

Susan realized suddenly what her cousin was thinking.

"Oh no, no, I'm not here to take over, or anything like that—"

Blossom said nothing.

"I'm here to ask for your help."

That was the right note to have struck. Blossom wasn't the sort to like asking for favors, or to be indebted, but she was always ready to do someone else a good turn. Blossom was even more pleased when she didn't get recompense for this largess. Susan knew this by instinct. Her own mother had been that way.

"Are you in trouble?"

"Yes," said Susan. "Fairly serious trouble, if you want the truth."

"Well then, you've come to the right place," said Blossom, "but let's get you inside before these two perish of the sun."

The Excelsior Ranch, née Dirt Hole Farm, consisted of one principal building with an office for Blossom, fourteen chambers for overweight women in the process of divorcing their husbands, a dining room, and three baths. The low old-fashioned kitchen was entirely separate, and was presided over by a fat Indian woman and her fat seven-year-old son. A new building, well off to the side, had two bedchambers and a bath. One of the chambers was occupied by Wesley Goff, a rather anemic-looking, yellow-haired man from Worcester, Massachusetts, who was designated the ranch overseer. Wesley looked the type to be much more at home as a fitter on the fifth floor of Macy's than he did in this remote desert area of Nevada. And in fact, most of the heavy work at the ranch was done by Colleen, a brawny young woman with flaming orange hair and a perpetually burned skin. Colleen shared the larger chamber with Blossom, and neither woman seemed much to mind the inconvenience. In yet another building were the twin Indian sisters who did the cleaning, spoke only to each other, and seemed to have nothing to do with anyone but themselves. There were stables with a dozen horses, most of them as tame as Scotty and Zelda. An old storage house had been turned into a gymnasium. Here, with the most rudimentary of athletic equipment, Colleen put the divorcées through their paces. "Shed weight while you shed a mate," Blossom said to Susan, "that's what I tell 'em."

Blossom installed Susan in her best room, and after Susan had bathed and changed her clothes, she invited her cousin in. Susan sat on the edge of the bed, and Blossom leaned against the windowframe. Outside was the corral where three pale fat women rode around and around in a circle, while Wesley stood in the middle and gossiped with Colleen.

"Talk quietly," Blossom warned, "for the walls are thin, and the inmates are curious creatures."

Susan had debated how much to tell Blossom. She needn't have troubled her mind. She was too weary for anything but the truth, so she told it as best she knew how, beginning with her poverty after the Crash, not sliding over her decision to marry for money, her worry that she'd led Marcellus on, nor her unintentionally falling in love with Jack. She told of all the difficulties that had come after and ended with her seeking refuge and anonymity at the Excelsior Ranch.

Telling the truth was the right thing to do.

If Blossom didn't entirely understand, she didn't make judgments. Her only question was: "But if you didn't murder the man, why are you running from the police?"

Susan stared. "I don't know. I probably look even guiltier now, don't I?"

"Yes," Blossom said. "I would think so."

Susan considered the issue for a moment, then recanted. "No, I'm not running from the police, actually. I came here because Jack told me to come here. If he thought there was a good reason I should hide myself away, then I'm assuming that I'm doing the best thing."

"That's a fair amount of trust to put into the son-in-law of the man who was murdered."

"He's also the lawyer of the man who's divorcing me," Susan said, "and I trust him even after that."

"You're probably right to trust him, because I know already that you're no fool. And don't worry, I'll keep you here safe enough," Blossom said. "We'll give you a new name, and tell some story about you. I've heard enough of 'em that I don't doubt I can come up with something plausible. Even though Dirt Hole Farm won't be as exciting as Reno, you'll have company, and not bad company either." She laughed. "Up until three days ago we had a Russian princess here—"

"A Russian princess?" echoed Susan, startled.

"Princess Something Unpronounceable hyphen Something More Unpronounceable. I don't know if she's real or if she's bogus, but however that is, she still works behind the linen counter at some place called Wanamaker's. You know it?"

"Yes, and I think I know the princess, too. She tried to kill me last night."

"My, you do lead an interesting life, don't you Susan?"

Blossom laughed, but then suddenly she appeared troubled. "A friend of the princess's is arriving tomorrow."

"Oh no..." Susan's heart sank.

"Beauregard, was it?"

"Beaumont," said Susan miserably, and she wasn't a bit surprised.

CHAPTER TWENTY-TWO

"IT CAN'T BE A coincidence," Susan said dismally after she'd explained to Blossom that Barbara Beaumont, expected tomorrow, was the woman in the world Susan wanted most to avoid.

"It must be," Blossom argued. "She made the reservation three days ago. That was before you decided to come here."

"Actually," Susan corrected morosely, "it was even before I knew I didn't have anywhere else to go. When I was just a plain old future divorcée rather than a future divorcée suspected of murder."

"Maybe she knows we're cousins," Blossom suggested.

"The only person I told about you is Jack, just before I left for Nevada. Maybe he told her. It's perfectly like Barbara to go a fair distance out of her way simply to annoy one of my few living relatives."

"I'm eager to meet Mrs. Beaumont. She sounds like a piece of work."

"There's no one to stop her from coming?"

"No telephone here. No telephone at Pyramid either. I suppose I could drive into Reno and stop her..."

"That would be suspicious-making," said Susan.

"Then she'll be here in the morning," Blossom warned, "arriving by private car."

"If she comes here, I have to leave," said Susan with a sigh. It was getting even harder to be a fugitive. "Do you have any idea of where I might go?"

"You can stay here," said Blossom. "We'll just tie Mrs. Beaumont to a chair for six weeks."

Susan for a moment looked horrified, and then she realized that Blossom was joking. "I'd love to see Barbara tied to a chair for a few days, but I think it would constitute kidnapping."

"Susan, what I do to these women probably constitutes slavery and torture anyway, but there is a way for you to stay on here without the woman getting suspicious. There's a cabin a mile or two from here, and it's not near any of the trails we use. There's not much to it, but Colleen and I fixed it up a little, and sometimes when these females get to us, we'll say we're going in to Carson City to pay our taxes, and we hide out there."

"No chance Barbara will run across me there?"

"Is she the sort who crawls up rocky slopes that a mountain goat would turn up his nose at? Does she like places without running water or electricity—"

"I'll be safe," said Susan.

"Colleen and I will take you up there this afternoon— don't want Jack's wife showing up ahead of schedule and catching you here. One of us can stay the night with you if you like—it's pretty lonely out there."

"You're very kind," said Susan. "I can use a little kindness right now."

Blossom laughed. "You do own this place, you know, and you've never asked for a penny out of me for it."

"But all the work is yours," said Susan. "I had no right to ask you for anything."

Blossom shook her head. "Well, if you don't go to the chair, and you don't get to marry your lawyer, then you know you've always got a home. Even if you don't want to stay here with us, I'll make sure you get a portion of our profits here."

"Oh no, Blossom—"

"Don't thank me yet. The profits aren't much, but what do I have to spend the money on? Even if those thieving McAlpines in Pyramid had something I wanted, I wouldn't give them the satisfaction of paying them for it. It's just Colleen and Wesley and me here, and there's plenty to take care of us. We can take care of you and still not go without."

Susan discovered she was weeping.

Blossom pushed away from the window, sat down beside Susan on the bed, and laid that weeping head tenderly on her angular breast.

"You ride well," said Colleen admiringly.

"I'm surprised," said Susan. "It's been many years, and of course this isn't a bit like the Myopia Hunt Club."

Blossom led the way on her horse. Susan followed. Colleen brought up the rear. Blossom's and Colleen's horses were loaded with supplies, and Scotty and Zelda trotted along happily behind. They seemed to like this place, but perhaps they only mimicked Susan's mood, and Susan had already decided she liked this place very much.

"What will those women think—the ones who saw me come and leave so quickly?"

"I'll tell them you made a mistake and thought that the Club Excelsior was for putting on weight instead of taking it off."

Colleen laughed heartily behind her. "That'll make 'em swear!"

"That is very strange," said Susan, a thought occurring to her suddenly.

"What?" asked Blossom, glancing over her shoulder.

"Barbara is as thin as I am. There's no reason for her to come here."

"Which means," said Blossom, "that Mrs. Beaumont *does* know I'm your cousin."

"And she probably expects me to show up here."

"Don't worry," said Colleen. "I don't care if it was Eleanor Roosevelt and the Queen Mother who was arriving here to find you out—Blossom and me'll protect you."

The sun was lowered already behind the Pyramid Mountains, and their horses picked their way among the rocks in the purple shade. The way was so rough and winding that it seemed a distance much greater than a mile or two from the ranch to the isolated cabin. Even for Susan's fear of discovery, the place seemed sufficiently out of the way.

"We're almost there," said Blossom, and her voice echoed off the rocks. She turned sharply into a deep canyon cut in the side of the mountain.

Susan's horse followed into the canyon, which was in even deeper shadow. It was already evening here. Susan felt as if she were going between the ribs of a gigantic skeleton. The canyon made a sharp turn, and just beyond the turn was a low cabin fashioned half of stone and half of dark planks. It was pushed up against the rocks, and had two small four-paned windows, a narrow door, and a roof of corroded metal.

Susan had seen places just like it in western movies. It was the place where murderers took refuge from their relentless pursuers.

As the three women dismounted, Scotty and Zelda ran forward and took up places on either side of the door, as an earnest display of the protection they intended to provide Susan in this out-of-the-way place.

"It's not Park Avenue, you two, is it?"

"We done the best we could to fix it up," Colleen began in disappointed apology, "but I know it ain't what—"

"Oh no, no," Susan cried. "That's not what I meant at all. I'd rather be here—*much* rather be here than on Park Avenue, and I'm sure these two would as well."

By the way they wagged their tails, it looked both as if the terriers understood and agreed.

Inside was what the outside promised. Once Colleen had lighted the kerosene lamp, Susan saw a back wall of stone, with exposed stone and planks for the other walls. Two narrow hard cots. A hearth that served for heating and cooking. An open cupboard with cooking utensils, some crockery, a box of cutlery, and a shelf of books. A closed cupboard for storage of food. Two shotguns leaning in the corner. Some old-fashioned prints nailed to the wall—innocent children, gamboling pets, dewy-eyed actresses of the previous generation, and several signed photographs of current film stars.

"I write to 'em," Colleen said, blushing, "and they send me their pictures, for nothing."

It was better than a penthouse on Park Avenue.

"No," said Susan, "please don't think you have to stay with me."

"You might be frightened," Colleen protested.

"This place isn't any lonelier than the house in Albany—and as long as I have Scotty and Zelda to keep me company and frighten away the wolves—"

"It might be better if we did get back," said Blossom. "Don't want curious people asking where we spent the night, do we?"

Susan stood in the doorway and watched them mount their horses. It was dark now. Inside, the kerosene lamp cast a soft yellow glow over the cabin. Colleen had built a fire in the hearth for warmth, certainly, during the cold desert nights—but it also burned for comfort.

"Take my horse back," Susan said.

"That really leaves you here alone," said Blossom. "Could you find your way back to the ranch?"

Susan nodded. "But I'll be all right. Taking care of myself in New York for two years was probably a great deal more difficult than this is going to be."

"I'll visit you tomorrow," said Blossom. "And bring you news of your close friend, Mrs. Beaumont."

"You're sure we can't tie her up?" Colleen asked with a sigh.

"Good night!" Susan called. "And thank you!"

The horses disappeared around the sharp turn in the canyon, and were lost to sight. A few moments later the echo of their hooves on the loose rocks was lost as well. Susan stood in the doorway and watched.

"Good-bye!" she heard two voices call in the distance, and she wished they hadn't—simply because they sounded *so* far away.

Susan looked up at the sky, a narrow slash of stars seen between the high dark walls of the canyon.

She listened, and heard nothing.

Then a short rattling of loose stones somewhere.

Then nothing again.

She turned, and went back to the cabin, shutting the door behind her.

There wasn't time for her to be fearful of the isolation and loneliness that night. She extinguished the lamp, and without even having the energy to remove her clothes, fell instantly asleep on the cot nearer the fire. When she woke, Scotty and Zelda were waiting impatiently, but in complete silence, by the door. They were very glad to see Susan get up.

Susan had a breakfast of cheese and biscuits. She rebuilt the fire and made coffee. With Scotty and Zelda she ventured out to the mouth of the canyon. Behind her the mountain rose precipitously and moodily. She had forgotten to ask Blossom its name, but she was certain it was Dead Man's Mountain, or Mt. Superstition, or Dragon's Head, or some other appellation appropriate to its appearance. Before her was an uneven rocky plain, with scraps of brownish-green herbage that looked dismal and parched, even for desert vegetation. In the near distance was a small range of mountains as ugly as the one that rose directly behind her, and another range of uglier mountains behind that. She saw no trace of human habitation. In fact, she couldn't even see an indication that any human being ever came this way.

For a novice fugitive, she hadn't done badly in finding a place off the beaten track.

But how long would she have to remain here?

And, if she was safe and hidden from Barbara and the police, she was also hidden from Jack.

What if he didn't love her?

What if she'd been taken in by some perfidious bit of lawyerliness?

What if he'd sent her into hiding for the express purpose of intensifying the perception of her guilt?

What if Barbara's being in Reno were part of the sham, and she and Jack were not divorcing at all?

"What if I kill myself and just have done with it all?" she said aloud to herself. "And save the state of New York the cost of the electricity it would take to execute me?"

Scotty and Zelda peered up at her from the shade of the boulder where they'd taken refuge from the noonday sun.

"Well, I can't very well kill myself with two dependents, can I?" she concluded.

"She's everything you made her out to be," said Blossom. "Even if I didn't know what she'd done to you, I'd be more than half tempted to tie her up for six weeks on general principles. I never knew that any one person could cause as much trouble as that one woman did in her first hour at the ranch."

"Oh no," cried Susan anxiously. "She found out I'd been there."

"No," said Blossom, "she didn't mention you, and if she knows we're cousins, she didn't mention that either. She's just causing trouble out of pure meanness of soul. She had a fight with the man who drove her up here because he overcharged her and he scratched one of her suitcases in taking it out of the trunk. Then she didn't like her room, so I gave her another one. Then she pitched a fit because she had to share a bath. Then she had to have her first room back because it was farther away from the stables. Then she got Wesley *very* upset because she asked him if he'd mind fixing her hair after dinner this evening, and Wesley is *very* sensitive about his past and thought she was ridiculing him, so *he's* off in a purple funk."

"But she didn't mention me or make any snide references to murderers who also happen to be husband-snatchers?"

"Not to me," said Blossom. "But I'll keep my ears open, and Colleen will, too, and I hope you don't mind, but I told Wesley a little about you, and I think he'd do *anything* now to get back at Mrs. Beaumont." Blossom shook her head. "Wesley hasn't done hair in *years*."

"I hope—" Susan began, then left off.

"You hope what?"

"I hope you and Colleen and Wesley aren't going to be too—overt—in keeping watch over Barbara."

"She won't notice a thing," said Blossom with confidence. "She'll have enough to do to keep alive till morning.

There's already a cabal against her. The other ladies think she showed up for the express purpose of making them look fatter than they are. But Colleen or Wesley or I'll be out here at least once every day, bring you food and news. Food and news..."

Susan laughed. "What more could I want?"

CHAPTER TWENTY-THREE

WHAT MORE SUSAN could want was something to do during the days, which were very nearly as tedious as the hours she spent on Park Avenue in the first few weeks of her marriage. It was difficult to believe that was only a few months ago. She'd been lonely then, too, and not known what to do with herself, no longer fretting over the two dollars that would see her through the week. She didn't have to worry about the two dollars now because everything she needed was brought to her by Blossom or Colleen or Wesley in a daily visit about the middle of the afternoon. She wasn't as lonely now with Scotty and Zelda for company. The pair was the one thing in the world she was grateful to Barbara Beaumont for, and Susan was certain it would send the woman into paroxysms of frustration if she knew how much of a comfort the two dogs were to her.

Other than eating and walking about the confines of the narrow canyon, and talking to Scotty and Zelda, and reading the dreadful romantic novels that Colleen had collected for the cabin, there was nothing at all to do.

Susan waited for each afternoon's visit with an eagerness that seemed as strong as any emotion she'd ever felt. She dreaded the visit with almost equal intensity, for she invariably expected to learn that Barbara had said something or done something to indicate she knew of Susan's hidden presence on the ranch.

But Barbara never said anything about Susan.

"It's hardly surprising, however," Blossom said, "since nobody will talk to her. Most women, when they come here, manage to make friends. It makes the time pass more quickly, and, hell, there's nothing else to do in this damned desert."

"Barbara doesn't have friends," Susan observed. "She has acquaintances who haven't yet turned into enemies." She was silent a moment, and then asked, "You haven't heard from Jack, have you?"

Blossom smiled. "I would have told you, you know."

"I do know, but I just couldn't help asking."

"Do you think he's deserted you?"

"No," said Susan. "I don't. But it's hard being alone so much. I start thinking strange things. Even when I know they're not true."

"Find something to occupy your time," Blossom suggested.

"Out here?"

"Look over your property. Practically everything around here is yours. The invaluable and inexhaustible Dirt Hole Mine, in particular, of course."

Both cousins laughed.

"Oh, well then, I suppose I *must* go and visit it, for after all, the Dirt Hole has made me rich beyond the dreams of avarice. I owe everything I have to that hole in the ground, but I don't even know where it is."

"I'll draw you a map," said Blossom. "Or I'll take you out there day after tomorrow. Tomorrow I'm going to Reno to pick up a couple of new arrivals."

"No, no, draw the map. Please. If I spend another day as boring as this one..."

"Oh, it is boring out here after all."

"Well, it is now that I can imagine there's something else to do."

So Blossom drew out a rude map to lead Susan to the Dirt Hole Mine. "The place is a bit of a legend around here," Blossom said, "because the only thing that was ever brought up out of it was dirt. And the dirt had to be thrown away, because it was salty and killed anything that was planted in it. I wouldn't go far inside if I were you. The place hasn't been worked in twenty years, and whatever is in there can't be holding up any too well."

"I have no fondness for dark, enclosed places," said Susan. "In fact, I think I could safely say that I have a horror of them. I hate closets and train tunnels and cellars, and all that sort of thing. I'm always afraid I'm going to get trapped. You don't have to worry about my going too deeply into the Dirt Hole Mine."

"Good," said Blossom, "because if you did, and you got lost, I'm not the one who'd come in after you. I hate those places, too. I'll send Colleen out here with a horse for you tomorrow—the mine's only a couple of miles from here—but I'd feel a great deal better if you'd ride there instead of walking. Just in case you twisted your ankle or something."

When Susan acquiesced to this plan, Blossom prepared to return to the ranch. "And if there's a message awaiting me from your husband's lawyer—no matter how unpleasant it is—I'll ride out tomorrow evening and give it to you."

"I didn't want to ask," Susan confessed. "But I wanted very much to ask..."

Neither Colleen nor Wesley showed up the next morning with the promised mount, and Susan didn't want to put off the excursion to Dirt Hole Mine either. The canyon and the cabin within the canyon had apparently shrunk to dismally narrow proportions recently.

Scotty and Zelda came with her, of course. Susan took two canteens of water, food for herself and the dogs, a candle and matches, and a compass. Of what use this last item might be if she got lost, she had no idea, since she hadn't any conception of where she was.

The one other thing she brought with her—and the thing that seemed most important of all—was the hope that Blossom would find a message from Jack awaiting her at the post office in Reno.

She simply followed the outline of *her* mountain, as she'd come to think of it. She'd learned its name from Blossom, not Mt. Superstition or Dragon's Head, as she'd suspected, but the obvious yet entirely inappropriate Mt. Bright.

She felt exposed as she circled the base of Mt. Bright, even though she saw nothing living but a few large birds that looked to have carrion on the breath, a few tiny toads that looked shriveled and burned and unhappy, and now and then something furry poking up out of a hole in the ground.

The map led her to another canyon on the far side of Mt. Bright. It was shallower, narrower, and rockier than her own, but at the end of it a kind of ramp had been leveled out. This raw roadway led upward along the side of the mountain. So many rocks had slipped down from higher up in the last twenty years that the way to the mine was hardly recognizable as manmade.

The way was steeper than it looked. Susan's labored breath told her that, and when she stopped and looked around, she was startled by how far she could see.

She could see very far across the desert, but there was little to hold her attention other than that range of ugly mountains, and the uglier range of mountains behind that.

She continued to climb. The road hairpinned, and Susan found herself walking into the sun. She bowed her head so that the brim of her hat would shield her face. She'd blistered once since she'd been here in Nevada, and didn't want to go through that torment again.

Scotty and Zelda walked inches behind her, employing her as a sunshade.

She came across something metallic and glinting—nearly buried in the earth. She kicked at some earth around it and saw it was a length of narrow rail.

She was getting closer, and she ventured to look up into the sun.

She was already there, it turned out. Here was the entrance to the mine. If there had once been a sign, it was gone now. The entrance was only a natural cave opening that had been widened sufficiently to lay the tracks inside.

She looked around and saw evidence that this was indeed the Dirt Hole Mine. Sun-bleached boards from some sort of exterior buildings. The crumbling cement foundations for those buildings, nearly buried now, too, in the earth. A twisted piece of metal, a rusted wheel, more bits of twisted metal, broken fragments of something that had been painted green, shards of green glass from beer bottles.

Susan shaded her eyes and peered into the entrance to the mine.

It was less than inviting, and looked rather like the hideout of a fugitive being pursued for murder—a fugitive who was guilty and quite deserved to die a miserable death trapped in such a place.

That seemed a good reason not to go inside.

She went inside anyway.

It was very black, so she immediately turned around and looked back out into the sunlight.

"If I can do it, you can do it," she said very loudly.

Scotty and Zelda crept forward into the cool darkness of the cave.

Susan went a few feet farther in. She ran her right foot along one of the rails, figuring that this would be the string to lead her out again if she got lost in the three or four yards she'd decided she'd venture in.

"This is probably a very stupid idea," said Susan aloud.

Scotty and Zelda, simply by the fact that they did not follow her any farther into the interior of the mine, appeared to concur with that assessment.

Susan stood still and allowed her eyes to grow accustomed to the darkness. Then she could make out the beams and supports here. To her relief, they didn't appear rotted at all. In fact, many of them had been reinforced, and the metal reinforcements gleamed in the light from the entrance as if they were still new.

She was more fearful of her own fear than of the mine itself. How was she going to cope with the rest of her life if she stopped ten feet into a cave that had probably been formed a hundred thousand years ago and hadn't collapsed yet?

She struck a match and lighted the candle she'd brought. She held it up and looked around.

If I see bats, I'll go back, she promised herself. *Bats carry rabies.*

Disappointingly for Susan, there were no bats, either rabid or simply filthy and disgusting in their own healthy right. She really would have preferred a dozen or so bats flying in her face than to be forced to continue her progress.

Four more feet in. Again she shone the candle around.

No bats. No rotted supports. Behind her, she could still see the entranceway, a smaller arch of light than before. Scotty and Zelda had not moved.

"Get over here," Susan said to the dogs.

They came reluctantly, and she watched their progress.

"You're not very brave dogs, are you?"

Zelda lowered her head in apparent shame and brought it up again with something in her mouth. She offered it to Susan in appeasement for her shortcomings in the way of canine courage.

From Zelda's mouth Susan took an empty cigarette package.

Susan examined it by the light of the candle. The package had contained twenty Spud cigarettes, and it looked new. She held it to her nose and could still smell the tobacco inside. The price was marked on the side of the paper in blue ink—twelve cents. Last year—when she'd been singing at the Villa Vanity, and knew of such things from the inane chatter of the cigarette girls—cigarettes, which were normally twenty cents a pack, were dropping to twelve and even ten cents, on account of a tobacco war in North Carolina. This meant that someone had been in the mine since the beginning of the year—very recently indeed.

That seemed reason enough not to go any farther inside. Just in case the someone who had dropped the Spud cigarette package was anywhere beyond, and just in case that supposed party was someone Susan did not care to meet.

This was a very silly fear, Susan decided.

The Spud package wasn't *that* fresh.

She took a few more steps deeper into the mine. Now she came to a turn. The rails went off to the right down a wide passageway. Off to the left was a much smaller, cruder shaft. Here the beams and supports had not been reinforced. The supports bowed dramatically inward, the ceiling beam bowed dramatically downward. A passageway that had originally been six feet wide and six feet high was now not more than four feet high and perhaps a yard wide.

She went a few feet off to the right, along the much wider passage, going just far enough to lose sight of the entrance to the cave.

This was genuine bravery, Susan decided, and she'd had quite enough of it.

"I'm sure you'll be happy to hear," she said to the dogs, "that it's time to go back…"

The dogs wagged their tails in apparent agreement.

But Susan didn't get very far, for a voice called out quite stridently from around the corner she'd just turned. "Hello! Hello, is anybody in there?"

The voice was Barbara Beaumont's.

I might have known, thought Susan instantly, and without thinking of the consequences, blew out the candle.

The consequences were that she and the dogs were plunged into darkness.

It was on a par with the rest of Susan's luck in the past month or so that the one day she ventured out of her cabin, the one day she had the courage to venture into a space that was close and dark and possessed of only one exit, should be the day that Barbara Beaumont decided to make what was probably her first visit ever to a worthless and abandoned mine in a place that must be considered, even for Nevada, fairly remote. Yet somehow the circumstances, once they'd presented themselves, didn't seem surprising at all.

Barbara's voice came again: "I know you're in there! But I'm not coming in, you have to come out!"

Susan slowly shook her head. The choice between remaining in a dark cave and meeting Barbara Beaumont in the sunlight was not an agreeable one, and was possibly on a par with having to decide whether to enter hell by subway or by taxicab.

"I'm not going to wait all day!" Barbara screeched.

"Shhhhh!" said Susan to her dogs, but they knew when to be quiet and the command was entirely superfluous. "She won't come in," Susan whispered, "she'll go away."

"Get out here!" Barbara shouted. "Or I'm coming in after you!"

What am I going to do? Susan wondered.

Going deeper into the mine was an unattractive idea, but it was preferable to meeting Barbara. So she turned that way—but this wasn't going to work either. For in this direction, in the blackened shaft leading deeper into the mine, she heard a masculine voice calling, "I'm on my way!" Then she heard footsteps, and a moment later, in the black distance, she saw the gleam of a lantern.

Barbara wasn't looking for her at all.

Barbara was looking for this man who had ventured far deeper into the mine than Susan had.

When he wiped his brow with the hand holding the lantern, Susan caught a glimpse of his face. The visage was familiar, but she couldn't immediately place it.

Then she did place it.

It was Malcolm MacIsaac, the private detective from Albany.

He was coming toward Barbara, and Barbara was coming toward him.

Susan was in the middle.

CHAPTER TWENTY-FOUR

SUSAN GRABBED UP Scotty and Zelda, whispered "Shhhh!" once more for good measure, and then backed across the dark corridor. Glancing toward the entrance, she saw that it was indeed Barbara Beaumont waiting for the detective—Barbara in all her desert splendor of whipcord jodhpurs, white silk blouse, and knee-length leather jacket in forest green. Barbara peered into the cave, but Susan stood in darkness and could not be seen.

In fear that Mr. MacIsaac's lantern would catch on her pale skin, or some of her clothing, or the dog's eyes, or any little thing that would alert him to her presence, Susan backed far into the secondary shaft.

Taking a deep breath, she crouched down and backed under the bowed supports and beams.

It grew narrower quickly, until she could feel the walls on either side of her at once. Yet because she still feared she might be within reach of the detective's lantern,

Susan continued to back up, squeezing herself and holding the dogs even more tightly against her breast.

They were utterly silent, and she blessed them in her heart.

She continued to back up until she felt the sinking roof of the passage against her shoulders and back. It was rock, but the rock was crumbly, and sand and bits of gravel spilled down the back of her neck.

Mr. MacIsaac passed. His lantern light flashed on the walls of the narrow passage, sooty as lampblack, but it did not touch her, and he did not even glance her way.

She released her breath in a long sigh.

"I didn't hear you at first, Mrs. Beaumont," she heard MacIsaac say. "Sound travels only so far in a place like this, and then it just stops dead."

"That is a scientific fact of undying interest to me," said Barbara, "and I will be sure to note it in my diary tonight. I will also be sure to..."

Then they passed out of Susan's hearing.

Susan waited in the silence and darkness a full minute more before moving—just in case MacIsaac came back into the cave.

She attempted to put the dogs down, but the walls of the cave were so narrow, she could not move her arms. She tried to waddle forward.

She couldn't move. She'd wedged herself in.

She nearly screamed from fear.

This was exactly what her worst nightmares were like.

She tried to twist sideways. She couldn't. She was stuck. She whimpered.

Scotty and Zelda whimpered in sympathy.

She drew in her breath, and then found she was in so tightly she couldn't even fill her lungs.

This made her feel even worse, but it also gave her an idea.

She slowly exhaled *all* her breath.

Without worrying that she might break her nose, she simply pitched herself forward and slipped out of her stifling corner.

She threw out her elbows to keep from crushing Scotty and Zelda beneath her. This saved the dogs, saved her nose, and only tore open the sleeves of her shirt and abraded the skin of her forearms.

She released the dogs and crawled forward until she could stand upright. She took a deep, full breath, and then peered toward the entrance of the cave. She saw no one outside.

Hugging the walls, she crept closer to the entrance of the mine. The dogs followed at her heels.

She stood just inside the entrance and listened. She heard nothing.

Then a harrowing screech.

She startled so that she slipped and fell forward onto the ground, expecting the worst—whatever that might be.

But the harrowing screech was only that of a bird of prey wheeling overhead.

No Barbara. No MacIsaac. And no sign of anyone else.

Susan was glad now, very glad, that the horse hadn't arrived in time that morning. For its presence outside the entrance of the mine would have given her away.

She returned to her cabin the way she'd come, but her progress was even more cautious now. Having seen Barbara and MacIsaac in the Dirt Hole Mine, she wouldn't have been surprised now to run into anyone at all.

She entered her own canyon with trepidation. The sun was now on the other side of the mountain, and the crevasse lay in early shadow. If Barbara and MacIsaac knew about the mine, they might also know of this place.

Susan sent the dogs ahead as scouts.

"If there's anyone there, don't bark—just come back and let me know."

The dogs ran as fast as they could to the end of the canyon, disappeared around the little bend, were invisible for a few moments, and then returned, running as quickly as they'd gone.

"Well?"

Zelda and Scotty sat on their haunches before her and made no movement or sound.

No one was there, Susan was certain of it, and proceeded.

As she was about to turn the corner, she heard a sudden loud scratching in the earth. She stopped dead, turned, and glared at the dogs.

"I thought you said no one was there," she hissed.

But there was no help for it now, so she simply sauntered around the corner, hoping it was Blossom, or Colleen, or Wesley there.

It was not.

It was, however, the horse she had been promised that morning. The animal was tugging at the stake to which she'd been tied, and was just about to pull it loose from the ground. Evidently, this horse didn't care for the boredom of the canyon days any more than Susan did.

"Oh, thank God," said Susan. "Thank God it was you, whatever your name is, and thank God it wasn't Barbara Beaumont, or Mr. MacIsaac, or the police, or Mr. J. Edgar Hoover himself who was here."

It suddenly occurred to Susan that Barbara, the detective, half a dozen detectives, and the head of the FBI might *all* be inside the cabin—or just any one of them. But she boldly pushed open the door and went in.

The cabin was empty. Apparently Colleen had brought the horse, for she'd also supplied Susan with yet another dreadful novel.

She saw no other disturbance to the cabin. If either MacIsaac or Barbara had been there, she was certain there would have been some evidence of it.

That was a relief.

She fed the horse and brought water from the supply in the covered barrel in the corner of the cabin. She fed the dogs, combed the spurs from their coats, and tickled their ears. Then she made her own little dinner—warmed stew from the night before and a warmed tin of peas—and as she ate, she wondered about what she'd seen that afternoon.

She wondered how Barbara knew about the mine at all, much less its location.

Wondered how Mr. MacIsaac knew about the mine.

Wondered what the detective was doing so much deeper down in the mine than Susan had dared go.

Wondered what business they had together.

Wondered if that business had anything to do with her.

It was this last question that had the easiest answer, for it almost certainly *did* have something to do with her. For, after all, it was Susan's ranch, Susan's mine, Susan whom Barbara was accusing of murder, Susan who was the ostensible reason Barbara was in Nevada at all. And Mr. MacIsaac had already been involved with Susan once, providing the photographs to prove Harmon's infidelity.

Susan was certain now that those photographs had been faked. Which meant nothing except that, in the pay of Marcellus Rhinelander, the detective had been willing to fabricate the evidence to prove what the lawyer had wanted to believe. That suggested that MacIsaac was here now to fabricate more evidence—this time to prove that Susan was responsible for the death of Barbara's father.

But even if this was a correct deduction, it didn't tell Susan what Jack's place was in all this.

Jack.

Blossom hadn't heard from him. If she had, she would have come to tell her by this time.

It was only seven o'clock now, however. Perhaps Blossom hadn't yet returned from Reno.

Susan made a fire, sat in front of it, and hoped that Blossom would come with a message from Jack.

Then she berated herself for simply sitting and hoping and sitting and hoping and sometimes just sitting, exactly like the dreadful young women in those dreadful novels that Colleen had stocked in the cupboard.

It was nine o'clock. Blossom hadn't come. She certainly would have returned from Reno by now.

Susan decided she should check on the horse.

The horse was well, and asleep, and Susan looked at the horse, and then looked up at the stars. Then she decided that as long as she was outside, she might as well go to the mouth of the canyon, where she could see more stars.

At the mouth of the canyon she not only saw more stars, she watched the moon rise above the ugly mountains across the way. It was not bright enough to read a newspaper by perhaps, but bright enough to ride a horse a mile or two over level ground.

She went back to the cabin. At their places before the fire, Scotty and Zelda raised their heads in silent greeting.

"I'll be back in a little while," said Susan, trying to sound cheerful and confident, and succeeding just about as well as she had succeeded in everything else she had tried in the past few months.

The dogs looked so dismal at Susan's decision that she instantly repented of it. After all, it *was* a terrible idea.

She took up one of Colleen's novels and began to read it. Despite her intention, she grew very interested in the plight of the young heroine, who'd been born rich but who'd become an orphan and lost all her inheritance to a wicked uncle. But when she became engaged to the man who was patently wrong for her and studiously ignored the gentleman who was patently right for her, Susan hurled the book into the fire.

She plucked it out again instantly, remembering it wasn't her property, but Colleen's.

Thinking of Colleen made her think of Blossom, and thinking of Blossom made her reconsider her decision *not* to go to the Excelsior Ranch tonight. Certainly Blossom should know as quickly as possible of what Susan had learned. Perhaps Blossom would see something of the matter that Susan couldn't see herself.

"I'll be back in a little while," said Susan again, and this time she wasn't swayed by the dismal looks of Scotty and Zelda.

After two in the morning, danger of being seen by Barbara or any of Blossom's other guests was past. The moon was still bright and clear above, and the way there was unmistakable, even though she'd traveled it only once.

She threw on an extra sweater, and threw a jacket over that. Outside, she wakened and saddled the horse, and led her to the mouth of the canyon. Then she mounted and trotted silently a hundred yards or so out into the desert. No one was going to be out so late at night—Susan had never even seen anyone there during the day—and the horse's way would be easier here than among the stones at the base of Bright mountain.

The night was beautiful. Clear, dry, and chill.

But not silent. Loudest, of course, was the rhythmic noise of the horse's hooves on the baked ground. Beneath that she heard the horse's breath, her own breath. She heard crickets. The coo of some nightbird she didn't know but had heard in the cabin as well. She heard the scurrying of small frightened creatures across the desert floor.

And she heard the noise of a motor behind her.

More accurately, behind her and *above* her.

She looked over her shoulder and saw nothing at first. But she followed the sound, and then discerned a black shadow moving across the field of stars.

Moving across the field of stars directly above.

It had no lights, and it was impossible to tell anything about it as it sailed over her.

However, she saw it in somewhat more detail when it banked around and came back.

It was a biplane, old-fashioned and rickety. The moonlight glinted off the propellers.

It continued to come closer, and its altitude dropped. It roared down at Susan so fast and hard, she was certain it intended to hit her, but at the last moment it veered off to the left.

At the same time, however, Susan's horse, whinnying in fright, veered off in the other direction. *With good reason,* Susan thought. She didn't like it anymore than the horse that an unlighted plane was playing practical jokes in the middle of the night in the middle of the Nevada desert.

Susan somehow suspected this wasn't a practical joke.

She snapped the reins and headed the horse to the mountain. There was no shelter there, but they'd be less visible against a wall of rock. The horse was a dark roan, and that helped. Susan's white jacket didn't. She awkwardly shed it, transferring the reins from hand to hand as she did so, and then tossed the garment to the ground.

The plane had circled round again. It came still lower.

"Giddap!" Susan screamed.

She heard the plane directly at her back. It sounded very low and close.

She leaned forward till her head was pressed against the horse's neck.

The horse neighed in fright, and while the plane suddenly swerved upward, narrowly avoiding a collision with the side of the mountain, the horse reared up every bit as violently.

Susan lost her grip on the reins and the horse's neck. She grabbed at the mane, but the horse reared again and she was thrown through the air holding a fistful of coarse hair.

Sailing through the air was a peculiar sensation. She saw the stars and the moon, bright and clear.

Then she felt something hard and coarse and uneven at her back—and then the stars and the moon seemed dim and blurred.

Then, before she'd lost total consciousness, she had time for only one more thought in a single syllable.

A name.

Jack.

CHAPTER TWENTY-FIVE

"JACK," SHE SAID, but this time aloud.

"No," replied a woman's voice. "It's Blossom, Susan."

Slowly she pried open her eyes. Blossom smiled down at her, an angular, trembling, tentative smile.

"I must have been dreaming of him."

"You weren't asleep," said Blossom. "You were unconscious."

Susan looked around. At first she couldn't focus beyond Blossom's face. Then her surroundings became more distinct. She wasn't in her cabin. She didn't recognize the room.

"Reno?" she asked.

"What?"

"Are we in Reno?" Susan asked.

"No, we're at the ranch," said Blossom. "This is my room."

"Unconscious," she murmured, closing her eyes again. "You said I was unconscious."

"This morning when Wesley got up, he found Coral outside the stable, so we knew something must have happened. Colleen and I found you halfway between here and the cabin. Why were you out riding so late?"

"I was coming to see you—" She couldn't talk more. Her head hurt very badly.

Blossom poured water into a glass and raised Susan's throbbing head. She gently poured the water into Susan's mouth in tiny sips.

"And how could you have fallen off Coral? She's the gentlest mare we have."

Susan pushed the water away. "I didn't fall," Susan whispered. "She threw me."

Blossom's eyes widened.

"A plane swooped down at us and Coral was frightened—"

"A plane—?"

"Yes," said Susan, "the pilot was trying to kill me."

Blossom stared at Susan.

"No," said Susan, reading her cousin's thoughts, "I didn't dream it."

"But—"

"And I didn't dream about Malcolm MacIsaac being in the Dirt Hole Mine yesterday either—"

"Who is—"

"The detective that Marcellus Rhinelander hired to prove Harmon's infidelity."

"A detective from New York?" said Blossom carefully. "You saw him in the mine yesterday?"

"Yes," said Susan, "he was meeting Barbara there. They almost saw me, but I hid and—"

Blossom shook her head like a doctor at the bedside of a favorite patient raging with a hallucinatory fever.

"No!" cried Susan. "It was all real. The plane, the detective, Barbara—I even remember what she was wearing—she—"

The door of the room flew open, and Barbara

Beaumont herself stood there, smiling broadly, carrying a large bouquet of desert flowers.

"Did I just hear my name mentioned? I hope you were saying something nice about me, Susan!"

Blossom stood up from the bed. "How did you know she was here?"

"Oh, news travels fast in a place like this..." Barbara strode forward and laid the flowers on Susan's breast, the way she might have laid flowers on her father's grave. "Susan, I hope you're not *too* much hurt. I trust there's no *permanent* injury to your brain. It really is the most incredible coincidence, your being found practically dead in the desert not two miles from where I'm staying."

"It's not such a coincidence," said Susan, giving Blossom a glance. *Follow my lead*, it said. "Blossom is my cousin."

"You *are* joking," said Barbara with affected astonishment.

Susan knew it was affected, because if this information had truly been unknown to her, Barbara would have moved heaven and earth not to show surprise.

"No, Barbara, it's the absolute truth. In fact, you may be even more astonished to learn that I own this ranch."

Barbara put her hand to her breast and drew back several feet. *"No..."*

"It's true," Blossom concurred with appropriate drama in her tone and gesture. "Absolutely *true*..."

"Of course," Barbara went on, coming back to the bed and placing her hand on Susan's wrist as if surreptitiously searching for a feeble pulse in a wasting victim. "You know I've been looking for you all *over* Nevada."

"Yes?" said Susan.

"I even hired a detective to find you," Barbara went on.

"Mr. MacIsaac," said Susan.

"This is *beyond* coincidence," gasped Barbara. "You *must* have the powers of a medium!"

"Well, now that you've found me, I suppose you'll

want Blossom to drive you into Reno so that you can telephone the Albany police."

"Whatever for? What*ever* for?"

"So that they can start extradition proceedings against me," said Susan.

"Oh, what nonsense, Susan. That's exactly why I've been trying to find you. I know you didn't murder Father. It was all a silly misunderstanding."

"You mean your father isn't dead?" Blossom inquired.

"Oh no, not that part," said Barbara. "Father really is dead. The part about Susan's having killed him."

"If I didn't," Susan asked. "Who did?"

"It was an anarchist plot," said Barbara smoothly, rather as if she were explaining why she'd been late for a luncheon appointment, "timed to coincide with the inauguration of the President. Some Socialist friend of Richard Grace's apparently," she explained, shaking her head as if to say, *That naughty chauffeur of ours...*

Susan said nothing. On general principles, she disbelieved everything Barbara Beaumont said. Only thumbscrews or the promise of immediate financial gain could make Jack's wife tell the truth. Anarchistic plots against Marcellus Rhinelander seemed implausible, to say the least. Susan didn't know what to believe, so Susan said nothing for the moment. She was glad, however, that Blossom pursued the matter.

"They've arrested the man?" asked Blossom.

"It was a woman," said Barbara, and laughed gaily. "I was right about that part at any rate! So everything's turned out happily—for everybody."

"Except for your father," Blossom pointed out, "who's still dead."

"And except for you and Jack, who are getting a divorce," said Susan. "And except Harmon and me, who are also getting a divorce."

Barbara laughed another little laugh, gayer than the last one. "I realize I was wrong about you and Father—*and* about you and Jack. So there's no reason for Jack and me to get divorced—so of course we're not. I really do adore the man, you know." She sighed, as if contemplating the object of her adoration. "And since you *didn't* kill Father, there's no reason for Harmon to divorce *you.*"

Susan and Blossom exchanged glances.

"This is very strange," said Blossom.

"It's just us giddy New Yorkers!" Barbara laughed.

"Whether or not Harmon still wants to be married to me," said Susan, "I'm not at all certain that I want to remain married to him."

"Don't say that," cried a familiar voice just outside the door.

A masculine voice. Harmon's.

Susan sighed. It would be.

Harmon sauntered in with a bouquet of flowers even larger than Barbara's.

"I've been a fool," he said. "An absolute fool. I don't know how I could *ever* have imagined—what I imagined. Susan, please forgive me. Please come back with me to New York."

Blossom said to Susan, "I don't know where he came from. I don't even know who he is."

"He's my husband," said Susan to her cousin. "How did you know I was here?" Susan asked Harmon. She was not only bewildered, but, looking at Harmon now, embarrassed that she could have been such a fool as to marry him. She felt rather like one of the dreadfully obtuse heroines of Colleen's novels. It was obvious, too, that Blossom didn't think much of him.

"I didn't know you were here," said Harmon. "But I came to Nevada to look for you, of course, and believe me, I would have gone to Alaska, or Timbuktu just as readily, and when I got to Reno, I couldn't find Barbara, I couldn't find MacIsaac, I couldn't find anybody, and then finally I ran into the princess, and she told me where Barbara was, so I came here in hope she could shed some light on the business and"—he stopped in apparent embarrassment—"and truth to tell, the flowers were for her, but it looks as if you deserve them more."

"What I really need now," said Susan, "is a little rest."

"I can't go—and I *won't* go—unless you tell me you forgive me," said Harmon. "And say you'll go back to New York with me."

Susan smiled the sweet smile of an invalid. "Oh yes, if you'll wait a little while, till I can get out of this bed, I'll be happy to go back to New York with you."

"Oh," cried Barbara in a little ecstasy all her own, "we're all going to be so happy again! We'll have to take bridge lessons! I met the Culbertsons at a party once, and they said, 'Barbara, if you ever decide—'"

Harmon interrupted her. "Barbara, let's go. Susan just told me everything I wanted to hear. Now the only important thing is for her to get well, so that we can all go back to New York and live happily ever after."

"And take lessons from the Culbertsons?"

"Yes," said Harmon, "anything."

Blossom, startled by all this beyond the power of speech, was readying herself to leave as well, but Susan detained her. "Stay with me, Blossom, till I fall asleep. Please?"

"Of course," said Blossom uncertainly.

Harmon kissed Susan on one cheek, and Barbara kissed her on the other, then left the room. Blossom closed the door tightly after them. She turned around, leaned against the door, and stared at Susan in the bed.

"So what do you think of my choice in husbands?"

"Truthfully? Not much."

"You don't think he truly loves me?"

"I don't know anything about men," said Blossom. "And I can't always tell when they're telling the truth...or when they're lying out three sides of their mouths at once. But it doesn't matter what I think about him, does it, really? You've already agreed to return to New York with him."

"When I get out of this bed, I will," said Susan.

Blossom looked disappointed in her cousin.

"Of course, I fully intend to be in this bed for the next three weeks and five days. Then the divorce becomes final, and I'll be happy to go back to New York with Harmon. As long as we're in separate cars on the train, of course."

Blossom laughed. "You didn't believe him either?"

"Not for a minute," Susan said. "There's something to all this, and I just don't know what it is. But at least I'm not still wanted for murder."

"If you ever were," said Blossom.

"Quite right," Susan said, thinking of that possibility for the first time. Perhaps Barbara had fabricated the incriminating evidence of Susan's crime just as Mr. MacIsaac had fabricated the evidence of Harmon's infidelity. "But the question is, who tried to murder me last night?"

"Barbara?" suggested Blossom.

"Barbara has a fear of airplanes. And whoever flew that plane certainly knew what he was doing—"

"Your husband?"

"If he's so adamant about staying married to me this morning," said Susan, "he wouldn't have tried to kill me last night."

"That detective?"

"If he was hired *both* by Barbara and Harmon to find me, it wouldn't be him."

"Maybe it was just some lunatic in a plane," said Blossom. "Someone who—"

Her voice was suddenly drowned out by the noise of a motor somewhere directly above.

"Oh no," said Susan, cringing in the bed. "Whoever it is, he's coming back."

Blossom rushed to the window, and Susan staggered to her feet, realizing for the first time that her body ached almost as much as her head.

"He's landing," cried Blossom. She grabbed Susan to keep her from falling.

Together they stared out the window at the biplane that was landing on a stretch of plain ground just beyond the corral. A dozen frightened horses neighed in their stables.

"Is that it?" asked Blossom. "Can you tell?"

"Yes," said Susan, "that's the plane. I'll never forget the sound of *that* motor."

The plane hit the ground, rolled on, slowed, and turned around, at last stopping at the side of the corral. The horses in the stables were frightened anew.

"He probably thought you were killed," said Blossom. "And now he's coming back to make sure. The nerve..."

They watched grimly as the pilot hopped out of the cockpit and took off in a run around the corral fence toward them. He wore gray trousers, a dark leather jacket, and goggles.

He got close enough to the window to see Susan and Blossom, and he waved frantically, pulling off his goggles.

"I'll get the shotgun," said Blossom, "and this time I won't load it with salt."

"Don't," sighed Susan. "It's Jack."

Part V

JACK AND SUSAN

CHAPTER TWENTY-SIX

THAT SUSAN WAS at the Excelsior Ranch was proof she loved him.

He'd sent her a single telegram, telling her to come here. No explanation then. No telegram, no telephone call, no letter since then. And still she was here, safe and waiting.

That was trust.

Trust like that came only from love.

He supposed that the woman standing in the window next to her was her cousin Blossom.

Blossom didn't look like a Blossom. Edwarda, maybe.

Both women disappeared from the window. He stopped and waited for Susan to run out and greet him.

Perhaps he'd even get an embrace. Even though they were both still married to others. He dared not hope for a kiss, but he thought that an embrace was entirely within the bounds of possibility.

What he got was Blossom with a shotgun.

"Inside," she hissed. With nothing that approached friendliness. "Quick, quick, before anybody sees you."

She poked the barrel of the shotgun in his back.

"You *are* Miss Mayback, aren't you?" he asked uncertainly, but moving forward all the while.

"Yes," she hissed, and prodded him through the door of a small low building with gray stucco walls. "And don't waste your breath telling me who you are, because I know."

He wondered why she seemed so displeased to make his acquaintance. Perhaps he'd landed the plane on some particularly valuable piece of land that only *looked* like cracked and lifeless desert.

The rifle barrel guided him down a short hallway, and then through an open door into a bedroom. He didn't need to be guided farther. Susan lay in the bed and regarded him with a cold eye.

"You look terrible," he said automatically.

"There's a reason," said Susan.

"Are you ill?"

"She's not feeling her best," said Blossom, coming in with the shotgun. Holding it beneath her arm, as if she were reluctant to put it down within Jack's reach, she carefully shut the door, fished a key from the pocket of her dress, and locked it. She turned and regarded Jack with a beady eye. "Someone tried to murder her last night."

"Oh my God!" cried Jack, staring at Susan in the bed. "Oh my God, who—"

"When did you take up flying?" Susan asked.

"What?"

"When did you learn to fly?" she repeated patiently.

"In the War?" Blossom asked sarcastically.

"No," said Jack, mystified. "But my father flew in the War. And he taught me. Who tried to kill you?"

"Why didn't you ever tell me you knew how to fly a plane?" Susan asked then, coldly ignoring his question.

"Because the subject never came up," said Jack, more and more mystified. "Why are you asking me these questions?"

Susan still didn't answer.

"Because someone tried to murder her with an airplane last night," said Blossom, and looked at Jack with a look that was full of suspicious meaning.

"A biplane," said Susan.

"*That* biplane," said Blossom, pointing out the window with her shotgun.

Jack looked out the window as if to make certain Blossom was pointing to *his* plane rather than some other biplane that might be about the vicinity of the corral. Then he looked at Susan, who didn't contradict her cousin's extraordinary statement and who returned his gaze levelly and without apparent emotion. Then he looked at Blossom, who was patently waiting for some sort of reply.

"You were wondering—I suppose—if I was the one flying the plane as it was trying to murder Susan?"

"Something like that," said Blossom.

"No," said Jack. "It wasn't me."

"Good," said Susan cheerfully as she straightened out the covers. "I didn't really think it was."

"You believe him?" asked Blossom.

"Of course," said Susan. "Don't you?"

Blossom looked at Jack a long time.

"Yes," she said at last, "I believe him. Or at any rate, the other one is such a liar that it makes me think I'd believe anything this one would say."

"What other one?"

"Harmon," Susan explained.

"You know Harmon?" he asked Blossom.

"I met him once," said Blossom. "About ten minutes ago."

Jack blinked. "Harmon is here?"

"He came to visit Barbara," said Susan.

"*Barbara* is here?" said Jack, blinking harder.

"She brought these flowers," said Susan, shoving Barbara's bouquet off the bed and onto the floor. "And Harmon brought these," she said, tossing them on top of Barbara's.

"What is Barbara doing here?" said Jack.

"Fulfilling her residence requirement," Blossom said, still a little sharply. She hadn't given Jack her entire trust yet, evidently.

"When I was in Reno," Jack said, "I never left my hotel room for fear I'd run into her. I spent two days trying to find a woman named Blossom who ran a ranch north of Reno. I was on the telephone, talking to a lawyer, asking him, while the chambermaid was making my bed. The lawyer didn't know, but the chambermaid did."

"That must have been Enid," said Blossom. "Enid got into trouble a little while ago, and I did what I could to help her. Sweet girl."

Jack nodded absently. "What is Harmon doing here?"

"Looking for Barbara, hoping she knew where I was," said Susan. "He was looking for me so that I could forgive him, and go back to New York with him, and start our happy life all over again."

Jack stared.

"Are you going to do it?"

Susan laughed. "You idiot. It's perfectly clear—to you, to me, to Barbara, and to Harmon, that you and I are in love with each other."

Jack stared.

"I shouldn't have said that, I suppose," Susan said, shaking her head at her own impetuousness.

"Yes, you should have," Blossom interjected.

"But I'm tired, and my head hurts, and everything is *very* confused right now, and there's no point in being confused about *this*. So I'm right, am I not—you are in love with me, aren't you?"

"I am," said Jack quickly. "Very much. I love you very much. I love you more than anything else in the world. And I didn't try to kill you last night."

Blossom finally put the shotgun aside, standing it in the corner.

"And I love you, too," said Susan briskly. Then, in case she had been too brisk, she added, "Desperately."

Susan, Jack, and Blossom sighed a sigh in unison. At least *something* was clear.

There was a knock at the door.

Susan?

Harmon's voice.

Are you all right?

"Yes," Susan called weakly.

May I come in?

"Not now, Harmon." She thought quickly. "The doctor's with me."

Is that the man who came in the plane?

"I sent for him!" Blossom called.

Doctor?

Blossom and Susan looked at Jack.

Jack fisted his hands, and then pressed them against either side of his neck. Then when he answered "Yes?" his voice sounded lower and hoarse.

Is my wife going to be all right?

"With rest, Mr. Dodge!" Jack called.

Let me speak to you before you go!

"Can do!" called Jack.

I'll be back!

Then his footsteps retreated from the door.

Jack sighed with relief. Harmon hadn't recognized his voice.

"Quick!" cried Blossom. She grabbed Jack and pushed him over to Susan's bedside so that his back was to the window.

"Bend over," she commanded.

Jack leaned over as if he were examining Susan.

The precaution was well taken. A moment later there was a rap at the window, and Harmon appeared there. He waved in at Susan, who pretended to be breathing deeply for benefit of the examination.

Jack placed his hand on her breast as if listening to her heartbeat through a stethoscope.

Blossom pointedly drew the shade down over the window.

"I really don't understand what is going on here," said Jack.

Susan removed his hand from her breast. "Neither do I. But maybe together we'll be able to figure it out. There are a number of questions I need to ask you."

"Later," said Blossom. "We have to get him out of here before your husband sees him. Or your wife sees you." She grinned at Jack. "A piece of work, that one."

Jack blushed. "I don't want to go anywhere. I think I'd better stay here and protect Susan."

"*I'll* protect Susan," said Blossom. "I think you'd better stay hidden for the time being. If they've got secrets, then it's probably a good idea if we have a secret, too. You're ours."

"If I don't stay here, what am I supposed to do?" Jack asked.

"You have to take care of Scotty and Zelda," Susan laughed.

"Exactly," said Blossom. "We also have to get rid of that plane."

"But—" Jack protested.

"Time for buts later," said Blossom.

"Susan—"

"Later," Susan agreed. "You trust Blossom the way I trust you."

Jack sighed. He turned to Blossom. "Tell me what to do."

❊ ❊ ❊

"Are you rich?" Colleen asked him.

"Ah—not very," said Jack. First-time flyers were generally terrified. This young woman had no fear in her voice or countenance. She intertwined her fingers and cracked her knuckles.

First-time flyers who were not frightened into paralysis were invariably absorbed by the novel spectacle of viewing familiar landscapes from a different vantage point.

Colleen seemed to care for nothing but certain details of Jack's life.

"But your wife is rich?"

"Barbara? Ah, yes, she is. Quite rich."

"Your wife could use a poke in the chops," Colleen remarked. "Head that way," she pointed, off to the right. They were flying low over the desert, going west from the ranch. "Have you ever given her one?"

"A poke in the chops?"

"Yes."

"Not intentionally," said Jack. "But once at a dance at the country club, I slipped on—"

"Who spoiled her?" asked Colleen, no longer interested since the lick in the chops that Jack once gave Barbara had been unintentional. "You or her father?"

"Ah, her father."

"You mean she came that way, and you still married her?" Before Jack could frame a response to that remark, either to satisfy Colleen or himself, Colleen pointed again. "It's just over this rise. So look sharp."

A few minutes after Harmon had left, Blossom had gone to the main building, calling Harmon and Barbara into the dining room on the spurious excuse of asking what Susan's favorite foods were so that the invalid might be indulged. While these two were occupied, Colleen and Jack ran to the plane, and Jack quickly took off.

It was Colleen's job to show Jack a place where the plane might be hidden.

She guided him to a little plateau in the Virginia Mountains—the ugly range of peaks directly across the narrow desert from Mt. Bright. It was invisible from any place near the Excelsior Ranch.

The plateau was so tiny, Jack wondered whether he would be able to land safely. He circled three times before he had the courage to make the attempt.

Unconcerned, Colleen continued to ask him personal questions. Finally, Jack realized that Colleen had cast herself in the role of prospective mother-in-law and wanted to make certain that Susan would have a suitable mate in John Austin Beaumont. When he'd figured that out, it became a pleasure to respond to the inquiries.

"Who do you think is more beautiful—your wife or Susan?"

"Susan, unquestionably. If I'd met Susan before I'd met Barbara, Barbara would not have had a chance with me."

Colleen liked that answer. "And now you wished you *had* met Susan first."

"No," said Jack, "because I love her even more now, having been married to someone like Barbara." That was not exactly the truth, however. In precise honesty, he wished he'd never seen Barbara's face. But somehow Colleen, in appearance a young woman of consuming sensibility, had inspired him with a kind of romanticism. Also, he liked very much to hear someone talk of his love for Susan, and Susan's love for him, as the happy fact that it was.

Colleen sighed a deep romantic sigh, and the plane landed a good five feet before a precipice that dropped a couple of hundred feet onto another, lower plateau of jagged rocks.

Jack and Colleen climbed out of the plane.

Jack peered over the precipice at the treacherous rocks below. He thought of his marriage to Barbara.

He looked up at the cloudless sky, and the sun that burned in it, bright and hot and white and unflawed. He thought of being married to Susan.

He turned away from the precipice. "Have *you* ever fallen in love, Colleen?" he asked in the generousness of his good feeling.

Colleen drew herself up tall. "True gentlemen don't make personal remarks," said Colleen huffily, and turned sharply away.

CHAPTER TWENTY-SEVEN

Despite her new opinion that Jack was a creature undeserving of consideration, Colleen led him down from the plateau, a journey that was neither easy nor readily apparent. It involved, in fact, a good deal of scrambling and sliding and creeping and fearing for his life.

Finally they reached the desert floor, and Colleen, still huffy, led him a few hundred feet along the base of the mountain.

"Is this the way to the cabin?" Jack asked.

Colleen glared at him over her shoulder, as if to say, *Of course not, you fool.* Aloud she said, "Thought you must be rich."

"Why is that?" asked Jack.

"'Cause no girl'd fall in love with you on account of your looks."

"Colleen," someone cried, "you lie. You lie like a cheap Brussels rug."

Suddenly before them was a thin young man with yellow hair. He held the reins of three horses.

"I'm Wesley, Mr. Beaumont," said the young man, who, on closer inspection, wasn't so young. But his hair was *very* yellow. "I know *everything*, so you don't have to be reticent around me. Don't worry about Colleen," he said in a confidential but loud tone, "*everything* ruffles this bird's feathers."

He handed a pair of reins to Jack.

"I've never been on a horse," said Jack.

"Um-humh," said Colleen, as if her worst opinions of Jack had been confirmed.

"Help him on, Colleen. There's nothing to worry about, Mr. Beaumont. We don't have very far to go, and Coral is gentle as a lamb."

"'Cept when there's a plane after her," said Colleen under her breath. "And I wish there was one comin' now."

The sun was high and hot overhead. The horse was hard and smelly beneath. Jack felt as if he were straddling a railway arch during a prolonged earthquake. It might be better if Susan didn't want children, since after this ride he wasn't certain it would be possible.

When Wesley pushed open the cabin door, Scotty and Zelda hurtled out and didn't come back until Jack had had a couple of minutes to look the place over.

Then they looked up at him as if to say, *What have you done with Susan?*

"Susan had a little accident," Jack explained to the dogs. "But she'll be fine, and she's sent me to look after you and keep you company."

Wesley and Colleen exchanged a glance.

"Do you think they took all that in?" Wesley asked.

Scotty and Zelda trotted over to Jack and dropped down on their haunches on either side of him, as if to say, *Of course we understood him.*

"One of us'll be out with food and news every day," said Colleen.

"Food and news," said Wesley with a radiant smile. "It'll probably be me that comes. Don't get much masculine company around this place, and I'm due for a little conversation on the subjects that can't be broached around the fairer sex."

"Go on, Wes," snorted Colleen. "Get five women together, and you'd think you was in a sailors' bar an hour after the ship come in. I was raised by a widower uncle with five boys, and the whole lot of 'em worked on the railroad, but I *never* heard such filth before I came here."

Jack tried to get the two of them to tell him everything they knew—about the attempt on Susan's life, about Barbara's presence at the ranch, about Harmon's arrival, about everything that had been said, or done, or hinted at. Neither would satisfy him.

"From us, it'd be gossip," said Wesley. "Talk to Blossom. Or talk to Susan. For they know more'n either Colleen or me."

With that, they were off.

A week before, Jack had woken up in a bed on the fourth floor of an apartment building that looked out on East Sixty-eighth Street in Manhattan, the most crowded island in the history of the world. He'd shaved with a razor that worked by electric current. Over the radio he'd heard about a massacre in Madrid that had taken place only hours before. He'd damned the clamor of morning traffic. He'd complained to a neighbor that the elevator was always stuck on another floor when you called it. He'd cursed himself for choosing the slowest of two dozen lines of ticket buyers at Grand Central Station, and in his frustration he counted two hundred sixteen travelers who got their tickets before he did.

That was seven days ago.

Now he found himself in a cabin without electricity, running water, or improvements of any kind. That cabin was located at the innermost reach of a narrow canyon dug deep into the sides of a dark mountain, in one of the remoter parts of a state that itself was fabled for being the end of the world.

His wife was less than two miles away, and didn't know of his presence.

His boss was less than two miles away, and had no idea he was there.

The woman he loved was less than two miles away, but she couldn't get to him because she was in bed, trying to recover from an attempt on her life.

And all Jack knew about any of this was that it was his job to take care of Scotty and Zelda.

It wasn't a particularly complicated or onerous duty.

He filled two bowls with the dogs' stew that was warming on the fire. When they'd eaten that, he filled the bowls with water. Then he let them out again for a few minutes, and when one of them scratched lightly at the door, he let them back in again.

He lay on the bed and coaxed them up onto his lap. He gently tweaked their ears, something they seemed to like very much, and he talked to them about Susan.

He fell asleep and didn't wake till Zelda began to breathe hotly into his ear. He tried to push her away, but she came back.

Finally he sat up, grabbed Zelda, and planted her firmly on the floor. The fire in the hearth had nearly died out. It was only embers, but by that feeble light he could see Scotty by the door.

"Oh, need to go outside again?" he asked, and got up. He went to the door and pushed it open, but neither Scotty nor Zelda made any move to leave the cabin.

"Well, if you didn't want to go out, why did you wake me up?"

Because someone's coming, was his next thought, for now he could hear the slow *clop clop clop* of hooves on the stony ground.

He checked his watch. Two A.M.

He hoped it was Blossom, with good news.

It seemed more likely that it was Blossom with bad news. Or that it was Barbara or Harmon, whose arrival would only constitute ill tidings. It might even be whoever had tried to kill Susan the night before, at just about this hour, returning to finish that job, or else to start a new one out, with Jack as victim.

The visitor was none of those.

It was Susan.

"Oh my God," he cried, running out to help her down from the horse, "what are you doing out of bed?"

"I had to see you," she said, drawing in her breath painfully.

He wasn't actually helping her to get down so much as he was putting her in danger of breaking her ankle, which was caught in the stirrup.

"Please," she said. "I can get down by myself." After taking a deep breath, she did exactly that. "But if you'll bring out a bucket of water..."

"If you're thirsty," he cried, "come inside the cabin."

"A bucket of water for the horse," said Susan.

He rushed to do her bidding. When he came back, he found she'd tied the horse to a stake in the ground and was feeding him quarters of an apple as a treat.

Scotty and Zelda patiently waited to be acknowledged. Susan tried to bend over to them, but pain stopped her. Jack instantly snatched the dogs up and held them out to be caressed.

"Did Mr. Beaumont take good care of you?" she asked them.

They wagged their tails, and Jack breathed a sigh of relief. He half feared he'd done something wrong with them, in the way bachelors are reluctant to pick up a fragile infant.

"Now let me take care of *you*," Jack said. She nodded acquiescence. He led her into the cabin and laid her down on the bed. He placed every pillow in the cabin beneath her head, then he folded two blankets and shoved them under the pillows.

"Anything to eat? Anything to drink?" he begged.

"No. I can't stay long, and there are a number of things we have to talk about, and think about."

"Yes, there are. And the first one is, I love you."

"You told me that before. I believed you then. Though I don't actually much mind hearing it again."

"I love you. And I want to marry you."

"Oh dear," said Susan. "This time around I was hoping for a little more romantic proposal than I got from Harmon, but that's all right."

Jack started down on his knees for the romantic proposal, but she stopped him. "If you're down there, I can't see you, and besides, it's too late, I've already accepted. Though I don't know how much good that will do either of us. We both have to get divorces first."

"But you said you weren't going back to Harmon," Jack protested.

"I'm not," said Susan. "Even if you weren't in the picture, I'd divorce Harmon. But Barbara says that you and she intend to remain married."

"I'm astonished," said Jack. "I checked in Reno. She's filed papers."

Susan thought for a moment. "She lied about that, then. I suppose she also lied about the police arresting the woman who murdered Marcellus."

"What woman?" asked Jack, wide-eyed.

"Barbara said an anarchist friend of Richard Grace's..." Susan didn't even bother to finish the implausible tale. She shook her head sadly. "So I suppose I'm still wanted by the police."

"Nothing you tell me makes any sense," said Jack. "Why do the police want you?"

Susan stared at him. "For Marcellus's murder. The police searched the Quarry, and in my bedroom there they found wire cutters and a page from an instruction manual for the touring car, so now they obviously think I murdered him. Someone planted that evidence, of course."

"No," said Jack, contradicting her. "No one planted that evidence, because there wasn't any evidence to plant. The police never searched the Quarry. They don't suspect you of anything. At least not of last Friday, which is when I telephoned them."

"Then why did you send me the telegram, telling me to leave Reno?"

"Because I didn't want MacIsaac to find you. He got your address from the Graces, and was coming out here to find you—and kill you, I think."

It was Susan's turn to be mystified. "Why does MacIsaac want to kill me?"

"Because *he's* the one who murdered Marcellus."

"Are you sure?"

"No. But I think he did."

"So Barbara lied both about the evidence and about the real murderer being found."

"Apparently," said Jack. "No, not apparently. She *did* lie about it."

"Why did she lie, though? And even if MacIsaac murdered Marcellus, why is he trying to kill me? Was he the pilot of that plane last night?"

"He could have been, I suppose. I rented it in Reno, and the owner said that someone had taken it only the day before."

"Maybe he flew up here to visit the Dirt Hole," Susan suggested.

"The Dirt Hole?"

More explanations. For half an hour more, the two went through everything that had happened since they'd last seen each other, everything they'd feared, and everything they now suspected. They came to the conclusion, in itself simple enough, that everyone was lying.

But this conclusion provided no answers for all the other mysteries surrounding Jack and Susan.

Susan lay on the bed, half sitting up against the pile of blankets and pillows. Jack sat cross-legged on the floor, where it was easiest for her to see him.

"What now?" Jack had to ask at last.

"What now?" Susan echoed. "I sneak back to the ranch, and hope no one sees me. Tomorrow I play loving invalid, and I say very sweetly to Barbara, 'How is Jack? I'm so glad you two are going to remain together. Please give him my regards.'"

Then they both laughed. And then were silent.

Then Jack said again, "I love you."

"I love you," said Susan.

"I'd love to—"

"We can't," said Susan hurriedly, apologetically. "I didn't do anything to deserve this divorce. I know it's terrible of me, but I want to keep it that way."

Jack was silent.

"Aren't you going to make an attempt to talk me out of my resolution?" Susan asked at last.

"No," replied Jack miserably. "Unfortunately, I feel exactly the same."

They were silent a few more moments, then Susan said suddenly, "But I really do want to..."

"Don't let's talk about it anymore," said Jack hurriedly. "While you're playing invalid, what should I do?"

Susan evidently had something in mind, but she hesitated to say it.

"Go on," Jack prompted her. "If it will help, I'll do it."

"You might visit the mine and see if you can find out what MacIsaac was doing in there."

"Of course," said Jack. "I should have thought of that. Why did you hesitate to suggest it?"

"Because I hate the place. I hate places that are dark and enclosed and where I might get stuck and—"

"I hate high places," said Jack. "That's why my father made me learn to fly a plane. But dark places don't bother me. I used to love exploring caves."

Susan digested this a moment, then said, "Maybe I don't love you after all."

Jack looked stricken, and then realized she was joking. "If that worm MacIsaac can go down into the Dirt Hole Mine, so can I. Don't worry, I'll be fine."

"You have to be," said Susan. "Because if you get into trouble, I can't be the one who's going to come after you."

CHAPTER TWENTY-EIGHT

H E DIDN'T WANT her to leave, but she insisted, appealing to his lawyerliness. "You know I have to go. It's what's best for us."

She left at a little past four in the morning. Jack got to sleep at a little before eight in the morning. He got up at a little past nine, thinking he'd wasted half the day.

He made a hasty breakfast, more for Scotty and Zelda than for himself. He searched through the cabin, gathering up everything he thought might be of use in an exploration of the mine.

A candle and matches.

A compass.

A ball of twine.

A length of rope.

Some hard cheese and crackers.

He changed into corduroy trousers, cotton shirt, and sweater, and pulled on his hiking boots.

To his supplies he added a pen and some folded scraps of paper—just in the unlikely event he had to send a message.

This suggested that he ought to take Scotty and Zelda along on the journey, too. "Because if a message needs to be gotten somewhere, there has to be someone to take it," he said to the terriers. "Am I not right?"

He didn't need to use the map Susan had given him. The dogs apparently understood their destination, for they led the way without hesitation. The morning was bright and hot and it made Jack dim and sluggish, but he plowed on behind Scotty and Zelda, thinking, *These are not desert dogs. I'm not a desert man. But if this is what we can do for Susan and myself, then we will do it.*

Then he plowed on with renewed vigor, not quite so dim or sluggish as before.

At last he reached the entrance of the mine, which was exactly as Susan had described it.

The ground was too hard for footprints, but Zelda led him to a discarded cigarette. It was a Lucky, only half smoked, with cerise lipstick on the end.

He would have staked his soul that Barbara had been there first.

He peered through the entrance and saw nothing but blackness.

He stood still and listened. He heard nothing.

He called. "Hello! Hello!"

No one answered.

He ventured a couple of feet inside, motioning for the dogs to follow.

The dogs remained outside the entrance. Jack disappeared into the darkness.

Scotty and Zelda looked at each other.

"Come on!" Jack's voice called. "This isn't for me, this is for Susan!"

The dogs reluctantly trotted in.

❀ ❀ ❀

"Dreadful," exclaimed Barbara. "It's the only word for the way you look."

"I didn't get much sleep," Susan admitted.

"But you *have* to get better. For Harmon's sake. For *my* sake," said Barbara.

"For your sake?"

"I've treated you dreadfully. Abysmally. My back is positively criss-crossed with flagellation marks, all self-inflicted. I've *worlds* to make up to you, and I want to start on it this very minute."

"Let it wait a bit," said Susan. "Whatever it is."

"It can't, though. Harmon and I are going to pile the back of his car with every blanket and pillow on this ranch, and we are going to drive you to Reno, and put you in a *hospital*. We'll drive around till we find the most expensive one. No expense will be spared to make you well."

For some reason, it was apparent, Barbara or Harmon—or Barbara *and* Harmon—wanted her off the Excelsior Ranch.

"I don't want to leave," said Susan. "The doctor saw me yesterday and he said the best thing for me would be bed rest and fresh air."

"Quack," cried Barbara. "Quack, quack, quack!"

"I'm staying here, Barbara."

"No," said Harmon, slipping into the room. How long he'd remained unheard outside the door Susan had no idea. "You have to go, Susan. I insist."

"*We* insist," said Barbara. "Jack would insist, too, if he were here."

Susan shook her head. "The ride would be bad for me. I can feel that, in my bruised bones. I stay here. Of course, if you two are bored, there's no reason you can't go on to Reno. I'm afraid I'm not much company just now."

"I wouldn't think of leaving you," said Harmon. "I wouldn't think of it."

"I wouldn't either," said Barbara. "Harmon, you don't know it, but Susan and I are new best friends. I'd trust her with my life."

Susan sighed a sort of invalid sigh. "In my state right now, Barbara, that might not be a very good idea..."

Barbara was about to say something else, but at that moment Blossom hurried in, out of breath.

"Please, Mrs. Beaumont, Mr. Dodge—Susan needs her rest."

"Susan needs bright spirits around her," Barbara snapped. "Bright spirits who adore her and will tell her amusing stories of fashionable people. That's what Susan needs. At every minute. Until she's well and we can get her out of this hole in the ground you call a ranch."

"I also need a little sleep," said Susan weakly, and closed her eyes, the way Little Eva closed them so that she could see the angels better. Without further argument, Blossom shoved Barbara and Harmon out the door again.

I adore you! cried Harmon from outside the door.

Adieu! Barbara shrieked.

Blossom locked the door. "You have another guest," she said quietly.

"Who is it?"

Blossom glanced at a bit of pasteboard in her hand. "A Mr. Ramey. Lawrence Ramey."

"I never heard of him. Who is he?"

"He works for the government."

Susan dropped back on the pillow. "I wonder what crime I'm being charged with today. Kidnapping, you suppose? Treason?"

"He wouldn't say why he came."

Susan sighed. "I think I'd rather be with Jack right now. No matter how far he goes down in the Dirt Hole Mine."

Down in the Dirt Hole Mine, Jack simply followed the path of the rail. Even when dust and clods of earth fallen from the walls and ceiling obscured the tracks, he could follow them by dragging his foot along one of the rails. He hardly needed to look at it at all.

Scotty and Zelda followed cautiously in his wake.

The mine was in better shape than Susan's dire description had suggested. Many of the openings and beams were bowed, but even when they'd split, the walls hadn't collapsed, and the ceiling hadn't fallen in.

This principal corridor wound at random and only very gradually sank itself into the bowels of Mt. Bright. Off it were numerous smaller passages. Some had been dug experimentally, in hope of catching a meandering vein of silver or gold. Others seemed to be naturally collapsed openings into hollow chambers in the mountain.

Jack ducked into one of the latter and found himself in a large, naturally formed room. There was nothing here of interest, neither grotesque rock formations, nor bottomless pools of black water, nor vampire bats swooping down from the high and blackly invisible ceiling. Just a hollow in the mountain with walls of crumbling dirt, and a floor of dirt and dust.

Jack sneezed, and the dogs yelped in fright.

He continued his way along the principal corridor.

More dark passages going off to the right or to the left. A gradual descent which showed him only dust, and dirt, and crumbling earth, and never a sign that there had been anything else. It was no wonder the place had been named Dirt Hole. Susan's uncle must have been the richest and most sanguine of wealthy conceited idiots if he had spent the money it took to dig this far into Mt. Bright or to lay track for the little hopper cars that would never bring out anything but dirt and dust.

He calculated he'd gone about three-quarters of a mile into the mountain, when the tracks ended abruptly.

Jack kicked up the earth farther along, for the corridor itself did not end quite yet, but he found no trace of the rails.

Good and well, then.

He'd gone as deeply into Mt. Bright as it was possible to go, and he'd seen no evidence of recent incursion.

No new excavations.

No tools or supplies to excavate with.

No use of the tracks whatever.

No footprints or human detritus.

Jack didn't doubt that Susan had indeed seen Malcolm MacIsaac coming from somewhere deeper in the mine than she'd dared to venture, but perhaps the man was only as curious as Jack himself about holes in the earth.

Though from this vantage point of curiosity, the Dirt Hole Mine was the least interesting of all scapes. For there was nothing here but dust, and crumbling rock, and sterile earth, and—and something that went *click click click*.

The sound came from farther on, beyond where the tracks ended. A kind of quiet mechanical cricket.

Jack turned around and glanced at Scotty and Zelda, still the same two feet behind him.

They evidently heard it, too.

"You stay here," said Jack.

The dogs immediately collapsed on all fours, as if to indicate it would take a great deal to go against *that* particular command.

Jack went forward, following the *click click click*.

Two supports and a beam framed the final extension of the Dirt Hole excavation, and it was into this dark space that Jack ducked and moved forward, holding the candle before him. This allowed him to see that the walls on either side were growing narrower, and the ceiling was getting lower.

The *click click click* was louder now, and echoing.

Jack dropped to his haunches and eased forward as far as he could go. His head pressed against the dirt ceiling. Sand and dirt pressed into his scalp, crumbled, and spilled down his neck.

His arms were lodged between his body and the narrow walls of the corridor. He twisted so as to release the arm holding the lighted candle and pushed it forward as far as possible.

Something gleamed up ahead, close to the ground.

Some sort of machine, but that was all Jack could tell.

He continued to squeeze forward, like a finger pushing through a curious ring.

That was an unfortunate analogy for Jack to consider. For sometimes, when you did succeed in getting a ring past a troublesome knuckle, you never got it off again.

Jack squeezed through somehow.

When he reached forward with the candle to see what went *click click click* however, the walls were so close and tight that the burning wick brushed against a clod of earth and was extinguished.

Darkness is absolute three-quarters of a mile deep into a mountain.

Jack tried to reach into his pocket for a match, but discovered he couldn't move his other arm. It was wedged tight between his body and the wall.

His other hand held the candle. He tried to lower it to the ground, but he couldn't maneuver in that space and dropped the candle and its holder. They were of no use to him now anyway. They fell against whatever it was that went *click click click*.

He tried to move his right hand into his left-hand pocket. That was impossible, too.

He tried to back up through the narrow opening he had just entered.

This maneuver precipitated a shower of dust and dirt from the ceiling onto his head.

He was growing tired of squatting, so with one energetic move he kicked his legs out from under him, and fell on his bottom. His feet struck the opposite wall jarringly.

He began to understand Susan's dislike of the dark, enclosed spaces in which you might get trapped forever.

His legs were bent at the knees. His left arm was crushed between his body and the wall. His right arm was free, and he flailed it about, but it didn't hit anything but the ceiling and the right-hand wall. His back was blocking all but an inch or so of the hole he'd pushed through, and he had to bend his head forward so that air could get through to him in this tiny space.

In the blackness Scotty and Zelda whimpered again.

Using the opposite wall as a brace, Jack tried to push himself out through the hole by main force.

He succeeded only in pressing two three-inch footprints into the opposite wall.

Between his feet, the *click click click* went on. Regular, and exquisitely annoying.

He'd heard stories, as a boy, of greedy men who'd been trapped in mines by the lure of diamonds or gold or hidden treasure. He'd been trapped by something that went *click, click, click.*

Perhaps he could get out sideways.

He tried to turn over, twisting his legs first, throwing his right leg over his left, and attempting to turn the rest of his body after that.

This ill-advised plan dislodged a large portion of the right wall, which collapsed over the thing that went *click click click* as well as Jack's legs, his hips, his right arm, and most of his torso, with the result that all that remained unburied of Jack was his head and the collar of his sweater.

The only piece of good luck he'd had in the past quarter hour was that the dogs had not ventured into this space ahead of him. They remained unburied and quiet behind him.

"Scotty," he called softly. Softly, not because he thought he might frighten the dogs away otherwise, but because it was not possible to draw more than a few sips of air into his lungs.

"Zelda?"

The dogs came forward.

"I think you'd better go get help," said Jack.

The dogs scampered away. They might arrive at the ranch in a few hours, and perhaps someone would notice them and maybe mention having seen them to Susan. Then it was possible she would figure out that something was wrong and that he needed help.

Someone might show up in a few days.

If he was very lucky, he'd get a decent burial.

His predicament constituted interment, but in no way a decent burial.

His left arm, caught underneath him, was numb. So were his legs, beneath a weight of loose rock and dirt.

He could no longer hear the machine that went *click, click, click,* for the layer of earth over it. His left foot, however, was pressed against the device, and he could feel each clicking pulse.

He succeeded, with some difficulty, in freeing his right arm. He took a fistful of dirt, and with some greater difficulty, tried to toss it over his shoulder. Perhaps he could dig himself out.

He succeeded only in dropping a fistful of dirt into his face, clogging his nostrils, and stopping the passages of his throat.

He worked for some minutes staving off suffocation, and then decided he should wait for help, and do nothing at all.

The best way to pass the time was to sleep. He'd gotten very little the night before, and it would be fairly welcome at this point. Also, under the circumstances, sleep was the most painless way of passing through hours of discomfort and rather sullen hopes. He'd have to trust his body not to allow himself to be suffocated, and to wake in the event of another small landslide.

He fell asleep instantly.

He did not dream.

Later, he awakened instantly to full consciousness. Not because there had been another landslide. Not because help had arrived. But merely because he'd figured out the nature of the machine that shared his tomb.

It was a Geiger counter.

And that meant that the Dirt Hole Mine was—a uranium mine.

CHAPTER TWENTY-NINE

"A URANIUM MINE!" Susan exclaimed.

Mr. Ramey nodded. He was short and spare, and wore a dark blue wool suit entirely inappropriate for Nevada.

"I thought there was only dirt in that mine," said Susan, wondering.

"The uranium is in the dirt," Mr. Ramey explained, "and it has to be processed for extraction."

"I see," said Susan, and didn't particularly see at all. "What is it good for?"

"I'm—I'm not exactly sure of that bit," said Mr. Ramey evasively. "But I do assure you that the government has every interest in helping you to reestablish operations in the mine."

Susan blinked. "You actually want to *help*?"

"In any way that I can," said Mr. Ramey. He added a little self-deprecating cough. "You must understand that already, however, as I have gone to great lengths to find you. After I spoke to Mr. Dodge in New York—"

"Harmon knows about this?"

"Of course," said Mr. Ramey. "From what I understand, he's been accepting bids from mining companies already established in Nevada. This should prove a great boon to the area, I don't need to tell you."

"You do need to tell me," said Susan. "For I know nothing of this, and still don't know what to think of it."

"Well," said Mr. Ramey, "I'm sure if you'd just telephone your husband in New York—"

"My husband is here," said Susan.

"Well then," said Mr. Ramey, "I'm sure there won't be any difficulties then. We're only interested in having the mining operation set up as quickly as possible so that—"

"I understand, Mr. Ramey. I understand perfectly now," Susan said, sitting up in bed with a radiant smile. "Now, would you be so kind as to do a favor for a temporary invalid?"

"Of course," returned Mr. Ramey, confused.

"Go to the window there…"

Mr. Ramey did so.

"Open it as wide as it will go…"

Mr. Ramey complied.

"Now lean out and yell 'Blossom' as loudly as you can."

Mr. Ramey stared at Susan for a moment. "'Blossom'?"

"It's my cousin's name," said Susan.

Mr. Ramey leaned out the window and yelled, "Blossom!"

Blossom appeared in the doorway. "I was listening outside the door," she said unapologetically.

"Good," said Susan. "Now, did Harmon see Mr. Ramey come in?"

Blossom shook her head. "They were in here with you when Mr. Ramey came, and I brought him in the back way—just in case."

"Good," said Susan again. "Mr. Ramey, is there anything on your car that says you're from the government?"

"Ah—the plates, I believe."

"But it's behind the stables," said Blossom, "and Mr. Dodge and Mrs. Beaumont never go back there."

"Even better," said Susan.

"Mrs. Dodge?"

"Yes?"

"Am I to understand that—"

"All you have to understand, Mr. Ramey, is that from now on you must speak to me directly about all this. My husband has no authority in this matter. In fact, in three weeks he and I will be divorced."

"Mr. Ramey," Blossom asked, "if Susan didn't know about the uranium in that mine, and *I* didn't know about it, how did the government find out about it?"

Mr. Ramey smiled.

"A college freshman discovered it. A college freshman at Brown University, a boy who's never traveled out of New England in his life. In a course in geology he was given some specimens of earth to analyze—and one of the samples was from the Dirt Hole Mine in Nevada. He discovered that the earth was radioactive, and his professor determined that the soil sample contained a great percentage of uranium—nearly one-tenth of one percent."

"That seems like a very *little* percentage to me," said Susan.

"That one-tenth of one percent will make you the richest woman in Nevada within the year," said Mr. Ramey. "I can almost guarantee you that. If you don't believe me, I will be happy to introduce you to any number of people who'd be willing to take this place off your hands for a few thousand dollars an acre."

Mr. Ramey laughed, but Susan and Blossom were dumbfounded.

"At any rate," Mr. Ramey went on, "we very quietly sent someone out here to take samples of the earth from the mine—after all, the earth that had been analyzed at

Brown was about thirty years old—and the results this time were even better."

Blossom took Mr. Ramey back to his automobile. Inside the main house Colleen made certain that Barbara and Harmon were otherwise occupied. The government agent took off for Carson City, but said that he was available at any time if Susan needed him. Susan never even found out what particular agency he worked for, but there were so many new ones already that the name might not mean anything to her anyway.

However, there were many more important things to think about. Susan waited impatiently for Blossom to return. She needed someone to listen to her chain of reasoning and pick out the flaws.

"That man is the reason Harmon wants me to scuttle the divorce," said Susan.

"Looks that way," said Blossom, leaning against the window again. "But I thought he was already rich."

"I thought so, too. At least there was always plenty of money—of course after living the way I'd lived for two years, having five dollars made me feel like Croesus's favorite wife. But I never knew any details of Harmon's finances. Maybe he doesn't have as much as I thought he did."

"No matter how much he has," Blossom pointed out, "it's not going to be as much as you're going to make off this place."

"How much *we're* going to make," Susan corrected her. Blossom started to protest. Susan waved away her objections. "You offered to take care of me when I didn't have a penny or a prospect of a penny. Now you're going to let me pay you back for that kindness. That's all there is to it. But if you *really* want to help me, you can help me figure out what part Barbara is playing in all this."

Blossom and Susan considered this question for a moment.

Susan said, "It won't make any difference to her whether I'm rich or not."

"That's right," Blossom agreed. "But would it make a difference to her if your husband was rich?"

"I don't see why it should," said Susan. "They're only friends..."

Blossom looked at Susan meaningfully.

"Oh no!" Susan cried. "That's impossible. She's not his type. He only goes after singers, and hat-check girls, and girls who work in Macy's."

Blossom said nothing.

"Besides," Susan went on hurriedly, "Marcellus always *wanted* Harmon to marry Barbara. But Harmon didn't want to marry Barbara, and Barbara wanted to marry Jack. Barbara and Harmon grew up together. They were too close, Harmon said."

"But she got married," Blossom pointed out, "and he got married, too. Then they weren't so close anymore. So maybe then..."

Susan thought about this for a minute.

"Yes, it makes sense. It makes perfect sense. Harmon wanted to divorce me so that he could marry *Barbara*. And that's why Barbara wanted to divorce *Jack*. It also explains those photographs that Marcellus showed me. The ones that were faked. MacIsaac was working for Marcellus, but he was also working for Harmon. Harmon set up the photographs himself, hiring the girl from the Villa Vanity. That way Marcellus and I were supposed to think that Harmon was being unfaithful to me, but we would never guess that he was being unfaithful to me with *Barbara*, of all people..."

"Buzzards of a feather..." Blossom remarked.

Susan shook her head. "I feel as if I've been walking around with my eyes closed for the last three months. And poor Jack—I'm sure he doesn't know either."

"Still some things that don't make sense," said Blossom in deep thought. "Barbara inherited everything from her father's estate, didn't she? Once you'd torn up the will?"

"Yes."

"Then why does she care whether Harmon gets the money from this mine or not?"

"If Harmon's not as well off as I thought, maybe Marcellus wasn't either. Jack didn't even know how much Barbara inherited. She was very quiet about it, he said. Kept saying she couldn't understand anything the bankers or the lawyers said to her, but she wouldn't let Jack take care of it for her either."

"So if they both had less money than you thought they did, that would be a reason for both of them to stay married. You'd be rich, and they could still carry on. Of course, if anything happened to you—if, for instance, you were chopped up in the propellers of an airplane, then Harmon would inherit everything."

"Then Barbara could divorce Jack, and marry Harmon, and they'd live happily ever after." Susan shook her head, grieving for her own stupidity and blindness. She'd underestimated both her husband and Jack's wife. What she'd taken for insouciance, for deliberate superficiality of behavior and speech and attitude, was only a mask hiding deep-seated greed, selfishness, perfidy. In an odd way, she'd trusted their self-involvement, their laziness, their lack of passion or ambition.

She'd been betrayed in that trust.

Harmon and Barbara were wily, cunning, and avaricious. Compared to those two, she and Jack were babes in the woods, about to fall asleep forever beneath a blanket of leaves.

"I feel very stupid," she said at last to Blossom.

Blossom shook her head. "You're not stupid. Now that we've discovered the truth—and I feel sure that it *is* the truth—there's nothing they can do."

"Oh no, there's actually a great deal—"

Susan was interrupted then by two noises that sounded at once.

One was a friendly sort of knocking at the door, and two voices outside that pleaded, *Oh, may we come in?* Harmon's and Barbara's voices.

The other noise was that of barking dogs, just outside the window. Scotty and Zelda.

Susan leapt instantly out of bed and started for the wardrobe where her clothes had been put. "Jack's in trouble," she said.

"You can't go!" Blossom cried in a loud whisper.

"How can I *not*?" asked Susan. "Of course I'm going."

She whisked off her nightgown, threw on a blouse, and pulled on trousers.

Susan? Miss Mayback? Are you in there?

"Let them in," said Susan to her cousin.

Blossom shrugged, went over to the door, and unlocked it.

Barbara and Harmon sauntered in, and then stopped dead at seeing Susan perched on the side of the rumpled bed, at once buttoning the blouse, zippering the trousers, and pushing her bare feet into boots.

"You're well," cried Barbara. "I take back what I said—that doctor isn't a quack."

"This is splendid," said Harmon. "You look as if we'll be able to start for New York tomorrow."

"You and Barbara?" Susan asked. Blossom knelt at Susan's feet, helping her into her boots.

"No," said Harmon carefully, glancing at Barbara, "you and me."

"Residency isn't up for another three weeks," Susan pointed out. "I certainly can't return to New York before then, Harmon." She stood, her boots on, and turned her back in order to tuck her blouse into her trousers.

"Where are you going?" Barbara demanded. It was the old Barbara. Imperious and shrill.

"To see Jack," said Susan, turning around.

Barbara and Harmon stared.

"Jack?" Harmon asked.

"She's hallucinating," Barbara said to Blossom. "We ought to strap her down."

Outside, Scotty and Zelda started up another frantic round of barking. Susan went to the window long enough to gesture to them with a finger on her lips. They went instantly silent.

Blossom rummaged in the drawer of a rickety dresser. She pulled out a battery operated torch. "Take this," she said, handing it to Susan. "Here are extra batteries. I'll go saddle Coral." With that, Blossom hurried out of the room, leaving Susan alone with her husband and her new best friend in all the world.

As she hurriedly finished her dressing, Susan glanced in the mirror and saw Barbara and Harmon conferring with looks.

Oh yes, it all made perfectly wicked sense. She wondered why she'd never understood it before. These two had come much closer to each other than had she and Jack. Much, much closer.

"Jack is here?" Barbara asked at last.

"Yes," said Susan. "Didn't you know?"

"No, I didn't. Why is he here?"

"I believe," Susan said, "that he came here with the express purpose to tell me he loved me and that he wanted to marry me as soon as he had divorced you."

Harmon gaped. Barbara tried hard not to gape.

"So, when the divorces are final, I'll marry Jack, and, Barbara, you can marry Harmon. There's no way you could possibly know it, I realize, but, Barbara, I'll make you my confidante—Harmon is a splendid husband when the lights are turned out, if you know what I mean. Perfectly splendid. I just hope Jack is half as nice. This is very droll, isn't it? Talking about such things so frankly. Oh well," she laughed, "it's just us giddy New Yorkers, I guess. Then we'll all live happily ever after, I presume.

The only difficulty, of course, is that you and Harmon will be possessed of the combined assets of two fortunes, and Jack and I will be poor as church mice, with nothing but this worthless Nevada land to call our own. Life is unfair, but unfair or not, we have to live it out to the bitter end, don't we?"

Susan exited the room.

"Blossom!" she called. "I'm on my way!"

CHAPTER THIRTY

Susan brought not only the batteried torch, but more candles and matches, a spade, a trowel, two canteens of water, and a length of rope.

She'd left Blossom behind to make certain that Barbara and Harmon didn't follow. If they asked, she was headed for Pyramid, where Jack was ensconced with the thieving McAlpines, paying ten dollars a night for a room that wasn't worth seventy-five cents.

Wesley and Colleen actually were in Pyramid, and as soon as they got back, Blossom would send them on, in case Jack's trouble was direr than Susan was capable of alleviating alone. In the meantime, it was Susan alone...

The first disappointment was that Jack was not to be found just outside the entrance of the mine, having twisted his ankle, for instance, or suffered a mild case of sunstroke, or been bitten by a snake whose poison induced temporary paralysis of the legs.

While Susan was untying the spade from the back of the saddle, Scotty and Zelda barked and yelped and flew into the mine and then flew out again when she didn't immediately follow.

Susan nervously switched on the battery torch and went into the mine.

The first few yards seemed almost like home.

But Jack wasn't there.

She called his name, softly at first, then loudly. Then more loudly still. No response.

Scotty and Zelda eagerly pushed on, and Susan unenthusiastically but hastily followed, the handle of the spade bouncing and jarring against her shoulder.

Down, and down more deeply still.

Past crumbling walls, and bowing ceiling supports.

Following the metal tracks laid in the floor of the corridor.

There were times she could touch both walls at once.

Sometimes her head brushed the ceiling.

She shone her light on the walls, on the ceilings, on the supports.

She did not shine it into the holes and passages on either side. She only followed the dogs onward.

Down, and more deeply still.

If Susan doubted the depth of her love for Jack Beaumont before, she could not doubt it now.

The tracks ended.

The dogs stopped in their tracks.

"Where is he?" Susan demanded.

There was no reply.

She shone her light around, but saw nothing but the walls of dirt, the ceiling of dirt, the floor of dirt, and the two dogs.

"Jack!" she screamed.

No reply.

Then an echoed noise, low and rumbling.

Snoring.

"Jack!" she screamed again. "Wake up!"

Then his voice, low and confused, "Susan?"

"Where are you?"

"Here."

"Where is here?"

"I don't know. I'm trapped. Right in front of you maybe."

Because of the acoustics of the tunnel, it was not possible for Susan to tell exactly where the sound was coming from. Then she realized she had two excellent scouts with her.

"Zelda, where is Mr. Beaumont? Scotty, do you know?"

The dogs trotted through the last portal of wood, and Susan followed with the light.

The passage got narrower and smaller, which was a very nasty perception for Susan.

It was so dense and dark that the light she shone all around seemed dampened.

"Why did *you* come?" Jack's voice asked from somewhere.

"Because you sent the dogs."

"But you said if I got in trouble in the mine, you wouldn't come. I never expected you to—"

He broke off suddenly.

"What's wrong," she cried.

"Nothing," he whispered. "It's just a little difficult to talk with this mountain on my chest."

Finally she saw light reflected off a tiny patch of white.

"Jack, move your head."

The white thing was Jack's scalp.

"I see you," she said. "Thank God."

Then the batteries gave out, and Susan was left in darkness.

She closed her eyes and prayed a real prayer for the first time in many, many years.

"What happened to the light?" Jack asked from the blackness.

"It went out."

There was silence for a moment, and then Susan's voice sounded clearly in the darkness. "I'm quite certain," Susan's voice remarked, "that this is the most dreadful moment of my entire life."

"At least you're not buried in half a ton of dirt. Did you know, by the way, that you are owner of a very valuable property here?"

"Yes," said Susan, remembering that not only did she have candles and matches in her pack, she also had extra batteries for the torch. She lighted a match. "It's a uranium mine, I understand."

That dim yellow light made her feel a great deal better.

"If you knew that," said Jack, "why didn't you say something about it? It would certainly explain why Harmon doesn't want to divorce you."

She took out a candle and put the match flame to the wick. The light got brighter.

Susan's spirits rose proportionately.

"I just found out half an hour ago. Some man from the government dropped by, I think, to make certain I didn't sell the mine to a foreign power. You're quite right," Susan went on, dropping new batteries into the torch, "about why Harmon doesn't want to divorce me. But do you know why Barbara doesn't want to divorce you?"

"I've no idea," said Jack. "I honestly haven't thought much about Barbara in the past few hours. Other matters were more pressing." Such as the fact that he was buried under half a ton of radioactive soil, three-quarters of a mile deep in the earth, and on top of everything else, had an itch on his right knee that might turn out to be his final sensation.

"The only reason Barbara wanted a divorce from you," said Susan, brushing away a little dirt from the top of Jack's head, "is so that she could marry Harmon."

"Harmon?" echoed Jack, then added parenthetically, "That feels very good. Harmon *Dodge*. Barbara and *Harmon*."

"Yes," said Susan.

"I find that hard to believe."

"But if Harmon wasn't going to divorce me, then there was no reason for her to divorce you. It would be easier to keep their *liaison* secret if she were still married."

"Barbara and *Harmon*?" Jack repeated, trying to get used to the idea. Something hard and cold pressed in over his face, stripping skin from his nose. It was Susan's torch.

"I can't see anything but dirt in there," she said. "You really are buried."

"I also thought Barbara was too lazy to be unfaithful," Jack mused. "And I thought that Harmon was attracted only to hat-check girls."

"I brought a spade," said Susan. "Shall I dig you out?"

"Please," said Jack.

Placing the light to one side and a lighted candle to the other, Susan began to dig, tossing the dirt over her shoulder, first to the right then to the left. Scotty and Zelda hung back in the darkness, out of the way of the flying debris.

As she gradually cleared away the narrow opening, Jack's head, unsupported by the fall of earth, lolled backward. Finally he was able to see Susan's face, though it appeared upside down. At the same time, however, breathing became even more difficult for him.

"I'm going to try to widen this opening a little," said Susan.

"Not a good idea," Jack warned. "These walls aren't very stable. I might be buried completely. So might you."

"I have a rope," Susan suggested. "I could put it around your neck and pull you out."

"Also not a good idea," said Jack. "This is supposed to be a rescue, not a lynching."

"Then I don't know what else to do," said Susan. "You're blocking the opening, and I can't get past you to dig you out. I can't widen the hole, and you won't let me put a rope around your neck. This is still the worst moment of my life, I think."

"There is something you can do," said Jack.

"What?"

"Kiss me."

"What good will that do?"

"Well, if I never get out of here, at least I will have died happy."

Susan kissed him. They both felt better after that.

Susan looked around, at the meager lights, at the close, crumbling walls, at the ceiling that bulged down toward her head. "If I were an artist, this is how I'd draw hell. I just don't understand how I can feel so romantic at a time like this."

"We may never have another chance," Jack pointed out.

"Maybe we should wait till someone else comes," Susan suggested.

Jack sighed as great a sigh as his lungs would allow. "Not a good idea either. The weight on my chest and legs is heavier than before. I can't take much more of this."

"If I can't put the rope around your neck," Susan suggested, "maybe I could get it around your chest and under your arms."

"A good idea," said Jack.

"I even brought a rope," said Susan cheerfully, "which should make things a great deal easier."

Taking an end of the rope in her hand, she dug carefully out beneath Jack's head, and then clawed her way up under his arm, until she could feel his chest. Then, leaving that arm and hand in position, she began digging around his other side.

Her hair was pressed against his face, and he breathed deeply through it. On the whole, if he had to suffocate, he'd prefer doing it this way.

She dug and pushed and pressed until her hands were clasped around his chest, beneath the landslide of earth. She grasped the end of the rope in her left hand, and then carefully pulled herself free, leaving Jack with a rope underneath his arms and around his chest.

"I'm going to pull now," said Susan. "This will probably hurt."

"Please don't hold back on my account," Jack said.

Susan pulled hard.

Jack groaned. He twisted, hoping that would help. It didn't.

"Pull harder," he suggested.

Susan pulled harder. The rope burned in her hands.

Jack could imagine his head and shoulders being pulled free. He could also imagine his torso, hips, and legs being left behind with the ticking Geiger counter.

"Harder!"

She pulled even harder, turning away from Jack, with the rope over her shoulder, like the Volga boatman.

Jack felt his body shift.

He also felt a liquid warmth under his arms. His blood probably, where the rope had abraded through his shirt and skin.

"It's working!" he called. He twisted more.

Suddenly his head was free.

"Keep pulling!"

He twisted more. Susan jerked on the rope. Jack's left arm came free. He used it for leverage.

Susan jerked again.

At least two more feet of Jack came free: his shoulders, both arms, his lungs.

He filled his lungs with air.

"I can breathe," he shouted.

Susan dropped the rope and ran over to him. She kissed him again.

"I have to rest a moment," she said. "Do you mind?"

Jack breathed deeply. He waved his arms. He dug his hands into the earth and tried to pull himself out. "No, rest. Kiss me again. It won't take long to get my legs out. Maybe I can do it myself."

He started wriggling.

"Oh Jack..." Susan complained. She knelt behind him, hooked her arms underneath his, and then pulled.

Jack kicked and twisted.

Slowly he was pulled free.

For several moments he simply lay on the floor, his head in Susan's lap.

"I'm very happy," he said.

"I am, too," she said. "But this still feels like hell to me."

Jack slowly moved his legs around. "If you help me, I think I'll be able to stand up."

She helped him to his feet.

"Are you strong enough to walk back?" asked Susan. "Or should we just wait till someone comes?"

Clop, clop, clop.

"Here comes someone!" said Jack. "I hope they brought a litter. I never traveled by litter. I've always fancied it."

Clop, clop, clop.

"Colleen?" Susan called.

No reply. *Clop, clop, clop.*

"Wesley?" she called, directing the torch down the passage. "Blossom?"

It was none of them.

The narrow cone of light shone first on the face of Malcolm MacIsaac. Then Susan played it down the length of the rifle whose muzzle bulged into the dark cylinder of a silencer.

CHAPTER THIRTY-ONE

"CAN YOU FLY a plane?" Susan asked MacIsaac.

"Yes," he replied.

"That solves *that* question," Susan sighed.

"Did you cut the cables on Marcellus Rhinelander's touring car?" Jack asked.

"Want to get everything straight before you die?" MacIsaac cackled. "No, I didn't. I've never murdered anybody in my life. Yet."

"Then who killed Marcellus?" Susan wondered aloud to Jack.

"Your husband did," said MacIsaac. The barrel of the rifle wandered back and forth between then. "Are you two ready to die?"

"Half an hour ago," said Jack, "I would have said yes."

He stomped on Susan's electric torch, whose beam was still trained toward the hole where he'd been trapped.

At the same moment the torch was extinguished, Susan threw herself down on the candle.

All light was now extinguished.

Then briefly, the whole passage was lighted again— by the muted explosion of MacIsaac's rifle.

Jack felt air against his cheek.

Then all was darkness again.

"Scotty?" Jack called. "Zelda?"

"Attack!" cried Susan.

In the darkness they heard barks, growls, the scurrying of tiny feet, the ripping of cloth, and then a shriek.

Another explosion, illuminating the corridor like a bolt of lightning.

In that brief glow, Jack and Susan saw MacIsaac whirling around and around, the two dogs attached to him by their teeth and flung out horizontally by centrifugal force.

Then blackness again.

A crash, a groan.

Another shot, showing MacIsaac on the ground, but still holding the rifle.

One more explosion of fire, then blackness again.

A creaking of wood. A rumble of shifting earth. A hiss of sand.

"Oh my God," whispered Susan. "He hit one of the supports."

A splintering of wood.

In the darkness Susan flung out her arm and hit Jack in the chest. Then she grabbed at him till she had his hand. "We have to get out of here," she whispered. "Right now."

A louder splintering of wood.

A noise of slipping, sliding earth.

"Scotty! Zelda!" Susan yelled. "Run! Run!"

Jack and Susan ran also, despite the fact that their way in the blackness was barred by MacIsaac and his rifle.

"No!" the detective screamed. "You won't—"

Then there was an even louder noise of shifting earth and the threat was cut off.

Earth poured over Jack and Susan and knocked them backward onto the floor of the passage.

The black space was filled with a roar of tumbling earth.

Jack and Susan, still holding hands, scuttled backward across the floor.

The noise of falling earth continued.

They felt it spill over their feet. They went on backing up. The earth still tumbled over their feet.

In their progress, Susan shoved over the extinguished candle. She instinctively grabbed it out from under her.

Finally, they were pushed right up against an ungiving wall.

Jack stood and pulled Susan up beside him.

"This is the worst way to die that I can possibly imagine," said Susan.

"Sorry," Jack said, as if the whole business were his fault entirely.

"Oh well," Susan said, as the earth, having completely buried her feet and ankles, was now intent on burying her calves and knees, "it's not the *worst,* I suppose, with you here."

He squeezed her hand.

"Another kiss?" he asked.

She kissed him.

"I wish I could see your face," he sighed.

"I have a candle, but I lost the matches."

"I have some," he said, reaching into his pocket.

The earth had now buried them up to the waist. Jack lighted the candle and held it up between himself and Susan.

She smiled.

"I love you," he said.

"I love you, too," she said, "but I wish you hadn't lighted the candle."

She looked around. They were trapped in the base of a hill of loose earth. The passage back to the surface was entirely blocked off.

Earth continued to spill down from the ceiling of the passage, gathering around their waists.

"Maybe it will stop," said Susan.

They waited and listened. The earth continued to spill down.

"Let me look at you once more, and then I'll blow out the candle," said Jack.

He gazed at her. She smiled.

Jack sighed, and blew out the candle.

They were silent for a few moments, listening to the falling earth.

"I think it's slowing down," said Susan. "Or am I just fooling myself?"

Jack didn't answer, not wanting to hex it.

"It *is* slowing down," said Susan a few moments later.

"It's stopped," said Jack. The earth was up to Susan's neck, a little lower on the taller Jack.

They still held hands, just above the level of the dirt. "Shall we start digging?" Susan asked.

"I don't want to take any chances disturbing this hill," said Jack. "Besides, where would we put the dirt? There's hardly room for our heads."

"Then we just wait for Blossom," said Susan. "She knows where we are. We should be all right for a while, shouldn't we?"

"If the air holds out," said Jack.

They were silent a few moments more.

"I hope the dogs are safe," said Susan.

"I don't think MacIsaac made it, though," said Jack. "Do you think he was telling the truth when he said he didn't murder Marcellus—and that Harmon did?"

"Yes, I do," said Susan. She was silent a moment, and then asked, "Do you know how much money Harmon had, by any chance?"

"No, I've no idea," said Jack. "Is there some reason you ask that at this particular time?"

"Just curious. I have a feeling—"

"What sort of feeling?"

"Harmon always spent pretty freely," said Susan, "before I was married to him, and afterward, too. Maybe he didn't have as much as he'd like everybody to think he had. He handled Marcellus's finances, didn't he?"

"Nominally," said Jack. "I can't imagine he did it all himself. Try to push some of the dirt away from your stomach," he suggested, "it'll make breathing easier."

"Good idea,' said Susan, and started to push away as much of the loose earth as she could. "But perhaps Harmon really was handling Marcellus's money, and maybe he was stealing some of it, and maybe Marcellus found out, and maybe Harmon murdered him so that he wouldn't be caught."

"But if he were just doing all this for money," asked Jack, "why was he going after Barbara?"

"Did you buy all Barbara's clothes?"

"On my salary? You must be joking. Marcellus took care of Barbara's wardrobe."

"No he didn't," said Susan. "He told me so. It must have been Harmon. Barbara probably didn't care if he was stealing from Marcellus, so long as she could buy little leopardskin capelets."

"Always hated that cape," said Jack. "Made Barbara look like she had contracted some new strain of chicken pox."

I heard that, cried a muffled voice.

Jack momentarily let go Susan's hand.

"Was that Barbara?"

"Either that," said Susan, "or else we've already died and gone to hell."

I'm so angry with you two! came the muffled voice again.

"You're angry with *us*?"

The voice was suddenly clearer, and accompanying it was a beam of white light that shone down from somewhere near the ceiling into Jack's eyes.

Then it moved over to Susan's.

"Barbara? Is that you?" asked Jack.

"Of course it's me," she said. "And you two are holding hands."

The light shone on their clasped hands.

"Barbara," said Susan, "you're making the dirt spill faster. You're going to bury us alive if you're not careful."

"It would serve you two right," Barbara retorted. "You especially, Susan. Why didn't you warn me about Harmon?"

"What about Harmon?"

"He's a snake. A reptile. He killed Father. Did you know that? *He killed my father.* If I had known that, I certainly would never have asked him to seduce me."

"You *asked* him to seduce you?" cried Jack.

"You had those broken ribs," Barbara explained dismissively. She directed her light directly into Susan's face. "The only reason he was going to marry me was he thought Father was rich. And because he found me totally irresistible, of course. Then he found out that Father had spent all his money on smuggling in real liquor from Montreal, so there was no point in marrying me just because he was desperately in love with me. *Then* he found out that this mine was worth a mint, so he was going to throw me over and keep *you.* That *snake.*"

"Barbara," said Jack, "let me point out that you weren't married to Harmon. You were married to me, so you had no right—"

"Oh, shut up, Jack. This has nothing to do with you. This is between Susan and me."

"Barbara, did you see a spade over there? On your side?"

"I tripped on the damned thing."

"You think you might dig us out?" Jack asked.

"I couldn't possibly," said Barbara definitely.

"Why not?" Susan asked.

"I'm wearing suede."

Eventually, however, Blossom showed up with Wesley and Colleen, and the hill of loose earth that had trapped Jack and Susan was tunneled through.

"Mr. MacIsaac is under here somewhere," said Susan. "I don't think he was as lucky as we were."

"We'll find him," said Colleen, spade in hand. Digging up a crushed and suffocated corpse in a mine tunnel looked exactly like the sort of work that tested her mettle.

"Where's Harmon?" Jack asked.

"Wesley tied him to some piece of furniture or other," said Blossom vaguely, "and is now on the way to find somebody who's capable of making an arrest. You two go on now. We'll take care of this."

Jack and Susan walked slowly and wearily toward the entrance of the mine. Barbara sauntered along beside them, holding the flashlight.

"I heard him," she explained. "I was in the next room, quite by accident, I assure you, and I *heard* Harmon talking to that dreadful detective, and he told him to find you and kill you both. There were times, Susan, I admit it, when I wished that you were dead. But believe me, I would never have *paid* for the pleasure. But Harmon told the detective he'd give him ten thousand dollars if he did it." Barbara snorted contempt. "I asked Harmon for five thousand—*nothing*—for my summer wardrobe, and he told me he couldn't afford it. That *snake.*"

"How do you know he killed Marcellus?" Susan asked.

"Oh, they went on a bit about blackmail and that sort of thing." Barbara shrugged. "Harmon did it. He was up there that weekend. He knew exactly what was going on. And that will? You know that will? Father didn't leave you *anything*, Susan. It was a fake. Harmon forged it to make you look guilty. If you hadn't torn it up, he would have torn it up himself. He was going to blame the murder on you, and get you convicted to get rid of you—if he didn't murder you outright. I think he probably would have pushed you out a window. That's how I'd do it."

"I suppose I should thank you for saving my life," said Susan dryly.

Barbara was silent a moment, and then she leaned close, and whispered into Susan's ear, "You wouldn't give Jack back, would you? In gratitude?"

"Absolutely not," said Susan.

Barbara sighed.

"But remember," Susan added in the same confidential whisper, "I'm the one with money now. Jack doesn't have anything, and once Harmon goes to prison, he won't even have a job. So you'd be much better off letting Jack go and finding a rich man."

Barbara considered this for a moment.

"What are you two talking about?" asked Jack.

"Oh, nothing," said Barbara cheerfully. "Just girl talk. Susan and I are best friends now. There's nobody else in the world I would allow to marry my only husband."

"Barbara's going to find a new husband who's very rich and very good-looking and wants to be told what to do every moment of the day," said Susan.

"That's right," said Barbara. "And when I've found him, we'll all take bridge lessons from the Culbertsons."

The light at the entrance of the mine was dazzling. Scotty and Zelda stood there, waiting.

THE END OF
JACK AND SUSAN'S ADVENTURE
IN 1933